A Winter Ballad

⚜ BARBARA SAMUEL ⚜

HarperPaperbacks
A Division of HarperCollins Publishers

This is a work of fiction. The characters, incidents, and dialogues are products of the author's imagination and are not to be construed as real. Any resemblance to actual events or persons, living or dead, is entirely coincidental.

HarperPaperbacks   *A Division of* HarperCollins*Publishers*
10 East 53rd Street, New York, N.Y. 10022

Copyright © 1994 by Barbara Samuel
All rights reserved. No part of this book may be used or reproduced in any manner whatsoever without written permission of the publisher, except in the case of brief quotations embodied in critical articles and reviews. For information address HarperCollins*Publishers,*
10 East 53rd Street, New York, N.Y. 10022.

Cover illustration by Jean Monti

First printing: November 1994

Printed in the United States of America

HarperPaperbacks, HarperMonogram, and colophon are trademarks of HarperCollins*Publishers*

❖ 10 9 8 7 6 5 4 3 2 1

This book could only be for my sister Merry, the scrappiest, stubbornist, prettiest little sister ever born. It's also for Ian and Danny, each of whom wrought a miracle in his mother's life.

ACKNOWLEDGMENTS

Many thanks go to the network of romance readers and writers on Prodigy and GEnie, especially the ROOH and the Historical Fiction Gang. Very special thanks go to Sherrilyn Kenyon, the able and enthusiastic guide who helped me navigate the world of the Middle Ages.

A Winter Ballad

Prologue

Thick rain, cold and bitter, poured from a dark winter sky. Four men rode through the dankness, heads down in miserable silence.

A fifth man was flung over the body of a mule. Blood stained his hair. Rain wet the battered face. As this new woe penetrated, he groaned softly, but the others did not pause.

Steadily, though it was Sext, the day darkened. Jean-Luc de Ventoux, till late a farmer's fourth son and not yet seventeen summers, cast a wary look at the sky. An evil portent, that blackening sky—a dire warning to halt their evil.

But he growled the words to himself, fearful of raising the ire of the others again. They had laughed at his misgivings when they found the knight alone in the still of a cold evening, feeding carrots to a mule. Jean-Luc had quelled his nerves and joined in the ambush with vigor. It was Jean-Luc, he thought proudly, who'd delivered the silent powerful blow to the head that laid the knight low.

But even as the knight had fallen, a beast roared out of the woods, yellow eyes unholy as it leapt upon them with fierce, low growls, madly tearing at their clothes, so violent it took several long moments for anyone to react. One of the kidnappers suffered a long rent to his leg, and they lost another to a torn throat before Claude, their leader, kicked the beast squarely in the chest. It made a high-pitched yelp of pain as it flew, and landed in the grass of the meadow. There it lay, unmoving, tongue lolling.

By then, the marauders feared discovery by the soldiers camped not far distant, and bundled the body of the knight to the mule to make their escape. Claude wore the knight's sword hanging from his belt.

Now the sky darkened, more and more, ominously. Jean-Luc heard a snapping in the woods and peered nervously into the trees, unable to quell a finger of dread. He saw nothing.

The rain ceased, but still the sky did not lighten. Jean-Luc glanced uneasily toward the knight. There had been two men willing to pay richly for this man—one to have him dead, another to be borne back to France in secret. He was at the heart of some plot. Jean-Luc wondered what it might be.

All at once, the world was plunged into a darkness as dense as full evening. Jean-Luc cried out in fear, and could no longer hold his tongue. "'Tis an evil portent!" he cried. "Please . . . let's leave the knight before we are damned."

An uneasy murmur of half-agreement met his words, but Claude turned fiercely, holding to the stallion they'd stolen from the knight as it reared and

whinnied nervously. "Fools! 'Twill be your heads—
and your purses—that will suffer if you succumb to
this foolish superstition."

Jean-Luc swallowed. "But—"

"Enough!"

The knot of horses lifted their heads restively as
the stallion snorted and danced almost out of control.
As if in reaction, from the woods came a high, mourn-
ful howl.

The sound traveled around the knot of men and
horses. At first there was only the one howl, joined by
another, then another and another, until they were
surrounded with the eerie noise, echoing and bouncing, circling them. The stallion snorted, eyes wild.

In terror, Jean-Luc looked back to the knight, and it
seemed the golden hair glowed with some inner light.
Ropes about his wrists had made a chafed mark. And
with a certain horror, Jean-Luc saw that only the mule
was calm as the other animals danced and skittered in
response to the stallion's fear.

A great bolt of lightning cracked through the darkness and struck a tree nearby with a booming explosion. The stallion reared and screamed in wild terror,
then bolted through the forest in a frenzy. The other
horses followed.

Jean-Luc clung to his mount as the creature crashed
without grace through thick trees. He kept his head
low to the horse's neck, his fingers woven through the
mane. Around them was the wild pounding of the
horses through dense forest and the wolves baying—
surely the sound of hell, Jean-Luc thought in terror. It
began to rain again, hard. Lightning flashed in the
evil daytime darkness, and thunder boomed with a
rocking violence.

Jean-Luc's horse suddenly reared. He clung mightily, hearing a shout and a sudden, quick cry of pain amid the cacophony. Through the rain, Jean-Luc saw Claude had been thrown from the stallion, who bolted away through the trees. Furious, Claude jumped to his feet, brushing his clothes and cursing as he pointed after the beast, sending one of his men after it.

In the confusion, Jean-Luc saw his chance. Nickering gently at his mount to calm the beast, he steered the gelding from the pack and retraced their steps as well as he was able. The mule had not followed the wild bolt through the forest, but Jean-Luc found him calmly standing under the sheltering arms of an ancient rowan tree, as if to protect its rider.

Glancing over his shoulder, Jean-Luc dismounted, and with a grunt, pulled the dead weight of the knight from the beast. The man slumped on the ground, rolling to one side with a stuporous moan. He did not wake.

Jean-Luc took his knife from his belt and crouched to cut the ropes binding the knight's wrists and ankles. As the ropes fell free, a shout from the others reached him. "Jean-Luc!"

He jumped to his feet—and at that moment, the sky lightened abruptly. Stunned, he looked toward the brightness, letting the rain wet his face before he fell to one knee and genuflected.

"Jean-Luc!"

Taking the rope around the mule's neck, Jean-Luc mounted his horse and led the mule away. As he rode toward the others, an extraordinary calm filled him. Purses and heads were nothing in comparison to an immortal soul.

It was that thought that lent him courage to lead

the men in circles, far from the sheltering branches of
the rowan tree, when they went back in search of the
knight.

Defeated, weary, and not a little frightened by the
afternoon's events, the men at last headed home toward
Provence, leaving the body of the knight where it lay.

1

The body sprawled beneath the bare branches of a rowan tree. In the thick fog that laced through the trees and clung to the cold winter earth, it was invisible until Anya's black gelding shied and whinnied softly.

Geoffrey, Anya's page, made a frightened noise. "Is he dead, my lady?"

"I cannot tell." Anya dismounted and tossed back her hood. Warily, she crept forward, listening cautiously to the deep silence of the forest. There seemed to be no one else about. The horses stood quietly.

Anya eased closer, noting the quality of the knight's mail and the good condition of his hauberk. Any helm he might have worn was gone, and his head had suffered the loss. Blood, thickened by cold or time, clotted his hair.

Kneeling beside him, she examined him for signs of life, her hands clutched close in her lap. Tangled long hair the color of ripe wheat covered his face, and below the heavy leather on his chest, she could see no movement.

"Is he dead?" Geoffrey whispered loudly from his mount.

Anya lifted her shoulders, for it was impossible to know. Bracing herself for the eerie feel of dead flesh, she reached out to touch his hand. It was cold and marred with chilblains, but not dead-flesh cold. Nor stiff, either. Heartened, she reached forward to brush the hair from his face.

He moaned and shifted a little. Anya started and jumped back a pace, shooting an alarmed glance toward Geoffrey.

"See if he is armed before he awakens!" the boy urged.

"Why must I do all?" she protested. "You are to serve me, child!"

"But you are the older, my lady."

The knight moved no more, and Anya bent to check his sleeves for daggers. No belt or scabbard hung around his waist, though a shiny place on his hauberk showed where it would go.

The small shift of the knight had put him flat on his back, and now she could see his face. Blonds were often pallid and delicate. This wounded knight was neither. His flesh was tanned, the sharp cheekbones a touch sun- or wind-burned. A high brow and the straight clean lines of nose and jaw bespoke intelligence. His mouth, in his stupor, seemed peculiarly vulnerable.

She knelt again, no longer afraid, and probed his body for signs of injury. There were bruises along one side of his face, and the bloody cut on his head. One shoulder seemed cocked at an odd angle, but it was impossible to see what sort of injury made it so beneath the mail. When she pressed along his sides, he made no sound of pain. With both hands, she checked for breaks in his limbs. None.

"Come, Geoffrey. Help me get him on my horse."

The page stared at her.

"You'll not be much of a knight if a near-dead man frightens you so."

"What if he is a demon come from hell in the Great Darkness?"

Anya sighed. Two days before, the world had been plunged into an eerie, engulfing darkness at midday. Geoffrey had suffered nightmares both nights since. "He is only a man, child. One who will die if we leave him here."

Still he made no move to dismount. Exasperated, she put her hands on her hips. "Dismount and help me, young Geoffrey, or I'll see you sent to bed with no supper."

He obeyed. As he came to stand beside her, looking with some dread at the knight, Anya touched the boy's blond head gently. "Truly, Geoffrey, he is no danger to us."

The boy nodded. "What shall I do?"

Anya tossed her braid over her shoulder and eyed the man. He was quite large, though, thank the saints, slim enough. "'Twill be no easy task. We must take as much care with that shoulder as we can, and his head will bleed again." She sighed. "There's no help for it."

Between the two of them, they managed to drag and half lift, half throw the man over the back of Anya's mare. He groaned again, a low, agonized sound, but did not waken. Anya frowned. It would have been better had he roused. She held little hope for his life.

Once he was settled, Anya took the reins to lead her mare back to the castle.

Geoffrey suddenly screamed.

Anya whirled, heart pounding, to look for bandits. She saw nothing. "Geoffrey," she said sharply in reproof.

The boy pointed toward the spot from which they'd lifted the man. A lean, ragged dog skulked close to the place, his tail down. He sniffed the area and whined.

"A wolf!" Geoffrey whispered.

The creature looked as if it feared beating, but even the fear did not keep it from edging closer to the man on the horse. It whined again, a sorrowful sound.

"Not a wolf," Anya said. She thought it might be half, but would not give Geoffrey anything else to panic over. "'Tis only the knight's dog."

Gently, she reached out a hand, murmuring nonsense in an encouraging voice. She had a fondness for beasts of any sort. This one, though ragged and dirty, showed signs of great handsomeness. At her gesture, he crept forward slowly and licked her fingers. She touched his head, scratching below his ears. "I don't know what we can do for your master," she said, "but for you, there are scraps and a warm place to sleep tonight."

She straightened. "Geoffrey, I want you to put your hand on the knight's head, keep it from bouncing too much."

For once, perhaps because he felt sheepish over his myriad fears, the boy did not argue. They made their way through the forest back to the Hall.

At the gates, there was a stir over the wounded knight, but unlike Geoffrey, the men-at-arms did not argue with the lady of the manor. Female she might be, and ruined besides, but they recognized her authority. In the continued absence of her brothers, one on a pilgrimage to the Holy Land, another a canon at the cathedral in Lichfield, Anya was the only clear mistress they had. For five years, she had run the manor ably—far better, she knew, than her brother, who'd nearly ruined the fief in his sorrowing and drunken haze.

The men carried the knight to a chamber behind the Great Hall, close to the hearth, where it was warm and dry. They settled him on a straw mattress, then stood waiting. Anya dismissed them, except Geoffrey, whom she sent to the kitchens for the supplies she needed.

The dog crept in, head down, and when Anya didn't shout at him, slunk close to the knight's feet. "I fear your master has little time left to him," she said as she began to remove the hauberk and mail, gently as she was able. The knight groaned softly, shifting away from her hands. His flesh burned with fever, and Anya could smell the sour odor of illness about him.

A little pluck of regret touched her. The lean body, muscled and hard beneath his clothes, matched the extraordinary handsomeness of his face, visible even through the grime and bruises and days' worth of unshaven beard. She pressed her fingers to the high brow. "How long did you lie there?" she asked, knowing he could not hear. "How came you to our forest?"

A maidservant appeared with a bucket of water and strips of cloth. She set them beside Anya with a grunt, and her attention fell to the knight, naked on the straw mattress. A quiet murmur of surprise and pleasure escaped her mouth.

Anya looked at the girl, and caught the greedy gleam in her eye. "I will call you, Tillie, if needs be."

Left alone, Anya dipped her cloth in the warm water and began to wash the sweat and heat from the knight's body. First his face, so bruised and battered. One eye was swollen and a gash marked his jaw. She paused to look at the wound, but found it mending already beneath the caked blood. His lips were cracked, too, as if from thirst. He must have lain in the forest, wounded this way, for at least a day and a night.

Her estimate of his chances of survival plummeted again.

The head wound was deep and oozed with a muckish substance, but even it was not the worst of his injuries. She had prayed the shoulder had only slipped from its joint. Once she removed the mail, it was plain the bone above his chest was broken, and a great red bruise marked the place, as if he'd been given a blow.

Puzzled, she examined him more closely. Bruises marked him head to toe, darkest around his hips and legs. It seemed he had been beaten fiercely. Perhaps he'd been set upon by the bandits who owned the forest?

At his wrists, raw red rings marred the flesh—the marks of binding. One finger was swollen at the joint, and when she probed it, she found another small break.

There was no lack of strangers on the road to Lichfield, for pilgrims and knights and monks traveled the road daily. But few ventured from the road to the forest, and none ever came so far as the village of Winterbourne unless by intent.

Pursing her lips, she glanced at the dog, and suddenly wondered if its fear meant it, too, had been beaten. "Come here, my little friend."

The beast whined and, tail down, crossed the floor. Gently, Anya stroked him, feeling the long sinews of his body below oily gray-and-black fur. Her hand grazed a lump on his side, and the dog yelped, turning to nearly bite her. He stopped short of it, licking her wrist instead.

She rubbed his ears in apology. "They beat him senseless and kicked you aside, I think."

Anya called Mary, her most trusted servant, covering the knight with a fur before the woman came into the chamber.

"Bring me wine and rosemary, and a cup of ale," she said. "And a bone for the dog."

"Ye want me to fetch the priest, too?"

Anya straightened. "He'll not die."

"Aye, milady, but what if he does? Will ye send him to his grave with no—"

"No priest," she said firmly, and looked at the girl. "Just the wine and broth."

Mary scurried out. No doubt she would whisper this new story in the kitchen, to add to the others that made Anya's defiance of the church infamous. It mattered not. There were so many now, her fate was sealed. The priest himself had damned her—what more could the servants do?

Christian drifted. In his dreams, he stood at the mouth of hell, his skin blistered by the heat. Beyond, standing unharmed in the flames, the Beast laughed at his folly, and Christian tried to protest that he was the wronged; that it should be his father, not he, who should be burning here.

Hell shifted, became a cold battlefield, and he was

dying of thirst. An animal chewed his body. He
screamed, but it did not stop. Then he was walking
somehow, and each step shot agony through him, but
he could not find his dog. In his dream, he cried out,
"Ysengrin!" and at last, the dog appeared, licking his
fingers.

He had no idea how long he had thrashed and
wandered, but it was Ysengrin's tongue that roused
him slowly. He came awake by pieces, to a dizzy sort
of awareness. He lay in a bed, warm with furs and the
heat of a wall nearby. Flickering candles winked in
the dimness. Christian could see little; his head thundered, and his shoulder burned as if there were still
creatures tearing at it with their strong teeth.

In a chair nearby the bed was a woman, slumped
beneath another fur. Who are you? he wanted to ask.
How came I to be here? He had been so sure he would
die at the hands of the bandits. But his lips cracked
when he moved them, and all that came from his
throat was a dry croak that sounded not of words at all.

It was enough to rouse the woman. She came
awake instantly, tossing away the fur to stand up and
take his hand. She touched his head, and his cheek,
and reached for a cup. "A little water?" she said.

He found he could not even nod, but it was not
necessary. She cradled his head against her breast and
lifted the cup to his mouth. The liquid flowed over his
parched lips and tongue like a magic potion, silvery
and cold. Greedily, he gulped, closing his eyes to taste
it more deeply.

Before he finished, she took it away, and he wanted
to shout at her to give it back. As if she sensed his frustration, she murmured something soothing, and her
voice was deep and strangely settling. Her breast made

a plush cradle for his aching head, and her cool hands smoothed the heat from his cheeks. He thought she sang, but oblivion came to him too quickly to be sure.

The knight hung at death's door for several days. Between other tasks, Anya kept watch over him, patiently feeding him ale and broth and water, mere drops at a time. In the morning, and again at night, she washed him with cool water, head to toe, to break the fever that still raged wildly; then pressed cloths soaked in wine and rosemary to his bruises.

She accepted no help with the task, and could not say why. It seemed the strange, broken knight was her own atonement, a silent penance she performed. As each day took him further from the mouth of death, she began to revere the moments she spent tending him, and let nothing interfere with the intimate tasks.

He was long and golden, with strength in his arms and legs, and perfect symmetry in each thing—his feet were as beautifully made as his brow. Candlelight gilded the hair on his chest and legs until he seemed to glow like a god from another world.

She had never wanted a man, not any of them. And she told herself she admired this one only because he was purely under her control. He was weak as a babe, and needed her, as any of the helpless creatures of the fief might.

But it was a lie even as she thought it. Not even burning with fever was he helpless or weak. Even in the deepest stupor, he exuded a strange dormant power. Sometimes she found herself sitting for long, uncounted minutes, simply staring at him. In those lost minutes, she felt awash with a queer sense of her

own body, arrayed around her, made of flesh and
bones and empty limbs.

Then some sound would bring her again to herself,
only Anya of Winterbourne. Appalled at her yearning,
she bustled away, afraid some might observe her cov-
etous glances and make sport of her wish to have that
which would be forever denied.

By the fifth day, he seemed on the mend. Anya left
Geoffrey with him and went about her chores. The
accounts had to be watched carefully, for the wars
and floods and miasmatic winds had given them all
poor harvests this year. Not only Winterbourne suffered, either. All her brother's holdings were strained.
If the villages and manors were to survive, they could
tolerate no waste.

She was weary with keeping watch, a weariness she
felt in her neck and grainy eyes. Twice, while record-
ing the day's expenditures, she yawned mightily.

Stephen, captain of her men-at-arms, approached her
midmorning. "My lady, I would have a word with you."

She gestured for him to join her. Behind her in the
hearth, a fire burned and crackled, smelling of pine.
A multicolored young cat scattered rushes playfully,
digging below them in fierce delight. Anya chuckled
and scooped Esmerelda into her lap, taking a small
pleasure in the tiny bones and body against her hand.
The cat kneaded her kirtle, purring. "Is there news of
my brothers?" she asked.

"William has sent word he cannot leave the monastery."

She sighed. "Gave he a reason?"

Stephen shrugged. "The struggle between Lancaster

and the king has given the church much to worry
over."

Deliberately, she lifted her cup and drank of the ale
within, trying to rein her disappointment and temper.
"The piety of my brothers should alone win my
entrance to heaven," she said, setting the cup precisely
back in the ring it had left on the table. "A monk and a
pilgrim—and no one to feed the peasants." With a bitter smile, she looked at him. "'Tis well one of us was
not so deeply smitten."

Stephen shifted uncomfortably, turning his eyes
from her face. "My lady, it is not wise to flaunt your
unbelief so. There is talk—the priest may send word
to the bishop. . . ."

"The priest is a doddering idiot who cannot even
speak the Latin of the mass and drinks away the
villeins' tithes. My brothers are high placed and will
intervene on my behalf if it comes to that. You
needn't worry."

"Aye, my lady." He stood, but made no move to go.

"Is there more?"

He cleared his throat. "Think you it wise to bring
the stranger here so?"

Anya stroked the cat in her lap. "A Christian could
not leave a man in the forest to die."

"But he is unknown—perhaps there is a price on his
head! Nor can we afford the luxury of another mouth
to feed this season."

She met his gaze squarely. "Perhaps he is a saint in
disguise."

"But—"

"I will hear no more of it, Stephen. He will stay."

She could see he longed to debate the point. Instead, he inclined his head. "As you wish."

Geoffrey ran from the chamber behind the hearth. "My lady! Come quickly. He has awakened!"

Dropping her quill, Anya leapt to her feet and hurried after him.

2

Christian could barely move. There was no place on his body that did not hurt. Even his eyes felt raw, as if he'd been riding in a dust storm.

He stirred slowly. Before he alerted anyone to his waking, he meant not only to tally the state of his body, but also to garner what he might of his surroundings. His pallet was made of clean straw, and the furs over him held a scent of herbs. Beyond the small chamber where he lay were sounds of a busy household—the ordinary murmur of conversation and servants calling out and the clanking of spurs. The smell of roasting meat and onions hung in the air. A fair-sized manor, he guessed.

In the chamber itself, he was not alone. Nearby, someone repetitively spun a top over a wooden surface. Whir, clatter, whir, clatter. A boy, judging by the surprising sweetness of his quiet singing.

Slowly, Christian moved his limbs to gauge what

might be injured, what only weary from rough treatment. Feet and legs seemed sound. No pain in his groin, thank the saints. His head ached and his throat felt raw. Minor twinges in his wrists and hands—to be expected.

He must have made some sound, for the boy yelped. Christian opened his eyes, and the boy ran from the chamber, shouting. The noise pried loose the small check over his headache, and it thundered though his skull once more, temple to eye and ear to ear. He groaned and made to lift his hand to the place, but the movement sent splintering agony through his shoulder and chest.

Then the woman from before was bending over him, pressing her cool hand to his heated cheeks and brow. "Fetch more ale," she said over her shoulder to the boy.

Christian looked at her. In the bright light pouring through an opening somewhere above him, he could see her clearly. Not a specter, as he had feared. He stared at her in gratitude as she poured a cupful of ale from a tankard the boy brought, and knelt again to help him drink. Her elbow eased around his head and propped him just so, as if she knew it pained him to move. This time, she let him drink his fill before she put aside the cup.

There was a brisk ease in her movements that comforted him. He watched as she dipped a cloth in water and bent over him, pushing back the fur to gently wash his face and neck and chest. Hair the color of old gold coins escaped her braid and sprang into curls that tumbled freely around her cheeks and ears and neck. The face was made strong by angles of bone, and there was about her eyes an exotic tilt.

He tried to speak; managed only a ragged whisper. "What is this place?"

"Winterbourne, in Leicestershire. I am Anya, mistress of the fief at present, since my brothers—" She seemed to catch herself and shook her head. "My page and I found you in the forest not a mile from here."

Leicestershire. Christian closed his eyes, struggling to think how he had come so far. He did not remember all, only bleak snatches after the ambush in the borderlands. He had thought the men Scots warriors at first, bent on capturing him from the English army, but they'd been French.

French brigands meant it was his father who had ordered again Christian be killed.

Why, then, did he yet live? Why had they only beat him, not killed him, then dumped him in a forest so far from any he knew?

The thoughts tangled in the pain in his head, and he made a low noise of frustration.

The woman stroked his shoulder the way one might gentle a restless horse. "Whatever troubles you face will wait until you've mended, will they not? We are small in number, but the walls are sturdy, the men wary of strangers. None will harm you will you rest here."

Her voice was strange, he thought now, slightly husky and deep for a woman. Once Christian had known a man who had been near strangled to death who had a voice like that, and he looked at the girl anew. Not so young as he thought at first, though her skin was still fresh and her teeth were sound. "Where is your husband?" he rasped.

Carefully, she turned away and her gossamer veil dropped to hide her face. "I have no husband. This was my father's fief. I am caretaker while my brothers roam."

She looked back to him, her chin uptilted as if in defense. He gazed at her, glad to have some lighter thing to fill his mind. Strange she was, with the tilt of her eyes and angled bones. But the mouth was full and rich; her eyes the clear blue of a lake at midmorn. Her body was slim and womanly—and well he remembered the plump warmth of her breasts against his cheek.

He tried to ask if she were a nun, but the words garbled in his raw throat. "Vows?" he managed.

The sound she let loose could only be called derisive. "No." She tugged the fur more closely over his chest. "You must rest again."

Christian managed a small nod.

She smiled. "At least you are not stubborn."

When she made to turn away, he reached for her hand. In surprise, she looked at the clasp of his fingers around hers, then up to his face. The brisk and defensive manner dropped away for an instant, and he saw a fleeting vulnerability in her eyes. Then it was gone. She tried to tug her hand away.

Ill he was, and wounded, too, but he was twice her size and strength. It took little to tighten his fingers just enough to hold her.

He licked his lips and said as clearly as he could manage, "Thank you." He wished to add, *for saving my life,* and *I'm in your debt,* but that was too much and he left it for another time.

Anya hurried from the small chamber, eager to immerse herself in some task that would clear her mind. She made for the kitchens, but the cook had the evening meal well in hand, and Anya wandered out to the steps beyond.

A sharp wind, scented with woodsmoke and a hint of rain, blew in from the south. Low clouds grayed the sky, and the tops of the trees disappeared into their pillowy depths. Over the walls she could see the church spire of the village, and a cluster of sounds hung in the heavy air—the low grunt of a sow in the pen, a wavery screech of children playing, the cheerful complaint of gossip among the girls in the kitchen.

Her heart slowed a little as she stood there, breathing deeply. Sharp slaps of wind cooled the heat in her cheeks, and her hand began to feel again of itself, not the broad power of the knight's fingers. Such big hands. Anya had not realized until her hand disappeared into the flat palm how very large a man he was. She wondered now how she and Geoffrey had managed to lift him to the mare. God's grace, she supposed.

Restless, she lifted her skirts and descended the stairs, wandering toward the inner gates without much thought. Beyond, in the outer bailey, she found a favorite place on a small rise of winter-dry grass where her only view was the thick forest beyond the manor. Here it was silent, and she could forget the villagers who might starve before next year's harvest, forget her resentment of her brother John, who wandered some alien land to atone for what he saw as his lack of courage, forget the manor and all its needs.

The knight would live.

She tried to quell the thready trill of excitement the knowledge gave her, but could not. Even sleeping in the light of a single candle, he was more virile and beautiful than any man she had ever seen. More compelling than she'd ever dreamed a man could be.

Until today, she had not seen his eyes clearly. She believed you could judge a man by the light in his eyes, and in many years had not been wrong.

Her heart skittered again. The knight's eyes were just the shade of the sky overhead, the color of water-laden clouds. Deep and clear, fringed with black lashes uncommonly long. And like a window letting in light, the shadows in them changed and flickered and fled, then reappeared.

He had secrets. And he was intelligent. Those were the things she saw in his eyes. Both she had already known. His brow bespoke the intelligence, and why else would a knight be so far from his lord if he did not have some secret?

She had not been prepared for the shocking ripple of longing his open eyes would give her. Even with the growth of beard on his cheeks and his yellowing bruises, he stirred her.

She was not given to such swooning idiocy. For years she had listened to the titterings of maids and the lustful pantings of the guards, not understanding what moved them so. And she'd been thankful for the lack.

Now a stranger—who might be a criminal or a bandit for all she knew—had plucked the dormant music of her blood without speaking a word.

With a sigh, she lifted her knees and crossed her arms, then buried her face in the crook of her elbow. It was foolishness to feel this—but she could not overcome the sense that with the appearance of the knight in the forest, her life had shifted irrevocably.

The thought frightened her. At the hands of men,

she had known naught but pain and betrayal. It was only the helplessness of this one, who needed tending like a small beast or a child, that made her feel differently. It was dangerous to think elsewise.

Gritting her teeth, she forced herself to remember the grunting and painful pawing of the brigand who had raped her. She called up violent memories of his filthy odor and the grime on his lips and the way he had kissed her, thrusting his tongue into her unwilling mouth.

Familiar revulsion filled her. And when her thoughts crept toward making a comparison of the gilded knight and the vile bandit, drawing the difference between them, she forced her mind away.

When he next awoke, Christian first noted his head no longer ached. He opened his eyes at the lack of thundering between his ears, pleased he could see better, too, and the stiffness of his neck had eased.

At the crook of his throat was a tiny soft lump of warmth. When he stirred, the lump moved a little and rattled to life. A cold nose touched his chin, a soft head slid along his jaw. Christian chuckled, lifting a hand. A cat.

"You must be well treated to be so bold," he said. The creature was yellow-eyed with a multicolored coat. By the gloss of her fur and the flesh on her bones, she ate well. After a leisurely stretch, she curled again under his chin. Christian smiled. He must have been sleeping a long time for the cat to grow so comfortable with him. Lazily, he rubbed her ears, amazed to find such pleasure in so small an act. His life had been dangerous and filled with movement. Hitherto he could not remember when last he had lain still long enough for a cat to creep close.

In his sleep, Ysengrin made tiny yipping noises, and his feet began to dream-run. The cat lifted her head to see if she ought to be alarmed, but Christian could tell from her content that Ysengrin had let her have free run.

The door opened and the woman—Anya?—bustled in, not seeing that he was awake. She carried a bowl and dry cloths. Taking advantage of her unawareness, he watched her.

The veil and fillet were gone, and he could tell it had been a busy day. She wore a simple green kirtle with the long sleeves tugged up to her elbows. The garment fit loosely, as if she had lost weight since it had been made, but a stained apron tied around her waist showed there were still curves enough at breast and hip. The unruly hair had probably been braided in the morn and ignored since, for curls escaped around her face in beautiful, untidy tendrils. One trailed along her shoulder in a corkscrew.

He rubbed the cat's head lazily, watching the woman through half-open eyes. A deep sense of comfort enveloped him. She blew a strand of hair from her face, wiped her hands on the apron, put something in the water. The scent filled the room.

Not once did she look at him as she made her preparations. A busy woman, he gathered, and he was one more task she had to tend before she could find her own bed for the night.

As if girding herself, she took a long deep breath and turned toward him. Finding him awake, staring at her, she started visibly. "Oh!" Her hands suddenly gripped and worried each other. "You are awake!"

He smiled a little. "Aye."

Two deep angles of color slanted downward over her cheekbones and her gaze flickered away. "You might have warned me."

"Why?"

"So that—because I . . . 'tis no matter." With a distracted wave toward the water, she said, "I came to wash your wounds, but perhaps you'd rather eat? Broth can only hold a man your size for a little."

As if reminded, his stomach gave a sharp rumble. "Aye," he said with a chuckle. "I would eat."

She smiled—a calm and natural expression that sent the tilts of her face into a mischievous order. "'Tis time. You have lain here nigh on a week with only ale and what broth I could force between your lips." She moved to the door and called orders to someone beyond. "How much have you moved?" she asked Christian, returning to stand beside the bed.

"Little." He glanced at his near-useless left arm. "'Tis difficult."

"I will help you sit, at least halfway." Lightly, she spatted the haunch of the cat. "Go, Esme."

"Can you not move her to my feet?" Christian asked. "She gives me comfort."

The woman gave him an odd glance, but did as he asked. "Careful," she said. "She's a glutton for affection and will be your slave if you tend her too much." But as if to belie her words, she lifted the cat to her lips for a quick cuddle before she put her down. "Does not your dog chase cats?"

Christian glanced at Ysengrin. The beast padded over to lean against Anya's leg, giving Christian's hand a lick in greeting. "No. I found him when he was but a week old. He did not learn the ordinary habits of his kind."

She moved to his head, a rolled blanket in hand, which she lay beside him. "I will slip my arm behind you to help you up, but will need you to help me as much as you're able."

He nodded, bracing himself for the pain. Before it came, he found himself enveloped with the warm sweetness of woman-scent. Her hair brushed his cheek. He didn't move, but only looked up at her face, so close to his own. "Perhaps," he said with a smile, "I might just rest this way for a little?"

"You must indeed feel better if you're able to be so wicked. Come—help me." She slipped her arm beneath his head and urged him upward.

Now the splintering agony sounded. Against all his will, Christian groaned, shoving with his right arm to attain some semblance of sitting. The effort left him dizzy and palsied, but at least he was upright. The furs slipped down his chest and he glanced toward his broken collarbone.

"There was naught we could do for it—by the time we found you, it had begun to heal poorly. Other than breaking it clean again . . ." She lifted her shoulders. "It seemed unwise. You were so very ill."

Christian touched the uneven place. "'Tis clean enough," he said and looked at her. "My lady, you saved my life. I'll not quarrel over a badly set bone."

A servant woman bearing a trencher of meat in sauce and a tankard of ale bustled through the door. She was a young, handsome girl, with an overabundance of breasts and a saucy, rosy-cheeked health. "Ye getting back to yeself, eh?" she said with a broad smile. "Milady's been fussing over ye for better than a week and wouldn't let nobody help her, either."

Christian grinned and cut a glance toward milady,

who bent over the water, stirring it as if some sorcery was at work within. "Thank you, Mary," she said.

With a wide-eyed shrug that said, "See what I mean?" Mary flounced out, not without turning at the door to give Christian an expression he understood quite well.

Her departure left a small, awkward silence in the room. Anya stood at the table, her face turned away from him, and again he caught an odd vulnerability in the curve of her neck. He inclined his head and said as gently as he was able, "Lady, I am near to starving and your servant left the food too far from me."

"I'm sorry," she said and smoothed an escaped curl from her face with a fluttery movement. It promptly fell out of place again as she settled on a stool beside him. She handed him a wooden cup and he found within a good red wine. "To build your blood," she said.

He drank deeply, trying to think when he had last drunk wine. "By my measure I am already much in your debt," he said, handing it back to be refilled. "Now wine will muddle my weakened brain and I shan't be able to say it well enough."

He wanted to coax another smile to her lips, but she only bent over the trencher and settled it on his lap. "There's no need," she said. "God leads where God will. 'Twould have been my sin had I left you to lie there."

The meat was richly seasoned, in a thick gravy with bits of onion and apple. He savored it, closing his eyes and leaning back.

"Now you have your supper—will you share your name?"

Soberly, he looked at her for a long moment,

another morsel of meat in his fingers. "Who is your overlord?"

She raised her brows. "It matters not. I am mistress here, as I told you. I will answer only to the king for my actions in my brother's absence."

Christian measured her. Leicester stood in Lancaster's holdings, but the woman seemed to mean what she said. She would go to the king, not the earl. And the king, for all his troubles, was still Christian's ally.

The woman waited calmly, her eyes not wavering from his face. To buy a moment, he picked out another bite to fill his mouth, looking away from the straightness of that gaze.

"Have you some price on your head?" she asked.

"No," he said, for in truth, there was no legal ban on him. His father would kill him soon or late, but there would be no sanction for it. It would be done in secret and stealth, as the cardinal did all. "I am Christian de Morcerx," he told her honestly. "Late of Edward's army in the borderlands."

"How came you to be in these woods? That is a journey of some distance."

"I know not." Bleak flashes of memory skittered through his mind. He willed himself away from them. "I can tell you only there is a powerful man who wishes my demise," he said. "It seems he was not successful this time."

She stood and clasped her hands together. Before she spoke, he saw she measured him, and her words. A wise woman, then, as well as beautiful.

"My guards were unhappy when my page and I dragged you here," she said. "And with good cause, for there is some dispute over this fief and I have small hold on it. The season has been lean and I know not how everyone will be fed until next harvest." She paced as she spoke, but now stopped and leveled her dark gaze upon him. There was nothing mischievous about the angled face now, only a sober strength he found stirred him far more.

"If there is aught I should be warned of, I give you leave to tell me now. I'll not force you from this place until you are able to defend yourself, but if you have put the manor in danger, I would know it."

Christian sighed, suddenly weary. "In all fairness, my lady, I know not. I thought myself I had been forgotten until the knaves seized me at the borderlands." He pushed at the soaked trencher. "I have eaten my fill."

She removed it and poured more wine for him. "I have wearied you with my questions," she said and pressed her fingers to his brow.

Her cool touch soothed him and he let his head fall back, closing his eyes. "Who knows of my presence here?"

"None but the manor—and perhaps the villagers. More than I would like, but one cannot halt the flow of gossip."

There was a hint of bitterness in her voice that made him think she had some personal acquaintance with the evils of loose tongues. He opened his eyes. "How is it you have no husband, my lady?"

"The story is long and sordid," she said, smiling as one would smile at a child. "You are too weary to hear it now. Rest."

Christian disliked that tone, disliked that she seemed to see him as some pitiful thing to be healed, weak and helpless. He was a knight of Edward the king. With his sword, he'd laid low legions of men; with his smile, he'd seduced a legion of women.

And yet this one was unmoved because she saw him as weak and broken.

Her gaze caught in his. All at once, Christian saw there a long sorrow, at odds with the curve of her lips. For the space of a half dozen heartbeats, she did not look away, and he let himself drift in the unstill waters of her eyes.

Nay, she was not unmoved, only strong and wary, as was wise. He saw, too, the dormant pain there. A pain not unlike his own.

She moved away. "You must sleep," she said quietly.

He let her go, watching as she gathered the bowl and trencher, and felt lonely when he was again by himself with only a cat and dog for company.

3

William of Winterbourne, known to his fellow canons at Lichfield as Brother Simon, hurried across the courtyard of the abbey. A cruel wind cut through his habit and slipped below the bunched fabric of his cowl. At the abbot's office, he paused to catch his breath and wipe windblown moisture from his cheeks.

"You called for me, abbot?"

The abbot, a rounded man with a fringe of gray hair, motioned for William to enter. "Aye. There is news I wish to share."

"News?"

He turned toward the pale light falling through the thick glass of the window, holding up a leaf to study with his glass. "As you are aware, the holdings of the cathedral fared poorly at the harvest this year."

"Aye, as did the whole kingdom, it seems. I have

had a letter from my sister at Winterbourne, asking my help."

"Have you now?" The abbot turned, his blue eyes piercing. "'Tis that very Winterbourne I've asked you here to discuss—a rich fief even in poor times."

"Even they suffered this harvest, abbot. My sister fears the peasants will starve if she cannot find some way to help them." He folded his hands tightly. "She appealed to me for assistance."

The abbot smiled. "I trust you did not give it?"

"She refuses to allow John to be declared dead," William replied, not without a touch of anger.

"Foolish chit. Does she not understand her dubious position? No husband or father or brother? 'Tis madness for a girl to run such a wealth of land alone."

"But by the terms of John's pilgrimage, there is naught I can do without her. Unless she volunteers to turn the fief into my care, she is free to starve as she wishes."

The abbot flipped the leaf in his hand, deceptively calm. Few would have caught the involuntary blink of one eye, or the rigid stance of his spine. "Winterbourne is a fat little chicken, even if these lean times have thinned it. Surely," he said in a silky tone, turning to look at William, "she might be persuaded."

William did not immediately answer. The abbot had never met his sister Anya, had in his mind a vision of some frothy noble maid. Loath as William would be to speak it aloud, the girl daunted him with her sharp intelligence and fierce, stubborn ways. Well William remembered how his father had sworn that it was Anya who should have been his heir, for she alone held the spirit of a warrior in her breast. She alone had mastered the accounts and the subtleties of running a fief.

And always she had been the thorn in William's side. "What say you?" the abbot prompted.

William worried one thumb against the other. Long had the abbot lusted for the rich holdings of his family; it was the promise of those lands that had given William such quick advancement within the ranks. He found he had done well, in spite of his father's disdain for his lack of knightly skills. His future in the church seemed assured.

Winterbourne, a simple country fief, was the star amid the lands the family held. And as she always had, Anya stood in William's path with her fierce refusal to release Winterbourne to him. If the fief could not be delivered to the Church, William would spend his life in some remote outpost, his rich ecclesiastical career in ashes.

Finally he lifted his head. "Perhaps she can be persuaded." Stubborn she was, but never stupid. If she could not feed the manor, soon or late she would give in. At the moment, he did not see how to force it, but he would give the matter some thought.

Anya sat in the window seat of the solar, blinking hard in the fading light of late afternoon. Only three or four more stitches and the sheet—her last bit of mending for the day—would be finished.

But her eyes seemed unwilling to cooperate. Even when she lifted the rough linen into the gray light falling through the open shutters, she could not see well enough to take those last stitches. Her back ached with sitting in the cold spot, and her head pounded with a relentless dullness like the distant sound of horses on the road.

The week had been a long one. As if the struggle to stretch their stores through to next harvest weren't enough of a trial, the weather had worsened. Each morning Anya rose to thick mists or cold, pouring rain. Throughout the manor, the sound of sneezing and coughing became as common as the sound of logs crackling in the hearth. The rushes stank of dampness no matter how she ordered them stirred, and she kept a hawkish eye on the stores of grain for signs of blight.

With such dank weather, the fevers could not be far behind. By the Thursday following Candlemas, half the manor and a good portion of the village were abed. It seemed not to be a fatal disease, though one of the cotters lost a baby, and Ethelda the Old finally succumbed to the chest ailment that had so wearied her the past year. The rest fell to bed, sniffling and sneezing and shivering with fever, and there lay a week or ten days, then arose thinner but healthy enough.

The illness left great gaps in Anya's work force. She found herself one day baking bread and tending the ovens and hearths, another day lugging stores, yet another carrying slop to the pigs. All in addition to the ordinary run of her tasks.

This morning, she'd risen before the sun to collect nettles, supervised the meager dinner they'd eaten at midmorning, then turned the rushes herself since no one could be spared but a guard—and in such uncertain times, it was unwise to leave too few men at the gates.

Now she had been sewing for hours, her most loathed chore. With a low noise, she dropped her hands to her lap and leaned her head back against the stone wall. From the kitchens came the faint sound of Mary, laughing at the no doubt bawdy story some man told. The rain that had threatened all afternoon began to fall with soft intent to the already saturated earth. Anya rubbed her temples with cold fingers, thinking she should get up to find herself a tincture of Saint Benedict thistle and perhaps a wash for her weary eyes, but could not seem to give the order to make her legs move.

In the Hall, Geoffrey began to play his pipe and tabor, blowing sweet, light notes into the gray day. Anya smiled. Like her brother John, Geoffrey had an unerring ear for music. The piece he played now he'd heard only once from a traveling minstrel at Lammastide. His voice was sweet and pure. Often he sang and played for her on these cold winter evenings; but he, too, had been ill and only the day before had climbed out of his bed, wan and thin, but cheerful.

The lure of the sound roused her and she closed the shutters to the rain. Leaving the unfinished sheet in her sewing basket, she went in search of the boy.

In the Hall, servants were setting up tables for supper, and the smell of the meal was carried through the doors from the kitchen to pluck at Anya's belly. Barley soup and bread tonight.

The sound of the tabor drifted from the small room behind the hearth where the knight yet stayed. Anya smoothed her gown and tucked a lock of unruly hair back into place.

But before she could reach the room, a hated voice pinned her with an imperious, "My lady! A word."

The pounding in her temples trebled as she wearily swung around to face Father Gerent, the village priest. He waddled forward, his belly swinging side to side below his stained robe like the stomach of a pregnant sow. His nose and cheeks showed the mottled red staining of a heavy drinker, but for once the small, washed-out eyes were clear-sighted. He meant business.

Anya placed her body in the open doorway between the wounded knight and the priest, unsure what had brought him to the manor. "Father Gerent," she said drily, "what drags you out on so dank a day? Have you come for wine to replenish your stores?"

"I have not come to minister to the damned," he said dismissively. "But the villagers have told me of the knight you harbor here in secret. I have come to hear his confession, if he chooses to give it."

Anya didn't move. "I give no leave for your rituals under my roof."

"Will you damn all in your employ with your heresy?"

"I am no heretic," she said, lifting her chin. "Only mere woman who will not be cleansed. And I make no move to stop any here from giving you your due, in your church."

The priest stood on his toes to peer over Anya's shoulder. "Sir knight," he called, "would you say your confession and take the Holy Blood of our Lord?"

Anya fixed her hands on the threshold. "Not in my house," she said fiercely. "When he may walk, he will walk to you, I have no doubt."

At her side, Ysengrin suddenly appeared. As if sensing Anya's dislike of the priest, he let go of a soft, warning growl.

A strangled sound of laughter came from the knight. The priest's face colored, but when he spoke, his voice was surprisingly calm. "I will return when 'tis more fitting," he said.

Anya knew when to retreat. "Please do." But she did not move from the doorway until he had safely disappeared through the doors to the kitchen.

Servants, stunned into silence by the confrontation, stared at their mistress. With a frown, she clapped her hands. "What are you looking at? Get to work or we'll all go hungry tonight."

They hastily turned back to their tasks. With a sigh, Anya let go of the threshold and went inside the chamber. Geoffrey, his hair wild without brushing, sat cross-legged at the end of the pallet, holding his flute. The drain of the fever remained in the wan color of his cheeks, but his eyes were animated as he greeted her.

Propped against the wall, a coverlet around his shoulders, sat Christian. He smiled. Yesterday, Anya had washed his matted hair for him, and it gleamed as bright and pale as candle flames, falling in thick waves around his commanding face and powerful shoulders.

As ever, Anya's heart skittered at the sight of him. "You look well, my lord," she said, settling on a stool.

"All thanks to the good lady of the manor." His oddly pale eyes, which might have seemed frightening in another man, turned in friendliness to her. "'Twill not be long now, I think, before I'm wielding again my sword."

Geoffrey paused midnote. "You have no sword!"

Christian nodded in mock sobriety. "Aye, there is a quandary."

"There are swords aplenty here," Geoffrey said eagerly. "When you are up and about, I will show them to you. Perhaps one will fit your hand."

Christian glanced toward Anya, a glimmer of shared

and secret humor around his sensual mouth. "'Twould be a great kindness, child."

"Truly," Anya said, "the swords of my father and brother yet remain at Winterbourne—though a knight must grow attached to his weapon, you cannot leave us unarmed."

"Agreed." Ruefully, he touched his injured shoulder. "Though 'tis some time yet till that day."

Ysengrin slumped against Anya's leg. She rubbed the great head with a smile. "I am honored you thought to protect me, good beast." She glanced at Christian. "I've grown quite fond of him."

As if he understood the words, Ysengrin turned and gave her wrist an adoring lap of his tongue.

"Ysengrin, you traitor!" the knight said. "'Tis I who have tended you these many years and yet you desert me at the first touch of a noble lady's hand."

"He is only grateful that I dragged his master back to life, I think." Anya looked at Christian. "He was so sorrowful in the forest, I nearly wept—though Geoffrey here squealed like a babe at the sight of him."

Geoffrey frowned. "I thought he was a wolf!"

"He is a wolf," Christian said. He snapped his fingers and Ysengrin obligingly padded over. "I found him as a pup, caught in a hunter's snare. His mother had been killed by a boar."

"Do not people fear him?" Geoffrey asked.

"Aye, but so they fear a knight and his sword. Fear is not always so terrible."

"Can he tear the throats of renegades?" Geoffrey asked eagerly.

"Aye," Christian said, lifting his brows. "Their throats and faces and bellies. He's fierce, is my Ysengrin."

Anya laughed. "Geoffrey, he is teasing you! Do not always believe the tall tales of knights. Like troubadours, there is often more drama than truth in their stories."

Stephen, the guard, brought Anya a packet. "A messenger delivered this now, my lady."

"Let him sup with us before he returns," she said, and turned the parchment over to see the seal of her brother William.

Her weariness had faded with the simple conversation in this room, but now her headache leaked back. The note was terse: unless Anya would agree to declare John of Winterbourne dead from his long pilgrimage, William could give no help.

For an instant, she closed her eyes in painful disappointment, then turned toward the candle burning on the table. Grimly, she put the note over the flame until it caught, and held it in her fingers until it was nearly consumed. Without proof, Anya would not allow her brother John declared dead, and would starve herself before she allowed good Brother Simon to bully her into declaring it so.

She looked up to find both Christian and Geoffrey watching her. "'Tis no matter," she said. "Geoffrey, take your flute and play for the messenger. Tomorrow you'll return to your duties. This night, entertain a poor weary monk who has traveled far in dismal weather."

He hurried to do her bidding, pleased to escape for one more evening the chores he found so odious. As he departed, Anya watched him fondly. "I think he would like nothing more than to don a troubadour's life when he is able."

"'Tis not so bad a way," Christian said. Esmerelda, the cat, crawled into his lap, and he stroked her absently.

Anya thought of the wandering minstrels who sought shelter at the manor in return for a night or two of entertainment before they passed on toward the larger households along the road. "Aye," she said quietly, "but he will be a knight, as is expected."

"Such are the times."

The times. Anya sighed, filled suddenly with a bleak sense of hopelessness. If William gave no help, the stores would soon be gone. And yet, if she gave in, William would send her to a nunnery.

That she would not do.

"Is there some trouble, my lady? I can do little but listen—but I note well your revulsion for the priest, to whom another might take a weighty burden."

A flush of blood heated her cheeks as she thought of the confrontation Christian had witnessed. "Truly, if you wish to make your confession, I will send for the priest. I do not wish to keep you from your devotions."

In his mist-colored eyes she saw no censure. "It will be no burden to wait until I am able to walk to him myself, my lady." He chuckled. "The priest risks death by entering here, I think."

Ironically, she lifted a brow and smiled a little. "You miss little."

"'Tis the habit of a knight."

"Only those with more sense than blood lust." Unable to hold the bold, bright gaze, she flipped idly at the burnt parchment on the table. "My troubles are no different than any in the realm tonight. I am only weary, and can see no end to this dismal weather." She shrugged. "The harvest was poor, and the war with the Scots has drained us. Now Lancaster and the king . . ."

"Aye." He rested his head against the whitewashed stone behind him. "The king will have Lancaster's head for the death of Piers Gaveston. Edward lives to avenge his friend."

Curiosity piqued, Anya inclined her head. "Did you know the Gascon?"

"Aye, from the time we were children." His gray eyes twinkled. "A man with a tongue like a razor, and Lancaster could not bear it. I think sometimes the more it annoyed him, the more Gaveston attacked."

"They say Gaveston made fools of himself and the king, at the coronation and whenever he was able."

"Perhaps. I liked him—he made sport of the seriousness of the court, and he was the best knight I've yet seen."

Anya laced her fingers together, weighing whether she ought to ask the question on her lips.

Christian seemed to sense her hesitation. "You want to know if the rest is true—if there was an unnatural relationship between them."

She blushed, but could not deny her curiosity. She nodded a little ruefully.

"I cannot tell you, my lady. What I saw was the deep love of two brothers, men alike in their love for things beyond kingmanship. If Edward had been given it to choose his life, my guess is that he would not have liked to be king, but some simpler man. He has a great love of a laborer's life." His clear gaze met hers. "It matters little, I think, what passed between them in private."

Anya felt a stirring at the quiet dignity of his attitude, and a little ashamed of her own prurient desire for the intimate details of those in the stellar realm of kings. "You must think me the worst sort of gossiping spinster."

He laughed. "Nay. Many words come to me to describe you, my lady, but those are not among them." The laughter seemed to cause him pain, for he winced and reached for his shoulder protectively. Anya stood to give aid, but he waved her away. A grimace crossed his face.

In a moment, he eased back against the wall. "'Tis only natural to be curious about the doings of kings," he said. "And our Edward is not like many other kings of memory."

"True enough," Anya said, although she did not remember any king before this one. His way seemed kingly enough to her.

Esmerelda had been alertly watching Ysengrin's tail and chose that moment to pounce, capturing the feathery mass in her paws. The dog looked at her with a puzzled expression, then made a quiet whining noise in his throat. Anya chuckled and bent down to scoop Esemerelda into her hands, then deposited her back on Christian's lap.

It was only as she straightened again that she realized how intimate they were here, alone but for the creatures arranged all about them. From beyond came the usual bustling of preparation for the meal, and the light notes of Geoffrey's pipe, joined now by a viol and the low, warm sound of a man singing a ballad.

But here was silence.

Again Anya was seized with the powerful awareness of her own body, with the the movement of limbs and angle of neck. Her breasts felt bulky on her chest, as if she were newly come to her form. Since earliest youth, this strangeness had never come upon her.

It made her awkward, and conversely even more aware of the knight's body: the extraordinary, simple beauty of his arm, muscled and lean, covered below the elbow with a glaze of golden hair; his chest and waist and the presence of his legs below the coverlets.

All the awareness made her thick of movement and she clumsily backed away, bumping the table in her haste. The iron candle sconce rocked dangerously and she caught it before it fell.

Blushing, she clutched her skirts. "I will fetch your soup."

"My lady," he said quietly and even his voice caused her discomfort. It was a deep and cultured voice, and sent a rippling down her spine.

Anya halted but could not raise her eyes or speak a single word.

"I mean not to fluster you," he said gently. "I will not leap upon you, nor snag you and pull you to my bed against your will. In truth," he said with a hint of humor, "even if I did, you'd be sore disappointed in my abilities."

Amused and disarmed, Anya gave him a reluctant smile. "I have not been in the company of any such as yourself, my lord. I am a foolish woman and clumsy in such exalted company."

He laughed outright, showing his strong teeth and the long column of his brown throat. "Perhaps you might soothe another man's ego with such flummery, but you forget I have seen you moving hither and yon and ordering your servants and guards and accounts with the surety of a queen. Mere woman you are not."

He inclined his head, and a new expression crossed his face. "Nay," he said with an uptilted brow. "I think you would like to lie with me, and know not how to ask it."

Painful humiliation pierced her, mixed with disappointment that this noble and beautiful knight was, when he awoke, no different from any other man. "'Tis sure that men all believe themselves enchanting. I see you are no different."

"Nor did I claim elsewise," he said with a tilted half-grin that—curse him—had the exact effect upon Anya that he wished it to have. In the newly present expanse of her body, a tingling grew. His eyes, bold and promising, met hers steadily. "And well I note you did not say me nay."

Unwittingly, he had given her the tool she most needed—disdain. "I will, then, my lord. Men are either foolish or brutish creatures. They chase battles and angels and heaven, or trample all below their arrogant feet with no care for the life and dreams of others. They take what they will or shun it all for the sake of piety while the peasants starve and the land goes wanting."

She found her breath coming quickly and a dangerous emotion boiled her breast. "'Tis not that women are mere or foolish or weak. 'Tis just that you are so far below us, I have no use for you."

As she turned, he snagged her hand. As it had been once before, she could not free herself. She spared her dignity this time by refusing to try.

She was unprepared for the moist heat of his mouth upon her palm, unprepared for the jolt it gave her to feel his mouth pressed to flesh that had hitherto never felt gentleness but only work.

"I tender my deepest apology to you then," he said, and she felt the words brush her fingers on the whisper of his breath. "I only wished to take your mind from the troubles I see in your face."

"I would that my troubles were so easily forgotten," she said crisply, and tugged her hand from his loosening grip.

Rattled, she bustled from the room. That night, she gave leave to Mary to take the knight's supper to him, for she would not chance another encounter with him until the burning imprint of his lips on her palm faded.

4

Christian shifted restlessly on his pallet, dozing only sporadically. Through the small opening high in the wall above his head came the sound of rain pattering against the evergreen trees beyond. All else was silent in the manor, for long had the inhabitants been abed.

His fitful movements dislodged the cat curled on his belly. Unperturbed, she stretched and circled, settled again in a comfortable hollow of his body. Christian touched her delicate head absently, wishing he might curl up the same way.

Instead, he found himself staring again at the single candle in an iron sconce on the rough table by the wall. Anya had left it burning for him. It shone softly in the darkness, lulling him.

He dozed.

And dreamed of a brace of flickering candles. Against them his mother knelt, a shadow only, with a veiled head. Nearby her was a man, hidden by the gloom in the church. On the altar was a shining cloth woven with gold, and a reliquary shaped like a small cottage. The piercing aroma of incense filled the air.

The sudden movement of Esmerelda the cat jolted Christian awake. With a sigh, he opened his eyes, realizing sleep would not visit him this night.

By his count, he'd lain in this pallet for seven days, perhaps more, since he did not know how long he'd been unaware of his surroundings. Anya had told him it was nearly a fortnight. Nearly three weeks then. The lack of activity was beginning to wear on his patience.

It was time for him to test his strength. Three nights before, he had tried to walk around the small chamber. After so long a time abed, the exertion had been nearly beyond managing. His legs and body were sound, but the injury to his head made him dizzy; standing upright to walk for any distance made him feel faint, and though the pain in his shoulder had lessened, it was still none too kind.

Restless, he shifted the covers from him and swung his legs over the side of the bed. Cold winter air struck his body. The bracing feel of it chased away the lingering cobwebs of his fitful dozing. Slowly, he shifted to his good side, holding his left arm close to his ribs, and strained to sit upright. Ah, there.

He sat on the edge of the pallet, his bare feet against the cold stone floor, waiting for new flurries of pain in his shoulder to ease. Slowly, slowly, he stood up.

Ysengrin, slumped by the door, sleepily eyed his master, lifting his tail in a wag. "Aye, my friend," Christian said, "I will attempt again to be a man instead of a weak child."

The dog lifted his head and the tail wagged a tad

more enthusiastically. With a half smile, Christian took an experimental step, then another and another. A small, dull throb began low in his head, but 'twas not so much it could not be ignored.

He reached the far wall in five steps, hobbling hardly at all. Feeling a curious, broad triumph at the small victory, he grinned. "There!" he said to his dog. With a flourish, he turned and flung out his arms in victory—

And nearly buckled under the sharp splintering pain that cracked through his shoulder and chest. He cried out involuntarily, instinctively reaching up to protect the spot with his other hand, and leaned against the cold wall to brace himself. Ysengrin whined softly, and padded over to lick his knee.

Christian breathed slowly, waiting out the fresh onslaught, closing his eyes to reach for that bright brace of candles from his dream, a vision that had long been with him. He knew not what it meant, or whence it had come, only that he returned to it instinctively at moments such as this, when it was urgent he marshal his thoughts.

The door opened and Christian jerked his head up in surprise, for he'd heard no noise from beyond. He thought it perhaps the serving girl who slept in the loft nearby the hearth wall—a sloe-eyed beauty from the village who worked in the kitchens and some-times brought him food.

Instead it was Anya who poked her head in, looking first to the pallet where he no longer rested. Unable to move quite yet, he simply stood silent in the shadows, cursing his palsied, womanish weakness and the nakedness that made him feel doubly vulnerable.

"My lord?" she said quietly, poking her head in

further. A gilded mass of curls captured the illumination from the candle as she leaned in. He had never seen her hair loose before, and in spite of himself, wished for a long look.

Not now. "Go, Lady Anya," he said, still waiting for the fresh waves of pain to abate.

Instead, she came into the chamber, adorned in a loose belted robe. Below was her kirtle, made of some fine, thin fabric. The unbound hair tumbled like an army of sprites over her slim body, well past her hips. When she spied him, an expression of concern crossed her face. "Let me—"

"No!"

The rough shout halted her, but she did not retreat. Only looked at him with that patient gaze. "'Til now you've not played the stubborn male. Do not be so foolish as to do it tonight."

"I weary of this incessant coddling." He flung himself upright, gritting his teeth against the agony it caused, and drew himself to his full height, which was a head and more above hers. "Leave me in peace."

A glimmer of suppressed laughter showed in her eyes. Christian glared. He'd warrant the serving girl would not laugh. Women were not unmoved by his body, and yet this one stood there, arms crossed, one eyebrow cocked in amusement. Amusement!

He took a step toward the pallet, ignoring her. His hip bumped the table and a wooden cup fell to the floor. Briefly he thought of stooping to pick it up and knew he could not manage it. His face felt hot with effort and fury; when Anya stepped toward him, he jerked away and grunted at the pain. "Leave me!" he shouted.

She did not go. Christian made his way to the pallet, but found he had no wish to be abed again. For all his humiliation in being thus observed, the new strength flowing through his limbs was heady indeed.

"My lord," she said quietly.

He turned his head, cautiously this time, so as not to jar the wasps in his arm. She held before her a man-sized robe lined with fur. "'Twas my father's." Her lips quirked. "If you wish to wear it, you will likely be forced to accept more of my coddling, for I doubt you can don it alone."

She treated him like a brother, or a child. For a moment, he eyed her, weighing the choice. Without her, he would be forced to wrap himself awkwardly in the fur from the bed. With a noise of irritation, he turned, avoiding her eyes, and held out his good arm for the robe.

He smelled her as she slipped it on him. A warm scent of fire and woman. Her hair brushed his belly as she came around to tie the belt. Again annoyance pierced him. Had it been the serving girl with the sultry eyes, he doubted he would now be dressed. She would have helped him, aye, but not like this. He'd wager a princely sum that she would find a way to ease some of his frustration, injury or none.

"Such a scowl!" Anya chided lightly.

He looked at her, cursing again the simple, businesslike way she cared for him. "A man wearies of lying abed."

There it was again, that pixie's grin that tilted her face into a mischievous order, giving her dark blue eyes a glimmer of secret laughter. "So come, my lord, and sit by the hearth with me this night. There is little fire left, but the coals are yet warm. We'll have a cup of ale and play a round of dice and perhaps your ill humor will be cured."

"All right, then. Mayhap it will help."

"Dare I ask if you need lean on a mere woman's shoulder, my lord?"

Reluctantly, he grinned. "'Twould be a kindness, my lady. Unless you'd rather kick this horse's ass a bit?"

"'Tis tempting," she said. "See that you mind that surly tongue and I'll not be forced."

But still, for a moment, they simply stood there, she smiling up, he ruefully returning the expression. "I had not noticed you were so small," he said, reaching for her. "I'll have to kneel to lean on your shoulder."

"Pah!" she protested. "You are simply viewing all from a giant's height!"

She slipped her arm around his waist, not so near he could feel her contours, but only a hint of her warmth. Although he felt fairly certain he would need no assistance walking from this small chamber into the Great Hall beyond, he let his hand settle on her shoulder.

"Lead on, my lady."

By the saints, it was good to be upright! His head ached only a little and strength flowed back into his limbs with a great rush.

And yet he allowed her to walk slowly beside him, taking pleasure in the sway of her body, the simple sweep of her skirts against his foot, the chary brush of a breast against his side, the fluttering curls over his hand on her shoulder.

She settled him in a great chair by the man-sized hearth and tossed a fur over his lap. He flung it promptly aside. "I need it not."

With a shrug, she poured ale from a tankard into

wooden cups, one for each of them, then settled on a bench nearby the chair. A trio of fat candles burned nearby the table, casting uncertain light over all, catching in her hair. One long, exuberant lock lay in a thick coil over her shoulder and trailed down her arm. He found himself lifting his hand to touch it, and stopped, drinking deeply of the ale instead. "Why are you not sleeping, my lady?"

She gave him a small shake of her head.

"Worry," he guessed. "The peasants and your brother?"

"There is much to think on tonight," she said, but whether in agreement or not, he could not tell. "In truth, my father used to fret that I slept so little. I seem not to need the same rest as others."

And yet, weariness marked her. Burdens showed in the slant of her shoulders, in the taut look of her mouth and the shadows below her eyes. "But tonight, there are worries, yes?"

"Yes," she said on a sigh. "Without my brother's help, the villagers will starve before next harvest."

"That brother whose note you burned over the flame?"

She ducked her head, letting her hair fall forward, but it was not quite enough to hide the rueful grin on her mouth. "That was a foolish defiance, to burn it. But aye, that is the brother of whom I speak. Good Brother Simon, too pious to lower himself to save the lives of a score of villeins."

"He is a monk?"

"A canon at the cathedral in Lichfield. But he holds the rest of my father's lands in trust for my other brother's return from the Holy Land, and he could lend assistance to us here if he so chose."

"And he will not? Why?"

Anya took a breath as she chose her words, and Christian noted with a tiny portion of his mind the way her breasts lifted against the silk of her robe. "Of all the holdings, Winterbourne is most often richest—and would be so this year in spite of the poor harvests had not an army of knights trampled through the fields on some business of Lancaster's." She shook her head. "William—the good Brother Simon—wishes for me to declare my brother John dead so the fief will pass to the monastery."

"Where is this other brother?"

"Only God knows," she said. "He departed on a pilgrimage five years ago. We've heard no word of him since."

"Ah. So William means to starve you out."

Anya nodded, giving Christian a bitter smile.

It was a common ploy. A sense of admiration touched him at her simple, quiet will. A poor harvest and ruined crops, the threat of starvation, and some war with the church he had yet to unravel—few women would be equal to the challenge.

And in spite of all, when she stumbled over the body of a wounded knight in the forest, she had made room for him, too.

"You are a woman of rare courage, Anya of Winterbourne," he said quietly, inclining his head. "I think I've not a met a woman like you before."

"If your intent tonight is seduction, my lord," she said with more weariness than he could fathom, "I will see you quickly back to your bed."

"I spoke sincerely, my lady."

Distrust was in her eyes as she looked at him. "As do all men."

"Not all," he returned quietly.

Her gaze lowered to the rushes and Christian watched her, his curiosity stimulated. She stirred him. Candlelight illuminated the edges of her cheek and nose, and ran a capricious finger over the line of her lips, full even in repose. "You are a puzzle, I admit," he said at last.

Briskly she stood up to stir the coals. "Puzzles are often dull once solved."

He smiled as she bent to poke a glowing log. Fire flared up brightly, and against the new red light, the tantalizing outline of one full breast showed plainly. His body noted the fact with a leap of approval.

"True," he said lazily, admiring the sweet curve, knowing she would likely crown him with the poker if she knew his thoughts, "but often the delight of uncovering the secrets can be well worth the journey."

She straightened and Christian hastily raised his eyes. "'Tis hard to figure, for example, whether you be innocent or fallen, my lady."

A flicker of pain made him regret the impulsive words. "Both," she said. "Ask me no more."

The words stirred his curiosity all the more, but he thought better of saying so.

Both, she said. Both.

"Forgive me," he said. "That was rude intrusion."

She paused a moment longer, but relented. "'Tis pleasant to have a companion in these dark hours."

He extended a hand. "Come—I will fold my hands like the true and gentle knight of a ballad."

That brought back her impish and skeptical smile. "Dice?"

"Aye."

She had secrets. So did he. Well he knew the need

to protect them. He'd leave hers buried as she wished.

The resolve did not lessen his slow wish to bed her, but the least he might do to repay her kindness was be one thing she could count on her side.

With regret, he cast one last, longing glance over her alluring figure. Pity, he thought, and gave his attention to the game.

They played dice for a long time. Long enough that Anya felt her walls of defense against him crumbling and had to work hard once more to school her face and voice and eyes into some semblance of simple friendliness.

Oh, but it was a trial! She took deep pleasure in his company, and liked the cover of darkness and the sweetness of having a man to herself like this.

As they played their game, she said cautiously, "You are not married, my lord?"

His mouth quirked in a half grin Anya felt throughout her body. "Nay. I am only a poor knight-errant, and none would have me. All my riches were in my sword and my battle skills." In the low light, his gray eyes twinkled. "I used them to terrorize peasants and ravish unwilling women."

She laughed, in acknowledgment of her tirade on the evils of men a few days earlier, but sobered. "You must admit soldiers often leave a village less whole than when they found it."

"True enough, my lady." A grimness tightened his mouth. "I do weary of battle."

"Were you long with Edward's army?"

"Aye. I've been with him ten years. He gave me shelter when—"

Anya waited, but it seemed this was part of his past he had no wish to share. She wondered what his story would be, but did not push. Time enough later, if need be.

"I've served the king since the mass knightings at Westminster." He lifted his cup and Anya watched his strong, graceful hand lift with a greediness she tried to hide. "None who saw that day will forget it," he said with affection in his tone. "Such merriment!"

"You are fond of the king."

"For all that it is unpopular to admit such now, I am. He may not be all some wish in a king, but he is no demon, either." With a weary gesture, he put the cup aside. "He gave me shelter when I was most desperate, and has given me means to live these many years."

A pallor had grown under his flesh as they spoke. Anya stood. "Come, my lord. You'll not rise again for many days if you weary yourself much longer here tonight."

He did not pretend to dissent, only hauled himself to his feet. Anya took his arm carefully. There he stood a moment, as if gaining his balance, and she was forced to tilt back her head to see his face.

Light caught in the stubby whiskers of his unshaven chin, and without thinking, she lifted a hand to brush them with her fingertips. "We shall see to your shaving tomorrow."

At the look in his eyes, she snatched her hand back, appalled at her boldness. It was only that he had been in her care and she had not yet learned to give distance. After a fortnight of tending him, she was as intimate with his body as she was with her own.

With one long-fingered hand, he reached out to capture a curl from her shoulder. "I would that I were more of a man tonight," he said in a low voice.

A prickling awareness filled her, deepening the restless feeling born in her when she'd found him standing in beautiful splendor in the hearth room.

In defense only had she warned him away. He'd think her foolish beyond measure if he knew how she longed to explore the places of his body she'd tended so intimately, explore them with greater intimacy yet.

Now, aware of his chest so close to hers and the strength of his legs, she allowed herself to wonder what it might be like to be seduced by such a man, to lie with him.

The imagining made her grow lumpishly mindful of her own body, the strange weight of her breasts and a hot movement on the backs of her thighs . . .

Flustered, she reached for him, to offer her shoulder, but in her coltish awareness she bumped against his side and jarred the injured arm. His breath left him on a little grunt of pain. Contrite, Anya reached toward his waist to steady him. Instead, unrestrained as it was, an unmistakable sign of desire bumped her wrist.

Shocked, she pulled away again, turning in confusion. Her feet—even her feet were too big, too much, too new!—tangled in the hem of her gown and she stumbled, narrowly missing an embarrassing fall only by flinging out her arms. "God's teeth!" she swore.

Behind her, Christian chuckled softly. The sound increased her embarrassment by half again and she fought against the urge to bury her face in her hands. After a moment, he said quietly, "My lady."

When she did not respond, he took a quick step

toward her and snagged her arm just above the elbow. With steady strength, he drew her close.

"Aye, you rouse me," he said, and his voice was like the amber light of sunset. "'Tis no cause for shame. You are beautiful and charming and I've long been without a woman at all, save the whores in the camps."

She glanced up in surprise. It was not wise. Once again she was snared in those eyes, ghostly gray and made more so by the fringe of dark lashes. There was gentle humor there, and frank appreciation. How rare it was to see humor in a man's eyes! How rare that one would sit for hours with a woman in comfortable chatter. How rare it was that he held her gently, that there was gentleness all through him. She swallowed.

But, too, she must have moved, for all at once she was not standing sideways, but face to face with him, her neck arched backward. Anya wondered fleetingly how he could be so unconcerned with the evidence of his desire standing at such attention. The thought made her chuckle and she met his eyes more easily. "I wonder how it would be to be a man," she said.

His hand moved on her arm, lightly. "At moments such as these," he said with teasing around his mouth, "'tis very pleasant indeed. How is it to be a woman?"

As if to coax a particular answer from her, his hand slid up her arm and curled around her neck beneath her hair. His thumb caressed her throat.

Anya felt dizzy. "Let me help you to your bed, my lord," she whispered.

He laughed, and let go of her to shift his robe into more discreet order about him. "And once there, will you tell me how it is to be a woman?"

"That takes little telling," she said with a sniff, moving close to brace him. It was harder now than before to affect aloofness. He smelled of straw and warm male skin. Against her arm, his back and side were hard muscled. All the parts of him she had washed and tended now seemed alien and full of mystery. Her voice came out on a breathy note. "Women labor to serve men. 'Tis simple enough."

At the threshold to the small chamber, he paused, his arm lingering on her shoulders, and turned a bit to look down at her. "That tells me naught of how it feels."

She heard his voice through her ears, and it rumbled through his chest, too, into her body through his ribs. In surprise, she looked up—in time to see his head lowering as he trapped her there against the door with his big body, all angles and planes. A sharp, new pleasure pricked her. She could not have moved had she tried.

Her stomach ached as she gazed up at him in anticipation—of what she could not name. In extraordinary detail she saw the shine of his unshaven beard around his mouth, which seemed an oasis of tenderness amid those prickles. Her breath caught as the light glimmered over his eyes, showing a darkness and hidden danger she had not seen before.

By the saints, he was a beautiful man.

With a sudden move, he straightened. His jaw set in a hard line. "'Tis wrong to tease you so, my lady," he said gruffly.

Her cheeks flamed. Tease, was it? With a prideful toss of her head, she helped him to the bed and stayed still till he settled on the edge. Her robe had loosened in their journey. She let it gape as she reached for the furs—they would see who teased whom.

He made no move, but she saw his gaze slip over

the thin fabric of her chemise, then shift away. A flush burned on the high slope of his cheekbone.

Anya lifted a brow. "Forgive me, my lord," she said softly and pulled her robe together over her breasts. "'Tis unkind to tease you so."

She whirled, leaving him to his own devices, but not before she heard a chuckle rumbling low from his chest.

Men, she thought, making her way to her own chamber. What an arrogant lot they all were!

5

In the morning, the wet, gray weather broke at last. Sunlight, cold and wan but sunlight nonetheless, danced into the Hall beyond Christian's chamber. The sight of it made him ache to fill his lungs with the smell of the outdoors. Too long he had lain in this room.

Geoffrey, the young page, fetched a serving woman for him. Together the pair helped him don the robe Lady Anya had brought to him the night before, and led him outside to sit on a bench in the bailey. Once settled, he said to Mary, "I would bathe today." He touched his chin. "And shave."

She gave him a saucy grin. "I'll tell milady."

Christian frowned. The task lay in Anya's realm, that much was sure. And yet he felt a strange reluctance to be tended again by her. He disliked the roles they had taken, he the weak, she the strong. "So be it," he said gruffly, seeing no other option. "But make it when she has little to do. I dislike adding work to her day."

Mary laughed, showing strong white teeth. "Oh, ye needn't worry, milord." She lifted one straight black brow. "Tasks there are she dislikes, but you ain't one of 'em."

He winked in thanks, and it was only as she walked away that he wondered why he had not flirted a little more. He frowned. Tillie, the sloe-eyed kitchen maid, had this morning given him a deliberate and generous glimpse of her bountiful womanly charms when she brought his breakfast—and seemed a bit miffed when he showed no more than an appreciative smile.

Two women willing and, he was sure, skilled—yet his recalcitrant lust seemed fixed on another. On one who had a low opinion of men, who was both fallen and innocent.

His scowl deepened. 'Twas unlike him. He should beware such foolishness. Grateful he was that she'd saved his life, but it would be madness to let himself think his heart had been entangled.

Mary brought him ale and day-old bread, and gratefully he sat in the sunshine, leaning against the wall. Around him, the manor inhabitants bustled about on their morning chores. A boy shoveled out the stable. A girl dumped slops into a trough for the pigs. Chickens roamed free, pecking at the earth and clucking quietly in the morning.

Into the homey stillness came the sound of bells ringing out the hour of Tierce. With surprise, Christian realized the village lay just beyond the walls. He smiled. Winterbourne was a rustic village in the wilds of country England—and to his surprise, he found it uncommonly pleasant. It was a relief after so long a time of roaming and fighting. Always fighting.

He breathed deeply of the cool morning air, smelling the animals and a wisp of roasting meat and the simple, mingled scents of the forest beyond the manor. How long since he'd sat still enough, had been unburdened enough to savor such subtle notes in the wind?

A long time. Too long. And he had thought, through that long miserable ride over half of England, a journey he remembered only in broken bits, that he never would again.

The knowledge struck him anew: he was alive. What a wondrous accomplishment it seemed! Perhaps when he was a bit steadier, he would go to the village priest and make a proper confession. It had been long since he'd done so. Perhaps, too, it would draw the ire of the priest from Lady Anya. She played with fire, there. More than she knew.

He wondered where she was this morning. And, more wickedly, wondered if she could be coaxed into celebrating his return to life with him. If his lust was fixed so, he might as well indulge it where it lay if he could. If she were willing. Surely an unmarried woman past twenty had once or twice lain with a man.

He could not linger long here, that much was sure. Soon he would have to ride to France, to find what malfeasance his father was about.

His father. Christian drank of his ale, staring toward the bare branches of trees waving into a pale blue sky, and pursed his lips. His knave of a father.

There was no doubt Etienne was about some evil if he had tracked Christian down, but Christian still could not understand why he had not been killed— nor why, after ten long years, his father suddenly wanted him dead again. Archbishop d'Auch was a rich and influential man in France. Some even said he would one day be pope, which was certainly one of Etienne's ambitions. Christian well remembered that boundless determination.

But what could such a man fear from a knight-errant in the north of England? Why now?

Once before, Etienne had ordered his own son killed. At fifteen, Christian had fled France and found shelter with his boyhood friend, Piers Gaveston, who had grown close to the crown prince of England. Wise beyond his years, canny and skilled in the knightly arts, Christian had made a place with Edward. Christian's father had seemed to forget him.

The murderous plot Christian had uncovered so many years before surely held no sway now. Christian had learned with great bitterness how closely the church protected its own. High-ranking members like his father could confess and be forgiven any sin, even murder.

A crow fluttered to the ground in the courtyard and began a noisy squabble with a chicken over some scrap of food. Christian watched them, frowning. What, then, could his father fear so intensely he would risk hiring assassins to kill his son?

The puzzle made his head ache. Across the yard, he saw Anya come through the gates, Ysengrin at her heels. At the sight of her, Christian's uneasiness fled. A far more pleasant emotion took its place.

She looked fresh this morning for one who'd been to bed so late. But she had told him she slept little. It somehow did not surprise him. There was an excess of energy about her in all that she did. Even now, there was quick strength in her walk, a swinging purpose in her arms. The woolen cloak she wore billowed away from her body, showing the simple green gown that was a bit too large for her.

Geoffrey settled next to him on the bench. "Do you think she's beautiful?"

Christian roused himself. "Who?"

"Why, my lady, of course," Geoffrey answered with the air of one long-suffering. "She is the only woman in the yard."

"Ah, so she is."

"So do you?"

Christian eyed the long strength of her limbs, the unruly curls clinging to her cheeks no matter how she brushed them away. She had not seen Christian and Geoffrey sitting here, and so Christian had the rare chance to watch her unobserved. "Women at court do not look like your lady," he said, smiling.

"Oh." Geoffrey sounded crushed. Clearly he thought Anya quite beautiful.

"At court, the women wear jewels and fine fabrics and they would not work the way your Anya does." They would titter behind their hands at the simplicity of her clothes and the way she left her hair simply hanging down her back in that fat braid.

Christian glanced at the boy, who stared at Anya with a curiously pained expression. Christian smiled. "They are all twinkling little stars," he said, and looked back to Anya. "She is a great, shining sun, warming everything around her."

Geoffrey grinned and Christian saw in the dark blue eyes and narrow face something of the woman they discussed. "Have you been long with her?"

"She is my mother's cousin. I came to live here when I was small, too small to remember anything but this. My parents died of a fever. My lady is very kind to me."

"So I have seen."

"She is kind to you, too."

"Aye." Christian lifted a hand and pointed. "When you seek a bride yourself, boy, remember your Anya and how strong she is, how kind, and you'll not go astray."

"Do you like her?"

Christian grinned. "Aye. And I think she's beautiful. Does that make you happy?"

"Well, she is not married, nor even betrothed."

Ah, so the child played matchmaker. "Nor am I," he said quietly. "But your Anya deserves more than a knight who has nothing." Who also, he added silently, must seek out a murderer before that murderer killed him.

"She fancies you."

"I know." Christian nudged the boy to end the conversation. "Go help her finish her tasks so I might have a bath. This beard itches."

Mary relayed to Anya Christian's wish to bathe, and Anya sighed. After the night before, she did not trust herself to perform the task without foolishness, but there was no help. The task lay in her realm, and perform it she must.

There was no time until the midmorning meal, which he took with them in the Hall for the first time, had been served and cleared. Anya had to tend to the complaints of her bailiff and steward, and heard a furious complaint over some disputed field that had been overrun by a cow. Aware of Christian sitting in a com-

fortable corner of the Hall, listening, Anya felt exasperated. What difference did it make in a fallow field?

But as she had learned to do at her father's knee, she
listened with all appearance of serious gravity and made
settlement between them. Finally she found leave and
crossed the room. "Come, my lord," she said briskly.
"We should not tarry, else some other problem will
appear to delay us further."

"By the saints, I would not ask it if I were not half
mad with the itching," he growled. "If I so burden
you, let the servant do it."

At this display of ruffled male pride, Anya sighed.
"I've said I will do it and I shall. Come now, Mary has
made the tub ready for you."

With a hard set to his jaw, he shrugged off her help
and walked on his own, slowly to be sure, but on his
own, to the room behind the kitchen, humid and fra-
grant. A wooden tub filled with steaming water awaited.

Aware of sharp anticipation and dismay mixed in
almost equal measures, Anya sharpened a shaving
knife on the whetstone while Christian disrobed.
Mindful of his wounded dignity, she let him step into
the tub without assistance, but watched from the corner of her eye to make certain he needed no help at
the last.

He leaned on the edge of the tube with his good
arm and stepped in, gasping softly at the heat of the
water. For a moment, he only stood there, obviously
waiting for his skin to adjust to the temperature.
Anya was sorely tempted to drink her fill of the sight
of him, but demurely focused on the knife.

Mary popped around the door. "Will ye be needin'
anything else, milady?"

Anya glanced up in time to see the greedy glimmer in

the woman's eye. Frankly Mary appraised Christian's fine male form, and Anya saw Christian preen a little, his shoulders suddenly straight, his chin tilting up at an angle.

"That's all, Mary," Anya said, raising an eyebrow.

Mary let loose a bawdy laugh, but obligingly closed the door.

From below her lashes, Anya watched Christian, waiting for him to settle in the water. It seemed he would not for a long time, and each minute he stood, she was more tempted than ever to turn and stare. From beyond the door came the noise of the girls in the kitchen and the clanging of pots, the smell of good food. Within was only silence and the whisper of the knife against the stone.

Endlessly the moment stretched. Anya at last found herself tempted beyond help. Biting her lip, she lifted her gaze. His back was to her, and a long, muscled back it was, nicked with the scars of battle. His golden skin gleamed invitingly.

The shoulders she had already seen were broad, and his joints loose and gracefully made. But there in the humid room, her gaze snagged on his buttocks, high and round and firm. Not smooth like a woman's flesh, but hard and dusted with the same gilding of hair as covered the rest of him.

With a sense of congestion and shame, she tore her gaze away. "My lord, the sooner you settle, the sooner I may begin."

He shot her a glance, and Anya recognized the same wounded male pride she had seen before they came to this room. He had been waiting for her to admire him, as Mary had!

Smiling secretly, she bent her head. Vain as a cock

in the yard, she thought, and wondered why it so tickled her.

Evidently he realized he'd lost the battle, for he finally
sank into the hot water, leaning back with a groan.
"God's bones, that feels good."

Anya took a gauze bag of herbs from the table and
dipped it into the water, letting it warm. She pressed
it gently to his wounded shoulder. "'Tis marigold and
comfrey to speed healing," she explained.

"It stinks." He did not take it off, however, only
settled more fully in the water, his eyes closed.

Anya knelt beside him to soap his face with a brush.
The chin and jaw, the small strip between his nose and
upper lip. Then she shaved him efficiently, scraping
away the rough bristles of beard. Gently she washed
his hair, probing with two fingers at the wound on his
scalp. "'Tis healing well," she commented.

He only grunted, leaning forward at her direction so
she might wash his back. The bruises were all but gone,
faded to dingy yellow. Again she wondered what had
happened to him, but did not ask what, if anything, he
remembered of the attack.

When she finished, she stepped back, shaking
water from her hands, relieved she had managed to
perform the task without a single humiliating moment.
Her dress front was soaked, but that was usual and
she didn't mind it in this warm room. Bending over,
she lifted the bag of herbs and dipped it into the hot
water again.

"'Twould be best for you to stay here a little, with
this on your shoulder." Her hand below the water
grazed his hip.

He opened his eyes lazily. Flustered, Anya brushed
with the back of her wrist at the escaped curls cling-

ing to her cheeks and pressed the bag to his shoulder again.

Christian reached up and brushed the offending locks from her cheeks. "There," he said quietly.

Until that moment, Anya had managed to keep her yearning for the knight at bay. But now he looked at her with that languid expression, his skin dewed and freshly shaved, and the bright awareness of her own body rushed in anew.

As if he sensed the awareness, his gaze traveled over her face, pausing at her lips, passing over her neck and to the front of her dress. In reaction, as if he had touched her, Anya felt her nipples grow taut and pointed in the warm room.

He smiled.

She pushed away from the tub, managing somehow to keep from stumbling or otherwise creating havoc with her sudden clumsiness. "Rest there, my lord. I will send Mary to help you finish in a little."

"My lady," he said, and there was command in his voice. With panic, she heard him stand up, heard the water splash as his body dislodged it. "I am finished now."

For a long moment she stood there frozen with her back to him. Then, because to do elsewise would show her to be even more foolish than he'd seen already, she picked up the length of linen she had earlier cast over a chair, and turned around slowly to offer it to him, her eyes demurely lowered. Her hands trembled.

He stepped into the circle of the towel, covering himself. When she would have stepped away, he snagged her with his good arm.

With a small, pained gasp, she came against him, her hands splaying on his chest. A tremor passed through her body, but there was no resistance in her; she could not seem to give the order to her legs to move her away. He smelled of the herbs in his bath and she could feel the dampness of his skin through her dress.

"This time, I do not tease," he said, gripping her tightly.

Between them was the towel and her worn gown, all wet and quickly warmed by the heat of their bodies. "You would like to touch me," he said, quietly, bending his head to whisper the words over her mouth. The breath of air tickled her lips, and she found herself opening a little to the taste, aching for the feel of his mouth. He bent close and brushed her lips lightly with his own, just the merest taste. She weakened against him, her hips seemingly without bones.

"Touch me as you wish, my lady," he said in his amber voice. "I give you leave."

Then he was kissing her, suckling at her lips in the most delicious way, flickering his tongue over hers, urging her to open to him.

She parted her lips with sudden eagerness, a whirling excitement rushing through her. He made a soft sound and slid his tongue inside her mouth, gently at first, then with more violence.

"Touch me," he said and captured her mouth once more, as if to give her courage.

Anya lost all sense of herself as he coaxed her, and found her hands moving of their own accord over the planes of his chest, over his arms.

She thought of the long expanse of his back and moved her hands along his sides, reveling in the taut, sleek feeling of him below her fingers. She inched her way below his arms and around to his back.

Now he clasped her head in his great palms, tilting

her head to plunder her mouth. The towel dropped away.

She touched the narrow path of his spine, exploring the firm power of the muscles on each side, the small rise of bones. Against her belly she felt the nudging of that unruly male instrument, and it gave her courage. She edged downward, all the way down his spine.

There she paused.

He made an approving sound, urged her closer, kissing her more deeply. Anya let her hands drop, curve around the firm buttocks and found a delicious combination of textures, hair and flesh and hard muscle that shifted when he moved.

For long moments they were thus, kissing and touching in the warm room. Christian made a low, hungry noise as his hands roved over her shoulders, touched her hair, and Anya arched ever so slightly against him, hungry for things she didn't know how to name.

Abruptly, he lifted his head, and she heard the harsh grate of his breath as he pressed his forehead to hers. His hand circled her neck, restraining her.

Startled back to the moment, Anya realized how boldly she clasped him, and jerked her hands from his body.

He let her go. "Forgive me, my lady." With a move more dignified that she could believe, he retrieved the towel and wrapped himself in it, backing away. "I forget myself, forget your place. You are no serving wench, but a lady of the manor."

Anya brushed away a loose curl, trying desperately to regain her composure. And yet, when he moved away, she found her eyes clinging to the long beautiful length of his arms, muscled and damp and strong, with a kind of hunger she had never known she could feel.

"It would be well for me to heal quickly and leave this place as soon as I am able," he said. "Else I'll seduce you and shame us both."

Anya's chin tipped upward in pride. Once again, he had toyed with her. Once again, she had allowed it. "Aye," she agreed. "And henceforth, I will let Mary tend your needs."

She left him.

Long after the household was abed, Anya sat by the hearth in the Great Hall, bent over her account books. The light of a candle flickered unevenly over her work. She was not yet ready to sleep, but the close scribbling wearied her eyes. Reluctantly, she closed the bound pages and put aside her quill.

Through the embrasures that led to the bailey, she could hear the faint voices of guards on the walk. Gathering her shawl close about her, she wandered over to peek through the openings. Against a high, round moon, she could faintly make out their shadows, but no more.

This restlessness had long been part of her life. She knew not why she felt the need to roam while others slept, unless it was the quiet she found in these late hours. It was peaceful with all the world abed, and she had time to think and ponder subjects far and wide in ways she could not when all were clamoring about her, asking this and that, nagging for her opinion, demanding her judgement calls or asking for a key to the storeroom and spices.

Twice of late the cook had grumbled that she could

just as easily carry those keys as Anya—had she not been in the employ of the Winterbournes for nigh on twenty years?

Anya let her grumble and kept her keys on her girdle, measuring out herself the stores of grain and spices hawkishly. On feast days, she was generous, but in ordinary times, the manor could satisfy itself on simple, spare offerings. Better that than nothing when summer rolled about.

She longed to send out a hunting party, for a boar or hart, but knew not where Lancaster was these days and did not wish to lose her men to poaching charges. There were seven pigs, and some would no doubt fall to the cook's knife before summer's end, but the rest she wanted to save for breeding. Who knew what would come with the next year's harvest? 'Twas far better to prepare for the worst.

They survived well enough on the occasional brace of game birds or fish, the rabbits they kept in warrens in the baileys. Enough, if they did not let caution slip.

Settling the matters in her mind somehow eased her and she felt the pleasant languor of sleepiness flood her limbs. Carrying her candle, she headed for the solar, trying mightily to ignore the lure of peeking in on the knight, who no longer needed her each night.

But she had need of him, or at least the need of making sure he rested well. Cursing her foolish woman's weakness, she crossed the hall. The door stood ajar, and she pushed it with her fingers, holding her candle aloft to illuminate his figure on the pallet. From the embrasure above his head came cool moonlight.

He slept well, properly sprawled as men would do, in no pain that Anya could see. One great leg was thrown out of the covers, and his hair spread over the pillow like some magical fabric made by fairies. His face in such repose seemed youthful and less hard than when he was awake.

Feeling foolish but drawn, she crept into the room. To cover him, as she would Geoffrey. To look at him. The peculiar awareness of her body she felt in his presence came back, tingling over her skin. It was a pleasant feeling, once she'd grown used to it, one so pleasant she wished to feel it again and again, and only this wounded knight seemed able to bring it to life.

As she bent over to tug the fur from beneath his heavy knee and toss it over the exposed leg, she smiled, thinking of his temper in the bath earlier.

He was a large man, in all ways, and had to stoop to kiss her. The memory sent waves of shuddering weakness through her. She stared at his male beauty in the quiet and darkness with a yearning as vast as the sky.

How simple it would be to lift that fur and climb in next to him. His skin would be hot from the furs, not cool and damp as it had been this afternoon. He'd stir next to her, and waken. And then he might touch her breasts, or even kiss them, and she could taste again the deep, silky nectar of that mouth, hear him laugh in satisfaction when they—

Abruptly, before she could indulge the wish, she turned away, hurrying to the solar where she slept. As she curled into the thick warmth of her own bed, she realized she was quite lethally smitten with the knight. Mary, who snored richly beside her, had guessed, but she knew Anya better than most. If the rest of them saw—

Humiliation burned in her cheeks. Oh, what sport

they would make of her then! The dried-up mistress of the manor, swooning for the beautiful, straying knight. In her mind she heard the stories they would tell one another, the bawdy bed jokes they would make. Already, news of the knight's great virility was spreading through the village. Twice she had seen young village girls on thin errands to the manor, looking carefully about for him. Once they all caught clear sight of him, she'd no doubt be flooded with coltish, heated young things willing to offer him a little entertainment.

Shifting in the cocoon of her covers, she censured herself. No need being black-hearted about the whole thing.

Mary murmured in sleep and turned over, burying her face into the pillow. Anya peered at her in the darkness, wondering what Mary knew of such things as passed between a man and a woman.

Appalled, Anya hauled herself over, to face the wall with the shuttered windows. Cracks of moonlight fell on the floor, cold and lonely.

What would it be like to bed such a man? And once done, could she then go on as she always had, content with her life? Or would the new burning haunt her always, make her into one of the bawds she had seen on the roads to Lichfield?

A new flush of shame burned in her. It was sinful to even think such thoughts, and for all her quarreling with the church, she tried to live a moral life as well as she was able. Lying with him would be wrong.

And yet, he might be her only chance to know of such things. Already, his strength was returning. Soon he would be able to mount a horse and ride away from Winterbourne, and Anya would see him nevermore.

A tactile memory of his skin against her hands passed through her, renewing the restlessness in her limbs. She closed her eyes and thought of his mouth. Would tasting all of that male power be worth the loss of him, worth the tittering in the village, worth the sin against God? More, would it be worth the chance that all the rest of her life she would feel the lack?

She didn't know. And not knowing, it was perhaps best to avoid it. The saints knew well she needed no more trouble in her life. There was plenty as it was.

6

Anya pored over her account books. On scraps of used parchment, she scribbled plans and new balances, then scratched them out again, one after another. No matter what she did, how she juggled, there was simply not enough food to last through spring—much less summer, though once the land was green again, the people foraged well enough. The woods were full of things to eat.

With a soft grunt, she lifted a hand to her aching neck, and moved her head to ease the tightness there. It helped little, and with a sigh, she took a fresh sheet of precious parchment and dipped her pen.

Dear William,

Once more I appeal to your higher nature. And this time, brother, I am begging. On my knees, if that will help. The villagers we have known since childhood will starve if you cannot find it in your heart to assist us—as will I, your only sister. Can you not let the past slip away, forgive me the sins you feel I have committed? Name your price, and I will pay it, only do not ask me to leave the only home I have ever known.

Her stomach burned as she signed the missive. She hated having to ask again her stingy, ambitious brother, but there was no one else. Lancaster had not even given the courtesy of a reply when she'd sent word to him, and all his resources were tangled in his vindictive struggle against the king.

A gentle hand fell on her neck, a large hand, with a flat palm and strong fingers that kneaded deliciously at the tightness in her muscles. "So long a face, my lady," Christian said. "And so weary."

Anya knew she ought to duck away from the dangerous pleasure of the knight's hand, but she found herself unable to do it. Since the day in his bath, a week before, they had worked out a sometimes unquiet but careful friendship. She enjoyed his company too much to stay away from him completely.

A soft groan escaped her lips as the knots in her neck eased. New feeling flowed through her shoulders and arms, and even the threat of a headache slipped away. "Thank you," she breathed when he finished.

He straddled the bench next her and leaned sideways against the table, and gave her a grin. His bad arm was in a sling Mary had rigged for him. "'Tis the least I can do."

"You look well this morning," she commented, scattering sand over the ink to dry it.

"With good reason. Only my shoulder still needs healing. All else is well." He dipped his head to finger the place on his scalp that had been so noxious when she first found him. It looked clean and dry and nearly healed now. "You see what your wine and rosemary achieved?"

Anya nodded, smiling only halfheartedly. Her stomach made a noise and burned more fiercely. Wincing, she called to a servant to bring her a posset. "Would that my stomach were as well," she said to Christian.

He inclined his head, the strange gray eyes newly alert and wise. "I cannot leave this place, Anya, until I can ride and wield a sword. For all that I feel whole today, this shoulder will not mend for some time yet." He touched her hand. "Let me help you."

"Have you some spell to multiply the stores dwindling in the storerooms below our feet? Some miracle, perhaps, that will turn water to wine, or a heart of stone to one of flesh and blood?"

He looked at the letter. "The heart of stone belongs to your brother?"

She tried to keep the bitterness from drawing up her mouth, but did not succeed. "Aye."

"You say he will not help until you declare your other brother dead. What if you did that?"

"No."

"What would it change? If your brother yet lives, he will return whether or not he has been declared dead."

Anya drank the posset, hoping to ease the burn in her belly. "William will send me to a nunnery and the land will go to the church."

"Ah." He chuckled, and the expression gave his eyes a merry light. "And even I have seen how ill-suited you would be to the life of a nun."

Anya lifted one eyebrow and half smiled.

"What is this war you have with the Church, my lady? Or is it only the priest?"

She frowned. "'Tis dangerous to discuss the Church with a stranger."

Plucking the letter she had written from beneath her hand, he ceremoniously tore it in half. "I have my own war with the Church, my lady."

He had told her someone wanted him dead. She had heard tales of the harshness of the Church in France. With renewed interest, she looked at him curiously.

But since he had not pushed to learn her story, she would not push to learn his. Some things were better left unsaid. "Have you some plan?"

"Aye." A twinkle lit the pale irises. "I'm going to see the priest today."

"The priest!"

He leaned forward until the great swelling round of his upper arm brushed the slender length of her own. His hair, loose on his broad shoulders, seemed to capture all the light in the room. "Listen to me, Anya of Winterbourne. I have knowledge of these things, and I tell you open defiance will win you no friends."

Feeling betrayed, Anya narrowed her eyes. "Do not counsel me thus, my lord. I will make no confession, nor let that—that pig under my roof."

"I did not ask it."

"What then? He is no powerful Church official, of that you can be sure. He's only a drunken village priest."

"A priest all the same." Christian tore the parchment again, into four pieces. "What if word trickles back to your brother that some bold knight has come to the rescue of his sister?" He met her gaze. "A bold and pious knight, who will likely lead the straying Anya back into the fold."

She inclined her head. "Clever."

"Ah—I see you thought me only handsome."

She laughed outright. "What a vain sex are men."

Playfully, he touched her nose with one long finger. "Aye, and a wise woman never forgets it."

Geoffrey burst into the room, alight with excitement. "My lady!" he cried, skidding to a stop before the table, scattering rushes hither and yon. "Come quickly!"

"What is it?"

The elfin face beamed. "Snow!"

Anya laughed and hurried behind him. On the steps to the bailey, she paused to lay a hand on the boy's shoulder.

"Is it not beautiful?" he breathed, turning his face upward to the floating swirl.

Anya looked not at the weather, but at the child who so reveled in it. The flakes lit in his wheat-colored hair and in his lashes, and melted on his freckled nose. "Aye," she said, smiling fondly.

Sensing Christian beside her, she glanced up to find him watching her intently, an unreadable expression in his eyes. "I'll need a cloak," he said, "and a page to give me proper dignity since I cannot yet ride, even so short a distance to the village."

"Geoffrey," Anya said, pressing her fingers into his bony shoulder. "Fetch a cloak for my lord and one for yourself, and lead him to the village church."

"The church, my lady?"

"Aye," she said calmly. "He will make his confession to the priest. You will wait with him."

Eagerly the child raced to do as he was bidden, and Anya gazed after him with a smile. "He is smitten with you," she said to Christian.

"You're very fond of that child."

Anya swallowed, avoiding his sharp eyes. Beyond the walls, snow danced in the treetops and dusted all with soft silence. "He's been with me since he was small."

"Your sister's child?"

She frowned. "No, he is the child of my aunt, my father's sister. She died in a fever when he was three, and he was sent here to be fostered."

"He said his mother was your cousin."

A chill touched her. "Children confuse things."

"You spoil him a little. You should have children of your own."

Crossing her arms, Anya looked at him. "I have no husband, nor any wish for one. There it stands." She turned to go back inside. "I have work to do."

He caught her hand. "You are forgetting again, my lady," he said with a mocking tone.

"Forgetting what?"

"That men are vain creatures and wish hale thanks for each small task they perform."

A teasing smile curved his rich mouth, and Anya remembered with a sudden shock just how that mouth had felt against her own. A bloom of awareness touched her. "What thanks do you wish?" she asked softly.

He reached behind her. Anya felt a tug at her braid and he lifted her ribbon. "A token to carry with me." Playfully, he pressed the strip of silk to his lips.

Instantly, her braid began to unfurl. She caught the end in her hand. "Very well. If you will play champion, I can only gladly offer such a token."

He handed it to her. "Tie it around my arm."

Anya chuckled, but did as he asked. "There." She looked up to find him staring down with a very different sort of expression on his face. For a long moment, she was snagged in that gaze, with snow falling in thick flakes all around them, his lips soft as if he would kiss her, his eyes probing and hungry.

"You do not know it, Anya of Winterbourne," he said in a rich, low voice, "but you are a rare and beautiful woman. If I were not an honorable man, I would bed you before I left here."

She swallowed and stepped away. "'Tis well, then, you are honorable."

He smiled. "I wonder."

A thin road led from the manor gates into the village, following the edge of the community fields. Since Christian could not manage a horse, he and Geoffrey walked through the thick, swirling snow, passing a cow that wandered slowly toward the village, its bell ringing quietly in the gray day.

"Geoffrey," Christian said. "We are going to the priest to help your Anya. There are things I wish for you to do."

"My lord?"

"Simply be a page, as you might imagine one to be for the king. Speak for me, as if I find it beneath me to speak to such small folks as these."

Geoffrey brightened. "What shall I say?"

"Whatever comes to your mind. Do you know what it means to be haughty?"

The boy lifted his chin in the air and turned down his lips. With one hand he made a gesture of brushing away imaginary obstacles in their path. "Move along," he said in a disdainful tone.

"Good!" Christian chuckled. "Who do you know who is thus?"

Geoffrey rolled his eyes. "The boys from the monastery, when my lady's brother comes to stay. They will not even speak to me."

"Well, now you may put their ways to good use. The priest must believe I am a great and powerful knight who will stand with Anya against all comers."

"Will you?"

"As long as I am able."

Geoffrey gave him a quick look, but said nothing.

The church was the finest structure in the village, as well it should be, and was built along the lines of many of the churches of Christian's boyhood, indicating the influence of the French in this place. The stone walls had been newly whitewashed this past season, and some industrious carpenter had built new shutters for it as well. In spite of the poor harvest, the villagers had not stinted on the church. It spoke well of them.

As Christian and his page approached the church doors, they drew the curious stares of the ale mistress and the men gathered at her gates. Two small boys, barefooted and raggedly dressed, skittered behind them, giggling as they dashed behind a tree, then behind a well. Christian glanced with amusement toward Geoffrey, who smiled in return at the antics of the boys, but quickly rearranged his face into proper sobriety.

The porch of the church was recessed, made of dark wood. It smelled of earth and the fresh winter wind. Christian stepped up to open the heavy wooden doors and felt a flash of—something—only half-remembered. It struck him again, more forcefully, when he went inside. For a moment, he paused in the doorway, struggling with the nagging sense of familiarity. When had he seen this place? Into the gloom he stared, seeing a scattering of candles lit to the saint on the altar. To Geoffrey, he whispered, "Who is the saint there?"

"Saint Thomas à Becket."

Christian nodded. The martyred Becket, one of his favorites. It seemed a good omen.

From some dark recess bustled the priest. Christian had not seen him clearly when he came to the castle. The man was short and stout, with a bulbous nose made red with wine.

"Father Gerent," Geoffrey said, "I have brought the knight we found to you, at his request."

The priest's mouth turned down in surprise he couldn't quite hide, and for a moment, he gaped at the knight. He recovered. "Welcome to our humble church. What might I do for you, my son?"

"He wishes to make his confession," Geoffrey said, and Christian managed to keep himself from smiling.

"Indeed?" The priest puffed like a bird ruffling its feathers. "I went to the manor for just such an errand, but the lady would not let me in."

"And so I have come to you," Christian said, drily. "But I would be done by Vespers."

"Of course, of course." He waved them toward the confessional.

Affecting piety, Christian knelt before the altar. He said no prayer, but only moved his lips. Unlike Anya, he did blame God. What King would allow his subjects to abominate all his laws, let his most trusted servants rape the land and all the people? So God had done, in Christian's estimation.

In the confessional, he knelt and paused to consider his purpose and how it was best served. Having been more or less in the bosom of the church leaders all of his young life, he knew well the primary motives of most of them—greed and lust. This priest looked past lust for women, and perhaps had been celibate in that way, but he had greed aplenty if Christian were to judge by that reddened nose.

To give credence to his confession, he began with a host of petty sins committed since his last confession a year before, that one given to a parish priest in the borderlands after a gruesome battle. Christian had been caught in the fight, in the wild noise and chaos of horses surging and swords clanking against mail and spurs and stirrups, the thunk of metal piercing flesh of horse and man, the thick, heated smell of blood and sweat and fear, that once scented was never forgotten.

He'd been attacked from behind, and his horse started, whirling with him astride. The stallion bolted. Before he could calm the beast, he'd trampled a girl in the village to death. Not more than twelve, she had lain broken and innocent in a pool of her own blood, victim of foolish power struggles between kings.

Not even the confession had cleansed him, nor had he expected such. Now he spoke in a low voice. "As I heal, Father, I fear my manhood has seized control of my senses, and from morn to night I think only of bedding a certain woman."

"Ah, there is a coil," the priest murmured. "Have you spoken with this woman?"

Christian smiled. Church laws had forbidden priests from knowing the identity of women in illicit liaisons, for fear the priests would exploit the knowledge. In this instance, Christian wished the priest to know exactly toward whom his lust was directed.

"Daily, Father," he said. "She is like an angel with

her golden curls and eyes like a lake at dawn. My heart pounds—and I fear I will not always be able to restrain my impulse, much less my thoughts."

A long silence met this impassioned speech. At last the priest roused himself. "'Tis plain you must remove yourself from her presence."

"That I cannot do. The debt I owe is too great, and I fear I am not yet well enough to travel." He waited but the priest said nothing.

Christian frowned, wondering how close Geoffrey lingered. He peeked through the curtain and saw the boy near the front of the church, well out of earshot. "Father, 'tis urgent you give help so I do not soil my soul, nor that of this woman. I dream every night of her below me, and when morning comes, I cannot breathe for looking at her beauty." This last he said tongue in cheek. "Have you no advice for me?"

"Ah—mmm." Again the silence stretched. By God, the man was a dolt! "Perhaps you might stay in the village, far from the clutches of such a temptation." Primly, he added, "No decent woman would allow a man to stay who evidenced such lust toward her. Perhaps she is not so fair of heart as she is of face."

Christian grinned. "Oh, but Father, she knows not of my passion, for carefully have I hidden it. My only wish is to serve her, not sully her. Is there not some chant you might give? Some penance I might serve to remove my lust?"

Reluctantly, the priest at last offered a prayer for Christian to repeat at the moments of greatest temptation, and meted out a penance of Hail Marys. "In the end," he cautioned, "you would be well advised to remove yourself from her as soon as you are able."

"Thank you, Father, I will note your wise counsel."

Geoffrey rushed forward when they emerged, and ushered Christian through the doors of the church and into the square beyond. In spite of the snow, now falling in thick, fat flakes, there were villagers about, casually arrayed at the well or the alemaker's house. All turned as knight and boy emerged. Curiosity gleamed in their faces.

A girl no more than fourteen, with high round breasts and skin with the unblemished texture of rose petals, dipped her head coquettishly in his direction. Christian carefully ignored her, mindful of her mother hovering.

It was no vanity that women found him appealing, and Christian used it to his advantage when necessary. Men could not be charmed the same way, and he wished their support as well. Without abandoning the haughtiness he'd asked Geoffrey to affect, he nodded politely at several of them, then walked with clear, sure strides back toward the manor.

When they'd rounded a turn by a monstrous old pine, Geoffrey giggled. "Oh, in awe they were!"

"You did very well, young Geoffrey. Would that I had so quick and able a page."

The boy beamed. "Think you the priest will do as you wish?"

Christian raised a brow. "What do I wish?"

"For him to write to William?" He began the sentence as a statement, only rising to a question at the end.

Christian clapped his shoulder, his estimation of the boy's intelligence rising yet again. "Good." He nodded, picking his way around a muddy spot in the path. "Aye, I think he will worry now, and soon will send word that a brave and noble knight is smitten with Anya of Winterbourne."

Geoffrey laughed. "And he'll rush here to see for himself, and I will play page haughtier than any of those silly boys."

"So you will." Christian did not think it would be so simple as that. But it was a beginning.

Snow fell steadily into the night. After the bells for Vespers, Mary came to Christian's chamber with another fur for his bed. "The lady sent this to ye," she said, shaking it out. "The night'll grow chill and she don't want ye to take a fever."

"Send her my thanks."

Anya had avoided him since his return this afternoon. Finally weary, drained from even so small an errand as the walk to the village and back, Christian had retreated to this small room behind the hearth. Ysengrin padded after him and together they watched the snow beyond the embrasure high in the wall. It was restful.

He watched as Mary spread the fur over the already substantial pile. "Tell me something, Mary," he said.

"If I might."

"What happened to your mistress?"

A shuttered expression closed the open shine of her face. "Happened?"

"Why is she yet unmarried, so beautiful a woman as that? Why does she war with the priest? Was there some dishonorable man in her past?"

Mary pressed her lips together, staring hard at Christian for a long minute. She glanced over her shoulder, then crossed the room and closed the door. "'Tis better you hear the true tale than all the black rumors that are told."

"Sit, then, and tell me."

"Oh, no! She waits beyond." Clasping her hands in front of her, she said in a low voice, "My lady was raped by bandits in a raid when she was thirteen. Her parents were killed, and her brother John grievously wounded. The thieves left Anya and John for dead. Anya walked back here, naked as the day she was born, to get help for her brother. She couldn't speak, for the beasts strangled her, nor did she speak for months after, not until it was plain she was with child."

Christian closed his eyes. The simple seduction and desertion he had imagined paled in comparison to this. "Did the babe die?"

"Nay! They took it from her when it was born, as punishment."

"Punishment! For what?"

Mary kept her face perfectly straight, but Christian did not miss the irony in her tone. "'Tis well known a woman cannot bear a child if she did not enjoy the act. So said the priest when she came with child to him for sympathy."

He swore. How could such tales still be spread? How could anyone with a shred of humanity believe a thirteen-year-old girl, strangled and raped and left for dead, had found any pleasure in the act?

The story explained the enmity between Anya and the priest. And Christian was certain he would not care for William of Winterbourne. "So she yet harbors hatred for the priest, and he will not forgive."

"'Tis more than that. She would not go to the churching when her babe was born. Nor has set foot inside a church since."

From beyond the door came Anya's voice, raised and insistent, "Mary!" Then before either of them could move, Anya came through the door, annoyance on her pretty mouth. "How long can it take to spread a fur on the knight's bed? You have other work. Go to it."

Mary scurried by, color in her cheeks. Christian watched her go. "'Twas not her doing," he said. "I kept her talking all."

"I am no evil mistress, as you seem to think, my lord." She frowned. "The woman sleeps next to me, she eats well—as one can plainly see—and she has freedom to do as she wishes when I do not require her. But I see no reason she should stand about and gossip while I am working."

Christian heard her words, but over the fresh face and clear eyes, he saw a girl, silent with horror, with courage enough to walk naked through the woods to save her brother. Now he had the answer for her raspy voice. Like the soldier Christian had known, Anya's voice had been marred with strangling.

Dear God.

"Why do you stare at me so?" Anya asked sharply. She narrowed her eyes. "Was Mary gossiping about me?"

"No." He shifted, turning his face from her.

"Then what? Heard you some tale in the village? Did the priest tell you I am a witch who rides with Satan on the full moon?"

He laughed, in spite of himself. "No! I swear, Anya. I look at you only because you are a woman unlike any I have known."

She bowed her head. "Oh."

"Now I am weary. I bid you good even."

Without speaking, she closed the door behind her. Christian bowed his head and buried his face in his hands, a grief in his heart over all the ill the Church had spread in the name of mercy and goodness.

Innocent or fallen? he'd asked.

Both, she had answered.

In shame, he vowed he would not touch her, no matter how great the temptation—and much it had grown these past weeks. He vowed, too, that Anya would at last have her champion. She had saved his life. He would do what he might to serve her.

7

For more than a week, the snow stopped and started and the wind blew mercilessly in a wild, wet prespring storm. Around the manor, servants and guards began to sniffle and cough as they went about their chores, and from the village came news of another fever. Alarmed at the new illnesses, Anya called for larger portions to be served in the manor.

It was Christian who noted the flagging spirits of the villagers, and approached Anya with the notion of a single feast night. At first she resisted, too worried about the stores to even consider the notion. But when the weather continued, unbroken, she agreed. He promised his help, and gave it—gathering up men in a hunting party that brought back game birds and fish. A sheep was slaughtered and prepared.

So tonight, in celebration of nothing more than life itself, they feasted on rich pasties and stuffed capons, on subtleties and cheese. Wine and ale flowed freely.

Anya, weary as any of them of barley and sops, ate and drank with zest.

By happy accident, a trio of musicians bound for Lancaster's castle had appeared late last eve, weary and shivering, seeking shelter from the bitter weather. Christian had given Anya a great, teasing grin at that. "Even the saints approve our feast," he said. "They've sent minstrels for our pleasure."

Gladly had Anya admitted them for all that it meant more mouths to feed, for the bad weather would make the manor inhabitants restless, and good music went a long way toward calming bad tempers. Last winter, one guard had stabbed another a week past Christmas, when the weather had roared for better than a month, wet and gray and grim.

Stuffed near to bursting with the feast, Anya leaned back with a groan. "I cannot stuff another bite into my mouth," she said happily.

"Nor I," Christian replied. "What a splendid meal that was, my lady!"

Anya smiled. "So I see."

"'Tis well you do not serve such at all meals," he said, lifting his cup of ale, "or I'd be too fat to be a knight when I left here."

"No, my lord—for when you were able, I'd work the fat from you."

He chuckled. "And you would, too."

"Perhaps I yet will. The roof needs patching, and ill can I spare the men to do it."

"You seem willing to do all else, my lady. Why not the roof?" A teasing glimmer shone in his gray eyes. "Or have I at last uncovered something at which you do not excel?"

Anya tucked her lower lip between her teeth. She

leaned close and admitted quietly, "I cannot manage heights."

"Ah, I *have* bared a weakness."

"It pains me to admit it, but I cannot even walk the castle walls."

He lifted his good shoulder in a half shrug. "We all fear something."

"Is that so? What then do you fear, my lord?"

The animation fled his features and he gazed toward the leaping orange fire with a pensive expression. Anya regretted the turn of the talk, and wished to call back her words, to put that teasing light back in his eyes.

And yet she waited, admiring the play of torchlight on his straight nose and high brow, in the wheat-colored hair so thick on his shoulders. His jaw was hard.

"I fear a man," he said at last.

"The one who wants to kill you?"

He nodded, lifted his cup and drank. Carefully, he put the cup back on the table. "My father."

"Your father wants to kill you?" Anya asked, unable to hide her astonishment. "But how can that be?"

Christian shrugged, as if he did not know or care, but Anya caught a fleeting burst of sorrow in his eye before he shuttered it away. "A father is only a man. A man kills his enemies."

"Not his children."

He met her gaze soberly. "Yes—and I his only son."

"But then you are his heir!"

"It matters not. He needs no heir." Christian bowed his head. "Let's speak of it no more. Time enough to dwell upon what I face when I leave here. For now"—he inclined his head and she saw the effort he expended to reclaim his light charm—"I will renew my strength with this good food and the smile of a beautiful woman."

Anya let it drop, but a certain dread filled her. She did not look forward to his leaving, though she knew it must be. To know he faced such an evil as a father who would kill his own child made her feel ill.

To dull the sudden ache, she narrowed her eyes and tried to imagine what he might have been like as a child. Mischievous no doubt, and quick. She half smiled.

He caught her staring. "What?"

"I was trying to think what you might have been like as a boy."

He lifted a thick brow. She could see it pleased him to wonder. "And what did you decide?"

Anya lowered her lids and blurred the vision of the man. "Wild. Silly." She peered harder. "And you loved your mother very much."

"My mother?" A perplexed smile crossed his mouth. "There's an odd thought."

"You like women," she said. "'Tis the mark of men who loved their mothers, or nurse or a sister. Most often a mother."

He laughed. "Perhaps this has escaped your notice, my lady, but 'tis common for men to like women."

"Oh, no. 'Tis most uncommon, my lord." She gestured to a servant to bring more ale. "Men wish to bed women, that much is true, but most of them do not like us very much."

His eyes glittered. "I do like bedding them myself."

"Ah, but that is not all you like," she said, leaning toward him with a smile. "See how you sit and talk me with me all? And you do the same with Mary, who is no noble, but only a quick peasant. You like our company."

"That I do." His strange, pale eyes grew sultry, and his voice was low, thickly amber, like the precious mead on the table. "Perhaps I wish to bed you, my lady, and think the time spent talking well worth it."

Anya, against her will, felt a whisper of response along her spine. To cover it, she lifted an eyebrow in some amusement. "Perhaps you do. But perhaps you are simply loath to admit you like to spend your time in the company of something so foolish as a woman."

He said nothing, only met her eyes boldly, not bothering to hide now his lust. A growing heat lit Anya's limbs, as if he were caressing her shoulder to knee, his hands big and broad and gentle.

Slowly, he leaned toward her, until her face and his were mere inches apart. "I'd like bedding you, Lady Anya. I think you'd like it, too."

Disconcerted, she bowed her head, aware of a thudding pulse in her wrists. Too much wine had they drunk, and it made them reckless. "We weren't to speak of it, my lord."

"A feast and music and drink put a man in mind of other feasting." His voice deepened another notch. "I have long been without a woman."

Anya flushed and glared at him. "So take Tillie or Mary to warm your sheets. God knows you'd find them willing enough."

A duskiness rose in his face, a darkness that somehow frightened her, made him dangerous, unknown. Not the teasing lord at all, but a hungry warrior.

What did she know of him, really? Only that she had found him in the forest. Perhaps he was in truth a bandit or a robber, ousted by his own for some transgression she could only imagine.

He leaned another inch closer. "You say you think

I loved my mother and I like women—yet I frighten you. Why is that, my lady?"

"I know naught of you."

"No?" Below the table, his hand fell on her thigh. Anya started, but willed herself to resist the ploy. He meant only to show her he was a man like any other. And somewhere in the depths of her soul, she knew he was not—that he might be bandit or thief or knight, but whatever it was, he was honorable in his way, that he would live by the codes marking whichever path he followed.

His hand, warm and broad, moved on her leg, rumpling the fabric of her tunic. He began nearby her knee, and eased in small circles upward, lazily, his eyes still fixed on her face, flickering now to her mouth and back to her gaze, which did not waver.

The room dropped away. Dimly Anya heard the musicians start up in the corner, lutes and drums, and Geoffrey's pipe. Beyond the shuttered embrasures, snow fell and wind whipped. Around her at the tables, people laughed and talked and began to sing.

But only Christian filled her world, her vision. Her lips felt curiously heavy, and the tingling newness of her breast and limbs and hips grew nearly unbearable. His hand crept higher, higher, finally coming to rest at the crook of hip and thigh.

"Ah, you move me, my lady," he said in a rough, low voice. "Well I would like to teach you the secrets that trembling lip longs to learn." His eyes darkened. "But you have me rightly pegged—I did love my mother. It makes me honorable even when I wish it did not." He shook his head. "I would leave you whole."

When he made to draw away, Anya caught his

hand below the table. "You did not find me whole," she said, "and could not leave me less."

He turned his hand, palm up, to grip hers. "Anya—"

Someone slapped Anya's shoulder roughly from behind. Furious, she looked up, about to let loose of a tongue lashing. But it was Mary who stood there, and there was urgent warning in her face. She cocked her head discreetly toward the doors. Anya looked to see who it could be.

When she saw who stood there, her heart squeezed painfully and she dropped Christian's hand as if burned.

"Who is it?"

"My brother William." She took her skirts in her hands, and stepped away from the trestle table, but Christian seized her wrist.

"Show not your fear, my lady."

She lifted her chin. "I have no fear of a peevish monk."

But her hands shook as she crossed the room, and she found it difficult to arrange her features in a welcoming smile. Her brother stood regally by the doorway, his hair black around the tonsure, his lean sharp face arranged in thunderous order. Even in the low light of the candles, she saw the fury in his black eyes.

Anya stood on her toes to kiss his cheek. "Welcome to you, my brother," she said.

"'Tis a miserable day for travel," he grumbled, shedding his sodden cloak. "Call for a bath for me and feed these pages. We are weary."

"As you wish," Anya replied, turning to gesture to Mary. "I cannot think what would bring you out in such ill weather. What is so urgent that it would not wait?"

He lifted one sharply arched eyebrow, an expression so full of irony and ridicule that it had often made her cry as a child. "I heard news of a rogue knight in the keep and came to see if your honor was safe."

"A bit late for my honor," she said, taking the cloak.

He gave her a mean little smile. "So it is." With a long, elegant hand, he gestured toward Christian. "I would meet him."

"So meet him," she said and stepped back.

William smoothly stepped forward and took her arm in a hard grip. "Walk with me, sister, and graciously introduce me to your guest, or I shall see to it these peasants starve and you spend your life in a nunnery."

She narrowed her eyes. "How dare you threaten me!" With a quick movement, she broke his grip on her. "How dare you come to my house and order me about like a child!"

His lips curled. "Bold now, with that champion of yours."

Never had she openly defied this brother, no more than the barbs she had just planted, as always. But weary she was of doing all herself, of struggling and worrying alone, of William's manipulations. He treated her as if she were only some disposable pawn in his game of chess.

"You have done all you could to harm me as it is," she said. "I am finished fretting over your whims."

"Do not tempt me, little one." He glanced across the great chamber and leaned in close, smiling as if only whispering a family joke to his sibling. "For well I know what you hold dear."

Anya raised her eyes, but did not speak. The arrow was true, and William knew it. She tossed her head. "Come. You've not had the pleasure of meeting our guest."

The pipes and harps rose in a frenzy around them

as Anya crossed the room, her cheeks burning with fury, so angry she barely focused at all on Christian until they were nearly upon him.

So it was with surprise she saw how his visage had changed. No more did he appear the teasing man toward whom cats crept, or the smiling one a young boy could worship.

This was the warrior Christian. She knew it instantly. He had not moved, but his body looked coiled and ready to spring, his great shoulders taut, his thighs hard with muscle. In the pale eyes there now glowed a feral danger, as if in an instant he might turn from man to beast and tear limb from limb anyone who threatened. The still and disturbing expression was focused upon William.

"This is Brother Simon," she said without preamble.

Christian stood, rising from his seat to his great height to look down at the slim monk. "I am Christian de Morcerx," he said, and even his voice was different— not now the amber of sunset, but the harsh grating of winter night. "Late of Edward's army in the borderlands."

"Ah, Edward," said William. "Our beleaguered king."

"So some say."

Anya gestured toward the table, anxious to end the conversation between the two of them. There were undercurrents she did not like, a sense of evil brewing by their meeting. "Will you eat, brother? We have made a feast tonight."

"Aye," added Christian, "wine will take the chill from your bones." He smiled, but it was not a warm expression.

William cast his eye down the length of the table, toward the musicians in the corner and the stout tankards of ale littering the table at intervals. Anya saw it all through his eyes—the peasants below the salt, laughing, the guards dancing, the pages playing in the corners by the hearth. There was a festive air in the room, one well fed by good cuts of goose and fine bread.

"It seems famine will not visit this house tonight," William said with a tight smile. "From your letters, I expected the villeins to be bags of bones by now."

Again her temper rose, but this time Anya caught it in her throat before it could escape to do injury. "We are only feasting to stave off winter fevers," she said as mildly as she was able. "Will you not partake of it with us? On the morrow it's back to barley soup and black bread."

His black eyes swept again over the remains of the meal and his lip curled with faint distaste. "Have a wench bring me ale and a little bread to my bath."

Mary hovered nearby and rolled her eyes behind William's back. Anya felt her nostrils quiver dangerously, but she held back the laughter. "Mary, will you see to it?"

"Aye, my lady." With a demure folding of her hands, she said, "Will ye come with me, my lord?"

Water for bathing was stored in a circular metal barrel built into the manor walls, nearby the stove to heat it. As William sat, wrapped in a dry robe on the stone bench in the bathhouse, Mary and a kitchen maid William had not seen before lugged buckets of water in from the kitchen, pouring them one by one into the great wooden tub. The room itself was steamy and warm from the cooking and the fires beyond the walls.

It made him sleepy, and he watched the dark-haired cooking wench with no small pleasure, wondering if she might be persuaded to come to him later. Her breasts were high and round and he liked the blush on her clear cheeks. He liked women young and sweet like this. Rare were his opportunities in the abbey— and perhaps the joys of the flesh might ease some of his fury at being sent out in such grim weather. Later.

He dismissed Mary when the water was ready. From the purse on his belt, he took a silver coin and pressed it into the girl's hand. "There will be more in the morning."

The enormous black eyes shone as she stared at the coin. She smiled at him and lifted her hands to the laces on her tunic. He halted her with one hand. "Not now," he said. "Find me in the hearth room when all are abed."

"The knight lies in the hearth room," she said.

William frowned, wondering where then he would sleep. Surely his sister, for all her annoyance with him, would not give his bed away when he was in his own house. "'Twill be me there tonight."

She cocked her head coquettishly. "Mayhap 'twould be better not to wait."

He slapped her rump, suspecting the ruse to be an attempt to escape her kitchen chores. "Later."

When she left him, he immersed himself in the bath and let his servant scrub the vile journey from his body. All the way, William had been furious with the abbot for sending him out in such sloppy weather. Mud and muck made the going slow; the snow and sharp wind were a biting misery.

It seemed an indignity of the highest measure to be sent like a whelp on some minor errand on the word of the village priest, who raved about the knight come to save Anya.

The abbot had sent William to check the story.

And William was very glad he had.

Somehow his sister had found herself a champion. That was clear enough in the stance of the knight, in the evil glint of his eye, and even in the boldness with which Anya defied William. She thought herself protected now.

William smiled. At long last, Anya had stumbled. Finally, he held the cards and she only her bravado. For, in the instant it had taken to cross the Great Hall, moving toward the negligently smug knight, William had recognized him.

Oh, not him exactly. But his father. There could be no doubt Christian de Morcerx was the son of Etienne d'Auch, the powerful French cardinal, whom all said would next be pope. William had met him in Paris some years before on an errand of the abbey, as compelling and giant a man as his son, though perhaps blessed with more charisma. D'Auch was the sort to charm the birds from the trees. 'Twas the heart of his rise to such great power.

All knew of d'Auch's son, of the quarrel with his father and the youth's flight to England. That the quarrel was bitter was sure, but its source was unknown. It was even said the cardinal wished his son dead.

Bones warmed once more by the water, William waved the boy away so he might think in peace. Had the abbot heard some rumor that the wounded knight at Winterbourne was d'Auch's son? And how had the knight come to be in the forest at Winterbourne, so far from the borders where peace at last seemed to have won?

It mattered not. Sweet good fortune had smiled upon him at last. He knew not the exact way he would employ his newly gained knowledge, but one thing was sure. If he were clever enough, Winterbourne manor and village might be the least of the prizes he could claim when all was finished.

8

In spite of the wine she had consumed, Anya could not sleep. As always, the arrival of her brother filled her with fear—not only of William himself—but of hell. Of the consequences of her defiance of the Church. As she lay in the darkness, her heart pounded, and her mind paraded out every beast and torment of the Nether World, that place to which she was condemned for all eternity when she died.

Next to her, Mary snored like a great bear. With a shaking hand, Anya wiped sweat from her upper lip.

Weary of the tormented thoughts, she climbed from the bed and knelt in the corner on the cold stone floor where stood a small altar to Saint Anthony. Mute, she touched the foot of the statue. Her pounding heartbeat slowed.

She whispered a prayer, asking forgiveness and help. Surely Anthony, that most kind and gentle of saints, would intervene on her behalf. To him only did she pray since her rift with the priest.

Calmed a little, Anya tipped back on her heels. 'Twould be so simple to end this terror. She need only humble herself, cover her head and play the repentant woman to the priest. A hundred times she had nearly done so. A few times she had even been on the road to the village before she turned away.

But she could never do it. The Church—and all its pious men—had betrayed her. She had been naught but a child when the bandits had overtaken the family and their retainers on the way home from a fair in Lichfield. Before her eyes, they had slit her parents' throats and beaten John nearly unto death. And then, oh, then, they had turned on her.

There were no words for the terror she had felt—and none for the rage. Even now, that rage burned like a cauldron of tar.

And yet, for all that she'd been a child, for all that the horror and the strangling had stolen her voice for months, she had been raised in those dangerous woods, had heard tales not unlike her own all her life. 'Twas a threat one lived with. She mourned her parents and the loss of her innocence and the change the attack had wrought in her brother John, but in ways it had made her stronger, as fire tempers steel. She had survived.

When it became plain that she was with child, she had seized upon the babe with relief. It gave reason to the attack somehow. It seemed perhaps God had used it to bring the child to the world, through her.

Remembering, Anya felt anew the sorrow and confusion of those days—one euphoric and singing, the next in the depths of despair. Mary, only a little older, had proved her only comfort. John drank and stared into the fire, rousing himself only to give his sister baleful glances of apology. He blamed himself that he had not protected her honor and subdued his guilt in drink. At his neglect, the manor fell into disrepair.

Father Gerent, seeing Anya's swelling belly, told her to hide herself away, to take to her room for the shame of it. All knew a woman could not conceive without pleasure, he said furiously to her one afternoon. Would she so shame her family as to flout her sin?

At first, his attitude had stunned Anya. She had been the devout child of a devout mother. The Church, hitherto, had given only pleasure and peace to her.

And the priest himself had been the first to see her after the attack in the forest, had met her at the gates when she stumbled home, mute and trembling and naked but for the scraps of her gown she had managed to salvage for the sake of modesty.

At thirteen, she had not been as well versed in such things as she was now, but even then, she had known the sin of the child in her belly was not hers to repent. If she hid herself away, accepting the burden of such horror, she would not survive.

So chin uplifted, she did not hide, but took up the reins of the manor that her brother had let drop. The men of the village gossiped, as did some of the women. They whispered among themselves and fell silent when she appeared. The priest would not let her into Mass, so she did not go, and set up this statue of Saint Anthony for her own needs.

Even then, even then, she might have been able to make peace with the priest. But William, like an avenging angel, heard the tales and rode home in his new monk's robes. Seeing the disarray of the manor holdings, he pronounced Anya's willfulness the cause and locked her in the solar for the length of her confinement.

Even this Anya had borne, and when the babe came, easily for so young a girl, Anya had greeted him with joy, and suckled him from her breast all the night through.

In the morning, they had taken him—William and the priest—in spite of Anya's hysterical screaming. In spite of her begging to allow him to stay with her, in spite of her promise to do penance of any sort for her willfulness, they had wrenched the screaming babe from his mother and sent him away.

William returned to the monastery and the priest left her alone.

At the end of forty days, the priest came to her, humbly, to tell her that he would allow her to come back to the Mass if she would confess her sin and submit to the churching given women after birth.

Even now, after eight years, the scene made her tremble with rage. And it was that rage that would not let her give in. Saint Anthony would intervene on her behalf, or Anya would burn. Of her own will, she would not claim sins she did not own.

Pallets were spread all through the Great Hall when at last the revelry died down. Christian, seeing the struggle between sister and brother over the hearth room, offered to sleep along with the rest in the Hall.

And now, as the room quieted, he found it pleasant enough. The manor was silent, filled only with the snuffling of the assembled sleepers and an occasional snore. In the hearth, the fire popped and snapped.

Geoffrey slept alongside him, pipe clutched in his slim fingers, firelight glinting from the tangle of blond curls. In sleep, the child looked sweet.

Christian found it peaceful. Or well, peaceful enough. He longed to have a woman here in his bed with him, but it was a small lack with such a full belly and no worry but that of an aching head in the morning from the wine he'd consumed.

The thought brought a chuckle to his lips. Anya, he'd wager, would awaken with more than splitting head. Her capacity astonished him, and she'd seemed determined to get quite drunk once her brother arrived. It puzzled him. The monk was a waspish man, intelligent and cruel by the look of his mouth, but he seemed simple enough. After a meal, he'd even been rather expansive, sitting with them, chatting amiably. Christian did not trust him, but he seemed less of a threat than Anya made him out to be.

But Anya tautened with fear in his presence, and hatred burned like a lamp in her blazing dark blue eyes. She loathed and feared this brother beyond all reason.

What, Christian wondered, was the secret they shared?

A noise in the solar drew his attention and he turned his head lazily. The door was only partially closed. Within, a second fire burned, bright since it had only been recently stoked. He could see the shadows of the women on the bed, one of them a snoring lump below the covers.

One of the shadows crawled from the bed, outlined by the fire behind. It was Anya, her hair loose over her thin kirtle. He wondered what drew her from the warmth of the furs on so cold a night.

As he watched, she knelt before a statue of a saint. Her shoulders were bent and sorrowful, her hair pooling around her in untidy curls that captured the low light of the coals. He saw that she prayed.

A pluck of sympathy rang in his chest. Slim and sweet she was as she knelt, too young and good to carry such burdens. He thought again of what Mary had told him of her past, and his longing to comfort her rose unbearably.

He forced himself to close his eyes, shut out the sight of her. It would be one thing if her graceful form, so alluringly attired, stirred only his flesh to its usual attention. That leap of flesh was a man's curse, and one he learned early to control.

But it was not only his unruly manhood responding now. Even as he cautioned himself to fall back into the pleasant doze he'd left, he found himself turning to see if she still shivered in her kirtle on the cold stone floor. She did.

It was not his flesh that longed to go to her, wished to offer a shoulder for her to lean upon. Something nameless, deep in his chest, ached for her sorrows and wished to take them away.

He knew more than he had ever wanted to know of betrayal and loss of faith. Those were the great burdens Anya carried, too.

In the end, it was that shared pain that led him to toss away the coverlets and step over sleeping bodies to push through the small opening of the solar door. He wore only his shirt, and the stones were cold on his feet, the air sharp with renewed winter beyond the walls.

He had learned to walk silently, and so Anya did not hear him. She was bent into herself, shivering. He knelt beside her and touched her shoulder. "Anya," he whispered.

She started a little, but the face she turned to him was bleak. The cry of recognition in his breast warned him to run, quickly, before he found himself ensnared.

"I cannot sleep for thoughts of Hell," she whispered.

Wordless, he drew her to him, pulling her to her feet so he might envelop her small, shivering body in his arms. She let herself be drawn, pressing herself against his chest, and he cloaked her with his body as well as he could, rubbing her arms and back to bring warmth back to them, holding her close to him. "I dream of it," he said against her hair. "The Church has poisoned us all."

Around them echoed the simple sound of many bodies breathing. Christian grew aware of his own breathing, and of Anya's, and the way the act of each pressed her breasts, full and soft, into his ribs. That awareness led to others, to the soft whisper of her hair over his hands and arms, to her slim hips against his palms.

His only intent had been to help her rise, urge her back to bed. But now the silence and her womanly warmth made it difficult to remain aloof enough to do it.

"Anya," he said, thinking he was going to tell her to return to her bed. But she raised her face, innocently, and he found himself lifting one hand upward through the swirling mass of her hair, found himself cradling her head in his palm, touching one ear with his thumb.

He found himself kissing her. Lips like rose petals, sweet as mead, hesitant and willing, innocent and hungry. He willed himself to resist the wildness she unleashed in him with such simple hunger, and the effort made his hands tremble. He lifted his head minutely, and found her eyes open—he dipped again, once, twice, three times.

And with great restraint, put her away from him, swallowing his lust. "I—"

She seemed to need no more urging. Backing away, she bent her head and moved away from him, catching up her skirts with one hand. "Good night, my lord," she whispered.

He left her, pulling the door closed tight behind him, and settled again in his cold pallet next to Geoffrey.

In the darkness, he let go of a long, slow breath. He was aware of his lungs, taking in air, and of his heart, thudding too fast in the cavity of ribs, and the raging thrust of his manhood between his thighs. By all that was holy, he had to have her somehow.

And did not see how he could do it fairly.

The kitchen maid proved able and energetic, and William was well pleased. At the sound of the cock-crow, he gave her a coin. "My stay will last till the weather breaks. Can you come again tonight?"

She pressed the coin back into his palm. "I will come for pleasure only." Her hand moved on his stomach. "'Tis rare a man smells clean and tastes so fine—and gives such satisfaction!" She laughed. "I think you would have been better used in some other life besides that of a monk."

"There is little choice for a younger son," he said with regret. "Though well I love women."

She rolled on top of him, her hair cascading in

black waves around them, and moved deliciously. "'Tis plain you are well practiced."

He glanced toward the light. Wan, but growing. He would have her again tonight—'twas soon enough. Slapping her backside, he said, "Get dressed," and watched appreciatively as she did so.

"Tillie," he said as she laced her gown, "what can you tell me of the knight who sleeps here?"

A flicker of pique crossed her black eyes, but was gone quickly. "What of 'im, milord? He's not the man you are, I'll say."

William frowned at the implication of that, but dismissed it. What matter to him if she slept with every man in Winterbourne? "'Tis plain my sister is quite smitten. Do you think he'll stay?"

Tillie smiled. "No offense, milord, but he would not bed me, though I offered. Why would he take your skinny sister? If ye ask me, he's a man of unnatural taste, like his king."

William dismissed this last, putting it down to Tillie's pique at his refusal. "Not all men like the same sort of woman," he said quietly.

Nonetheless, he narrowed his eyes, disturbed more by the knight's refusal to bed the willing Tillie than by her sluttishness.

'Twould bear close watch. And Tillie, it seemed was a gift in that way. "Come again tonight, lass. Don't forget. I'll make up for what the knight lacks."

She gave him a saucy and promising smile.

Anya was in the kitchens early to unlock the spice cabinets and measure out the grain and other supplies for the morning meal. Cool winter light, pale with the clouds and snow, fell through waxed linen windows. "A hearty soup will give all some help this morning. Use the meat left from last night's feast to richen the broth."

The cook, a whip-lean woman from the village with thinning black hair and sharp blue eyes, sighed. "I do not see, my lady, why you must tell me all this way. Have I not cooked for all these twenty years? Did you lack as a girl? Was not your father a hale man, even at his great height?"

"There is my very point, Erda. You cannot cook as you have always done, or all of us will starve." Firmly, she locked the cabinet again. "'Tis a testament to your cooking that you do so well with so little."

As Anya turned to leave, a new girl from the village—come to replace one who at been married to a boy in a neighboring town—wandered in from the Hall. Her hair was mussed, though she'd evidently tried to comb it into some order, and there was about her face the sloe-eyed satisfaction of a woman come from a man's bed.

Erda said nothing to the girl, and Anya frowned. Here it was, already full light and the girl just wandered in? "Tillie," she said sharply when Erda still only stared at the floor.

The other girls paused in their tasks and Anya could see from their faces they were eager to see the girl reprimanded.

"Milady?" Tillie asked. In her eyes was a certain superior aloofness.

Anya looked from Erda to the girls in their rough gowns scattered about the kitchen, not one of them fair as Tillie by half. When she looked again at Tillie, the girl swayed side to side in a vaguely insolent way, her skirts swishing with the movement. "Save your whoring for beyond these walls," Anya said at last.

Titters sounded from the other kitchen maids, and even Erda lifted her head at last, pointing to a pile of meat scraps that needed boning. "Get to work," Erda said.

Tillie gave Anya a single, half-shuttered glance of fury, but to her credit, she swallowed it quickly. Head lowered, she took up the knife and attended the meat. Anya left them.

In the Hall, the pallets were being moved aside, though some revelers still slept in the dim morning, undisturbed by the gradual stirring around them. In a corner by the door to the solar were Christian and Geoffrey, leaning against the wall.

The light, high notes of Geoffrey's pipe danced sweetly through the room. Anya paused a moment to let two men carrying a bench pass, and watched the pair in the corner. Christian's hair was mussed this morning, and lay on his shoulders in rough disarray. His pure masculine beauty made her stomach ache. Without thinking, she lifted her hand to her lips, remembering the kiss he had tendered last night.

As if he sensed her gaze, Christian looked up and caught her staring. Hastily, Anya dropped her hand away. To her dismay, the smile he'd reserved for Geoffrey slid from his face, to be replaced with a very sober, very measuring expression. Regret.

Humiliated, she ducked her head and hurried onward to the hearth room. As she expected, her brother was still abed, and in the room she could smell the heat of lovemaking. As the door struck the wall behind it, he roused suddenly, sitting up. "What do you want?"

"Leave the kitchen wenches alone," she said. "It stirs up jealousy to have one so favored."

"Oh, ho! You can have your pleasures, but I may not have mine, is that it?"

"Hold your tongue, William, for you know not of what you speak."

His eyes flattened, turned to slits. "Nay, Anya, you hold your tongue. I will do what I like in this place, if you wish any help at all."

"Help?" She tried to keep her hope from rising, from showing in her face. He might toy with her for the simple joy of disappointing her all the more. And yet, perhaps the presence of the knight did jar his meanness a little.

"Why else would I come?"

"To see my champion yourself, as you said."

"That too," he agreed cheerfully.

Never did she find her brother even a remotely agreeable companion, but in this self-satisfied mood, she wished most heartily to strangle him. This morning, exhausted with lack of sleep and the wild tangle of emotions the knight stirred in her, she spoke too quickly. "You sicken me."

In a trice he was out of bed. He grabbed a fur to wrap about him, and leaned close. "Do not test me, sister."

"Test you." She shook her head, smiling bitterly. "How can one test a man with no code of honor or ethics? Is there anything you believe in, William?"

"Aye. I believe Winterbourne is mine, and I mean to have it, whatever it takes."

She met his gaze levelly. "'Tis mine—not only by John's writ, but by virtue of my work here. You care not for the villagers or the land, you want only to advance your own career." He was much taller than she, but she stared up at him fiercely. "I am mistress of Winterbourne, and for all that you've taken, you cannot take that."

"Can't I?"

She crossed her arms. "You do not mean to help me at all, do you?"

"Good husbandry dictates that there is no feasting when famine is imminent," he said, turning to don his robes. "If you so squander your small stores, why should I be moved to help you?"

"Squander!" She laughed. "That 'squander' was the first meat the household has eaten in two weeks, and I ordered it to build their strength in this ill weather. Fevers abound—to keep them from death, I feed them."

"If a few succumb to fevers, so many fewer mouths to feed."

She tried to keep her disappointment covered, but saw when the gleam struck his eye that he saw her sense of defeat.

"Do as you will," she said wearily. "I am through begging you."

Christian's restlessness came on him again as the day passed. By late afternoon, he was tired of the smoke in the Hall, the noisy games of the bored inhabitants, the dreariness of the light. No more snow had fallen, but no sun broke through the gloom, either. He tried to rouse Geoffrey into going to the stables with him, but the boy resisted, hanging instead nearby the musicians to learn their tunes before they traveled on. If no more snow fell, they would leave on the morrow, as would the monk, who had seen whatever he'd come to see and now absented himself in the hearth room.

Christian wanted to ride in the cold day, to race with his stallion through the fields—a feat he would not dare with any other animal. Nor could he yet manage a horse, even if his own had not been left back in the wilds of the border or stolen by the brigands who'd tried to kill him.

He wished to be useful again, for never had he been an idle man, and the weight sat heavily upon him now. But for the shoulder, he was healed from the ordeal. Surely there was something he might do.

Beneath all this restlessness was a sensual memory of Anya in his arms last eve. All day, he'd avoided her, on guard against the new lust he felt. 'Twould be great cruelty to bed her.

And yet, now, there was at least an hour before the evening meal. He had no books to amuse him, nor the use of a sword. Nothing to do. At last, he sought out the one person in the manor who might ease his boredom.

Anya sat in the good light of her solar, sewing. A blue wool shawl covered her shoulders from the chill, and her gown today was finer than most she wore—though it fit her as loosely as the others. A pattern of paisleys and feathers was woven through the blue wool, and a border of gold edged the sleeves and hem.

She did not see him at first, for he entered quietly, mindful of the solitude he would break once he spoke. Against the light, her curls glimmered softly, and her profile, bent over her task, was exquisitely wrought—the smooth, high brow, a straight and noble nose, the slant of cheekbones.

He must have made some noise, for she glanced up, frowning and blinking. "Christian," she said in surprise, her expression easing.

"Are you hiding in here?" he asked.

She smiled. "Perhaps—but 'tis not your company I duck." She gestured to the seat opposite her knees. "If you do not mind the cold, you may join me."

"I long for fresh air." He settled in the spot, and breathed deeply of the cold coming through the half-shuttered embrasure. Beyond, the trees stood out in stark relief against the snow and gray clouds, the black branches of oaks contrasting elegantly with the conical shape of pines and firs. "'Tis beautiful and still today."

She looked out, as if noticing it for the first time, and her hands fell idle in her lap. "So it is."

In the clear light, he could see the lines of strain in her face, the smudges of darkness below her eyes. On impulse he said, "Can you leave your work for a little and come walk awhile with me?"

"Walk?"

He smiled and gestured toward the forest. "Aye, walk and breathe. You look weary. Perhaps the good clean air would give some refreshment."

Anya bent her head over the sewing and took a careful, neat stitch. "What of my brother?"

"What of him?"

"Already he suspects I am your leman."

"But all here know there is no truth in that suspicion. Does his opinion matter so much to you?"

"I hate him." She sighed. "But he has power over me, and I worry he will use such stories against me."

He stood, disappointed but unwilling to cause her further worry. "Then I should not even be sitting here with you." He stepped down from the dais of the window seat, and paused. "Truly, Anya, he is far more afraid of you than you are of him."

"Nay," she said, lifting her face to look at him. "You do not know, Christian."

The strange huskiness of her voice struck him anew, and brought with it a piercing pain. Were there none to treat her kindly? Was there no champion for her?

Gently, he touched her cheek. "A coward always fears a warrior, my lady. And a fine warrior you are."

She lifted a hand and circled his. "I thank God for you, Christian. You have made these past weeks far easier to bear. It has been a long time since I could claim even one friend."

Her skin was softer than fur, and he found himself unwilling to stop touching her. With light fingers, he traced the line of her jaw and neck, smoothed a recalcitrant curl from her face. "And long has it been long since I could speak so easily with anyone."

The lakewaters of her eyes shifted as if swept by some wind of emotion. Her lips, so full and red and pretty, softened. He swallowed, resisting the urge to touch her mouth with his thumb, the urge to bend and kiss her.

"Come," he said, plucking the sewing from her lap. "Walk a little, just in the baileys. 'Twill ease you. I promise. And if we are there in clear view of all, who can gossip?"

She smiled. "I will fetch my cloak."

9

No one seemed to note their leaving, Anya thought as they passed through the gates to the outer bailey. The guard only smiled at her, as if understanding her need to escape the cares of the manor. The habit was not unusual. Long before Christian came, she had often walked alone in the safety and quiet of the place. Here were winter-naked fruit trees, stark against the clouded sky. Toward one end were the hives. Around a small pond in summer grew medicinal herbs and tasty greens used in cooking, and it attracted no small number of game birds, for isolated it was, and calm.

Wrapped in a great black wool cloak of her father's, Christian walked silently beside her. He scorned the hood, and his hair blew loosely in the cold wind, wind that stung color into his cheeks. His stride was long and powerful, graceful in the way of men comfortable with themselves and their place in the world. His broad-shouldered leanness gave her a feeling of security she liked very much.

At the edge of the pond, she stopped and tested the edge of the ice with her booted toe. "It has been too soggy this winter for skating," she commented. "Have you ever tried the sport?"

"No. 'Twas warm where I spend my boyhood." He smiled. "Vineyards were our playgrounds. By the time I came north, I was too old to tie skates to my feet."

Anya smiled. "And where was this warm place?"

"Gascony. 'Tis beautiful, though I have grown to love England." He gave her a rueful grimace. "At first, I thought the cold a great cruelty."

"No snow in Gascony?"

"No. Many places have no snow, nor even much winter."

"Mmmm. So I have heard." She bent mischievously to grab a handful of snow. It was very wet and heavy, and formed a satisfying snowball. Backing away, she said, "So you had little chance for snowball fights, either, I suppose?"

He had been gazing with a certain satisfied expression over the frozen pond. The snowball Ayna flung caught him unaware, exploding against his chest with a soft puff of air. He made a noise and lifted his brows. "Wench, for that you'll pay."

With surprising grace, he scooped the snow with his good right hand and patted it into shape with his other. Anya bent to form another, laughing. She baited him a little, but ducked at exactly the right moment, and the snowball he threw landed harmlessly against a tree. When she threw hers, he was hindered by his injury, though he ducked, and it glanced off his chin, exploding with gentle scatterings of snow down his chest.

He laughed. "'Tis no fair fight! I am hobbled."

"A girl against a knight? Even a one-armed knight should be able to beat a girl!" She danced around the pond a little further, catching a branch that dumped its load of snow over her head. Behind her, Christian laughed, and with a sudden plop a snowball hit her squarely between the shoulders.

Shaking the snow from her head, she felt her braid come loose and cared not. Christian had been right. The clean, cold air had revived her, and now her blood flowed warm and zesty through her veins. She formed and fired three snowballs in quick succession, laughing when two caught him well. The third landed short.

"Come, good knight!" she called, her voice carrying clearly in the still winter air. "Find me if you can."

She spun and dashed into the thicket of trees nearby the pond, a bit of forest that ended a few yards distant with the bailey wall, and continued again beyond it. Dipping to hide behind a great old pine, she made a little tower of snowballs, then ducked and waited for Christian to come so she could ambush him. Carefully, she peeked carefully through the branches.

He was gone. Not by the pond, nor coming through the trees. Their footprints together in the snow were impossible to decipher, so she could not even see which direction he'd taken.

Frowning, she crouched behind the tree and held her breath to listen. Nothing stirred. Faintly from the manor she could hear sounds of voices in the yard, the call of a guard to another, the thin neigh of a horse.

But here nothing save the whisper of the wind through the branches. She glanced over her shoulder and peered once more through the trees. No sign of him. Not anywhere.

She stood up, about to call for him—

And was ambushed from behind. A cold wash of snow fell in clumps below her gown, an icy shock down her spine. She shrieked, trying to pull away to shake the torment free, but another handful of the wet, sloppy snow landed in her face.

Blinded and laughing, she stumbled forward. Before she could fall, Christian caught her against him, and she heard his rumbling laugh. "That will teach you, my lady, that clever wins over anything." His grip tightened around her ribs. "Declare me King of Snowballs or I will torture you more."

Anya laughed, leaning against him as she brushed snow from her eyes. He was warm and strong along the length of her and with a giddy happiness, she slumped against the tree, secure in his loose embrace. "Oh, very well," she said, and suddenly spied a branch above his head, heavily laden with snow. "I declare you King of Snowballs!"

Before he could sense her intentions, she reached up and shook the branch, slapping her hands over her face as the load tumbled over them.

When it was finished, she opened her eyes. Snow caught in his hair and eyelashes, sprayed over his cheeks and eyebrows. In the midst of the glittering flakes, his mouth was smiling.

"Declare me Queen," she said, but her voice was soft and breathy, carrying a message she wasn't sure she wished to give.

He pressed closer, his clear gray eyes alight. So

close, she could see the darker circle of black that outlined the iris, making the color truly startling. As she gazed at him in wonder, those beautiful eyes hazed with a sensual awareness.

"I declare you Queen," he said in a rough, unfocused voice. His head dipped and Anya lifted her face, ready for his kiss.

His mouth touched her cheek, and his tongue swept away a morsel of snow. The heat and cold so mingled raised the shimmer of her blood, and she found her hands somehow on his chest, clutching the good wool of the cloak for support. His mouth nuzzled the corner of her eye, her temple, her nose, and at each place, the tip of that hot tongue lightly swept away snow.

She began to tremble, and clutched more fiercely at the cloak, afraid her spine would melt and she would sink like a masterless puppet to the ground if she let go. These light flickers, the startling heat and cold together, made her feel things she'd not known of, shameful, wanton, delicious things. She wished to kiss him, to taste again the pleasure of his mouth, but could not find the words to ask.

"Ah, you move me, Anya," he murmured against her forehead. "You are like some fierce, wild creature, and none have shown you gentleness." He pressed tiny kisses down the length of her nose, and paused in hovering heat over her mouth. "I long to show you the good that can be between a man and a woman."

Her breath came in quick shallow bursts as she waited, waited for his mouth. At last she lifted herself to her toes and placed her mouth against his. Softly.

He made a low, pained noise and turned his head

to slant his lips over hers, and then he was not so gentle. He kissed her fiercely, holding her hard against him, his lips moving, his tongue probing hungrily. His hands on her shoulders grew urgent, tight.

In a burst of passion, Anya lifted her arms around his neck and plunged her fingers into the smooth thick weight of his hair, now damp with snow. And imitating him, she moved her mouth, and her tongue, reveling in the taste of him. With a curious sense of long knowledge, their movements meshed until there was a perfect, graceful rhythm so rich and deep and right Anya felt drunk with it.

A sudden cry through the bailey shattered the moment. "My lady! Lady Anya!"

Christian abruptly lifted his head, but did not yet release her. For a moment, she stared at him, dazed. His eyes were heavy-lidded and Anya knew he was as moved as she.

"I long to lie with you, my lord," she whispered urgently.

She saw his throat move, and he closed his eyes, putting her away from him. "No, Anya." His voice was gruff, and she noted with a dizzy distance that his hands trembled. "You know not what you say."

"Lady Anya!" The voice—Geoffrey's—was closer, and Christian smoothed her hair.

"Come," he said. "We must act as if there is nothing amiss. He'll sense it elsewise." With a quick gesture, he threw a snowball through the trees.

Aching and confused, Anya dully knelt and picked up a snowball from the pile, her cheeks burning with shame. He wanted her. She could feel it. Why had he pushed her away, then? Had he heard the stories the servants told, those wild, mean tales of her past?

Why else would a man say nay to a woman well beyond the point her virginity mattered? There was none she could see. He wished not to sully himself with a woman so soiled.

She lifted her chin, fighting the pain the knowledge gave her. But she would not be so foolish again.

When the trio returned to the manor, it was to find Father Gerent sitting in the Great Hall, bent in cozy discussion with William nearby the fire. At the faint smile the priest gave her, Anya's temper, already strained, snapped. Her brother knew well her feeling toward Father Gerent and thought to thwart her even in her own Hall.

Well she knew how to get back at her brother today. Without a glance or a word, she stormed toward the kitchen.

"Tillie," she said sharply.

The girl, bent over a loaf of bread she sliced into trenchers, glanced up, obviously bewildered at the tone in her mistress' voice. "Aye, milady?"

The other girls looked up, eager for another confrontation that would humiliate the too-attractive one among them. Anya felt a prick of shame, and tempered her voice. "Come," she said. "I wish a word in private."

She led the way to the bathing chamber. Tillie followed, her head lowered apprehensively. Anya loosened her cloak in the warm room. "You will go to your mother tonight, and stay there until my brother is gone back to Lichfield."

"But milady, there are guests—Erda needs me!"

"Nothing I cannot do."

A mutinous expression darkened the girl's brow. "My mother will not allow me to go home."

If she had behaved in the village the way she had here, Anya didn't wonder. "Then go you to your brother. His wife will take you in."

Tillie held out her hands, imploring. "Please, milady, I did not mean to be insolent this morning—'twas early, and—"

"This morning has no bearing on this."

"Is it that your brother is a monk? Milady, your battle with the Church is well known—I did not think you would be so pious about such things!"

"Curb your tongue!"

The black eyes blazed, and a flush of color rose in her cheeks. "You are only jealous! We see you pining all for the knight."

Anya slapped her. The sound was sharp and loud in the still room. For a moment, both were stunned. Tillie pressed her palm to the place. Anya stepped back, her hand stinging, appalled that she had allowed her temper to carry her away, that she was petty enough to punish a peasant for her brother's transgressions.

She closed her eyes. "Forgive me," she said. "That was wrong." She lifted her chin. "I have no quarrel with your work in the kitchen, and what you do away from here is no concern of mine. But you'll not lie with my brother again."

Tillie stared at her with purest hatred, but abruptly lowered her eyes. "Aye, milady," she whispered. "Send word when the monk is gone."

Christian boldly settled by the pair of churchmen and kicked off his boots to put his feet up near the fire.

William cast a sour look his way, but Christian cheerfully smiled, as if too stupid to realize he was intruding.

"'Tis too glorious a winter day for such long faces," he said, tossing damp hair from his face.

"Not all men frolic with children in the snow," William said.

"Then those men are fools." Christian grabbed a tankard of ale from the sideboard. "God's world is a rich place, no?"

William declined to answer, only went back to the discussion at hand. Christian paid it little attention, since it concerned gossip about the abbey and high politics in the English Church. They were tales he'd heard too often as it was.

He shifted in the chair and leaned his head back, enjoying the pleasant rush of blood through his limbs, the good clean sense of exercise in his body.

Oh, and Anya. Anya. He'd not felt such a rush of infatuation for a woman since early youth. Watching her move through the snow, laughing and playing as her hair came undone, had given him such a wide sense of well-being it was hard to remember there was a price on his head, and a life he had known before he came here.

I long to lie with you.

Her words whispered through him, and he could still taste her skin against his tongue, the delicate softness chilled with snow. There was such a wealth of passion in her! He longed to stoke and fan that fever until she quivered with the power—then give it release.

Even the thought roused him enough he had to shift in the chair, and he caught sight of her bustling toward the solar from the kitchen, ignoring the men nearby the hearth as if they were trees in the forest.

For a moment, he thought to follow her, to ease the hurt he knew he'd delivered by refusing her offer.

Instead, he stared into the leaping flames beyond his toes, smelling the sweetness of burning pine. Esmerelda the cat leaped into his lap and flopped down on his thighs. Christian stroked her absently.

His emotion and reason warred. Much as he wished to bed Anya, to kiss her endlessly, his life was not his own. He sensed, too, a danger in the connection that flared between them. Just now, kissing her under the pines, he'd felt a unity unlike anything he'd known with another woman, a sense of balance thrumming through the passion.

But as if to bring home all the reasons he could not let that connection grow, he heard William speak a name. It leapt out, like an exploding bubble of sap in a log.

Cardinal d'Auch.

Lazily, as if the name meant nothing, he lifted his tankard and drank deeply. Cardinal d'Auch. Appointed by Pope Clement, who had made a practice of bestowing the purple on his fellow Frenchmen in an effort to more firmly establish the papacy at Avignon.

The ironies never ended. But for an accident of fate, Clement would have died at his coronation, by the order of Etienne d'Auch, whose genius had been well employed that day so long ago. D'Auch learned the route the pope would take—and ordered an old wall along the way to be weakened. 'Twas not so difficult to remove the mortar from the old stones, to weaken it so it might be tumbled at the right moment.

And but for the grace of God, the plot would have succeeded. A duke, the pope's brother, and ten others were killed. The pope himself was thrown from his mule, his crown rolling away in the dust—but God had chosen to spare him.

It was this plot Christian had uncovered too late to stop, the plot that had unleashed a river of loathing between father and son. It had sent Christian fleeing for his life to England, the only shelter he could think of, where he found his boyhood friend Piers Gaveston at court.

"Clement is old and weak," William said now. "There are many who say his ill health is punishment from God for allowing Philip to persecute the Templars so."

"Are they all dead?" Father Gerent asked.

"Dead or rotting in prisons." Spying Christian's gaze, William said, "By your voice you spent your childhood in France. Knew you of the Templars?"

Christian refused the bait to join, and only shook his head. "Matters of state bore me."

"And Church, too?"

Christian heard the careful challenge in the words and looked up. "Even more so."

William regarded him steadily, a superior expression in the mean black eyes. "There is word Etienne d'Auch will next be pope, though none of course can know for certain. Does it not interest you who the next Father of the Church will be?"

He knows.

"Nay," he said gruffly.

"I've had the good fortune to meet the cardinal," William continued. "'Twas many years ago—he must have been about the age you are now."

Christian set aside his cup of ale and met William's gaze. For long moments, there was naught but the knowledge between them. Christian could hear the unspoken words echoing there on the stone hearth, the words he had heard over and over: the resemblance was remarkable. Once his mother told Christian that she thought God had used the same mold twice, so much did son favor his father.

William knew who Christian was. It gave Christian little choice, as William well knew. To keep Anya and her manor safe from the thugs who would no doubt track him here once William's word flew to France, Christian had no choice but to leave Winterbourne as soon as possible.

The sharpness of his regret surprised him. Without another word, he stood. If he had only hours left in this place, he would spend them with her.

But as he moved toward the solar, a young girl rushed in from the bailey. "Father Gerent!" she cried. "You must come! 'Tis my brother—he cannot breathe."

Christian felt a fleeting moment of sympathy for the old priest as he rose heavily, his thick features arranged in heavy lines. "Last rites, I expect. 'Tis the fever," he said. "A quarter of the parishioners are abed with it."

William rose with the priest and walked with him from the Hall, murmuring quietly. The priest nodded. Christian stared at the lean, dark monk, and before he could return, left in search of Anya.

From the sanctuary of his chamber, William heard the village bells ring. He lifted his head to listen, and automatically whispered a prayer for the dead. It decided him—much as he wished to enjoy Tillie's company another day or two, he would satisfy himself well tonight and leave with first light.

He coughed, unexpectedly, and alarmed, forced a

second. It sounded dry and calm, and he relaxed. Aye, with first light he would be gone.

His reasons for being here were satisfied anyway—there was no point to a longer stay. 'Twas plain the knight understood his message, and Anya would soon be alone without her champion once again. With the poor weather and a fever on top of the ghastly stores she had to see her through the rest of the winter, she would soon capitulate.

In spite of his desire to win the manor and village from her at last, he had to admit to a sneaking admiration of her once again. How she managed to stretch such stores so well amazed him. And if it weren't for the fevers and the assorted other troubles she faced, he doubted even this challenge would break her. Of his father's children, Anya had been by far the brightest and quickest and bravest. His father had always said he'd borne only one true knight, and her name was Anya.

Perhaps, he thought in his mellow mood, if all went well he might leave her with this fief. It was all she had. If he wrested it from her, he knew he would have to watch his back the rest of his days, for she would not leave vengeance in the hands of the Lord. Not again.

And the truth was, she'd unwittingly supplied him with a far plumper prize than Winterbourne. The cardinal might provide handsome rewards to one who knew the secret of his bastard son. This plum he would hold for himself, however, and send a messenger on his own to France. The abbot need only know Anya's hold on the village was slipping.

He settled in to wait for Tillie, his high spirits enriched by anticipation.

10

Three times through the night the bells in the village rang. Death bells. Each time they jolted Anya from sleep. The fever had a dog's grip on the village. Even the thought of it exhausted her.

Just before daybreak, William burst into the solar, obviously in high temper. Mary had gone to the kitchens already, so Anya was alone when he grabbed her arm and hauled her from the comfort of her bed. "What did you do with her?" he shouted, his fingers digging into her arm.

"Who?" Anya shook free, and tugged the furs more closely about her, shaking her hair from her eyes. Reason dawned and she smiled bitterly. "Ah, Tillie. I warned you, brother."

He leaned forward. "And I warned you, Anya. Till now, I've shown you mercy because you are my blood, but henceforth I do not even know your name."

"Mercy!" she cried. "Locking me away, stealing my

child, letting the villagers starve? That is mercy?" Enraged, she shifted to her knees. "You are mean of heart and spirit, William. As long as there is breath in my body, you will not hold Winterbourne!"

She let go of a yelp of pain when he grabbed her again, shaking her in fury. "You have no power, you fool! You are a woman!" His fury was so fierce spittle dotted the edges of his mouth. "Mark my words, I'll have this fief and all that it contains, no matter what I must do." He flung her backward. "Now *you* have been warned."

Christian spoke from the door. "As you have warned me?"

Anya, trembling with rage and fury, silently cheered at the start his sudden appearance gave her brother. Christian stood in the door, his great chest bare, his arms rounded and shouting of the muscle there contained. And here now, was the warrior again, the warrior of fierce eyes and hard jaw, the soldier who had killed and might easily be persuaded to do so again. He advanced into the room, weaponless but for the fist balled at his side.

He did not cease until he stood toe to toe with William. "Do not touch her again."

The words, calm and deadly, were more effective than the worst threat. William, for all that he tried not to show it, was cowed by the sheer size and weight of the knight.

"Go to the slut, then," he said with disdain, and flicked his robes from Christian's path. At the door, he paused. "Beware, both of you. I am done with mercy."

Anya picked up a candlestick, lifting it to throw, but Christian plucked it from her hand. "Do not waste it," he said with a touch of humor.

She looked up. The manor was not yet fully stirring, and no sound came from beyond. In the quiet dawn light, he was mercilessly beautiful, as if created solely to give pleasure to women's eyes. A sliver of light caught along the edge of his shoulder, another fingered his long mussed hair.

She met his eyes, and saw there a hint of his lust, in the flicker of his gaze over her naked shoulders. Below the furs, her body began to shimmer with awareness of her nudity and his eyes knowing it, and his bare chest and the ease of bringing them together in the silence of morning. He stood close enough that she could smell the heat of his skin.

He sank down next to her, touching her arm. "He marked you."

"'Tis nothing," she said, reacting acutely to the brush of his thumb, gentle on the bruised place. She held herself very still, afraid to look at him. His hand did not move, but remained, warm and heavy, on the bare skin of her shoulder.

"Did you hear the bells last night?" she asked.

He nodded grimly. "And in the hall, there are two more."

"Dead?" She lifted her head urgently.

"No! No, I'm sorry." His hand stirred on her arm, soothing. "Only ill."

Anya bowed her head, struggling to remain unmoved by his nearness. Her hair fell over her face and she was glad of the shield to hide her expression. She clutched her fingers so tightly they ached. His broad palm skimmed the shelf of her shoulder, smoothed down the flesh of her arm, glided back up. To her shame, Anya felt her nipples rise below the furs.

"I must leave you soon, Anya," he said soberly.

She nodded. "I know." Only an inch and that stroking thumb could dislodge her covering, would leave her bare to his gaze. At the wanton wish, she felt a new wash of heat, heat she tried to hide with simple words. "But surely 'tis some weeks yet before you can wield a sword, ride a horse?"

"I cannot wait for that day. Your brother has my secret, and will use that to hurt you if I stay."

"What secret? Can you not tell me and let me decide if I think the danger great enough?"

Slowly, firmly, he shook his head in denial.

Pierced, she stared at him. "Christian," she whispered in protest, unable to say more.

Bending close, he touched his lips to her brow. Anya closed her eyes, saving for all eternity the warmth of his mouth, the weight of his wide palm on her shoulder. How bleak life would be once he left the manor!

His hand roved over her arm, over her shoulder, tangled in her hair. In the movements, Anya felt the same longing now welling up in her. She lifted her head to meet his gaze. No teasing now in his face, no light spark of humor in his eyes, only raw hunger.

"I am an evil and selfish man to want you thus, Anya of Winterbourne," he said in a low, strained voice. "But I vow I cannot bear to walk away from you this morning."

He kissed her, his fingers less careful now, grazing the edges of her furs where they were clasped to her body. She met his kiss half timidly, half hungrily, unsure of his intent, unwilling to show again her wantonness to him for his refusal.

His tongue swirled against hers, his lips questing and none too gentle. The hand on her shoulder slipped over her back below her hair as his kiss deepened.

With a low, pained sound, he pulled her closer. Anya kept her hands clasped close to herself, struggling against the wish to touch the broad shoulders so close, to bury her fingers in the hair that brushed the upper swell of her breasts. His mouth, traveling along her neck, now at the crook of her shoulder and the hollow of her throat, gave her the most peculiarly weightless feeling, as if she were floating, only linked to the earth through his heat and passion.

Gently, he pushed her backward into the softness of the bed, whispering her name. "I long to show you the true art of men," he said, his mouth brushing her lips once more. "So you will know the right way when another man comes to you."

She wanted no other man. Only this one, his hair shining like wheat in the dim light, his eyes so clear. Only this man, brave and powerful—and as beleaguered as she. In wonder, she touched the golden hair over his chest, first with her fingers, then with her lips. "Show me," she whispered, her heart racing.

With a ragged sigh, he took the coverlet from her fingers and tugged it away from her body. He closed his eyes with a sigh, then opened them again, lifting a hand to place it upon her breast. "You're beautiful," he said hoarsely, and kissed her nipple. "May God forgive me, but I want you."

Anya trembled as his eyes and hands washed over her torso. Slowly, he kissed her body—the tender lower curve of a breast, the edge of a rib, her belly.

"A man of honor never rushes," he said in that same ragged voice. "And he learns to pluck the music of a woman slowly."

Her breath came in soft, heated rushes. "And what," she whispered, "does a woman do?"

He lifted his head. The gray eyes darkened with want, and his fingers circled her flesh. "She responds."

"Oh," Anya breathed.

He pressed a tiny kiss to the aching tip of each breast at first, then a flicker of his tongue. And another. Anya clutched the blankets beside her, aching to—

His mouth opened over her, and descended with heat and suckling pressure. Anya could not halt the small cry that tore from her lips, and as if he'd awaited that signal, he moved over her, pressing his hips against her thighs, swirling his tongue over her in teasing, whirling flickers.

Anya could not bear to be still another moment. Urgently, she grasped his great head in her hands, her fingers curling hard around his scalp. "Christian," she said softly, knowing not what she asked, only that he held the answer.

With a pained growl, he pulled her close, covering her with his great size and power so he could kiss her again. At the furred brush of his chest against her, at the heat of his smooth muscled belly skimming her own and the sharp pointed arousal pressed against her thigh, Anya moaned. She welcomed the stormy, bruising kiss when he gave it, holding her head with restrained strength between his hands.

A kind of madness seemed to envelop them then. He kissed her with the lack of grace of a starved man, and opened for her to kiss him back the same way.

He lifted his head. "God, how I lie," he said roughly. "'Tis not for you." And he kissed her, pressing their bare chests together, his good hand caressing her back all the way down her spine to a place just above her hip so sensitive she nearly could not stand it.

He suckled her neck and her ear, his hips moving

ever so restlessly against her. And deep in her belly, Anya felt a thrumming in answer, a need she could not name. She pulled him closer, moving against him, feeling his unshaven beard scrape at her cheek. She kissed his ear and the thick column of his throat and laced her fingers through the fall of his hair.

Neither of them heard anyone enter the room, only the shocked, frightened gasp of Mary—"Milady! Your brother returns!"

"Oh, God!" Christian groaned and yanked away, hurriedly tossing the covers again over Anya.

Frantically, her heart racing with terror and unfulfilled passion, she pulled her tangled curls around her like a cape. "Mary! Close the door! Quickly."

Christian leapt to the dais by the window and flung open the shutter, standing with his back to her. She saw him grasp his shoulder as if it pained him, just as William strode back in the room.

"Rather spoils your dramatic exit to come back so soon, Brother Simon," Anya said with narrowed eyes. She wondered if he could hear the ragged breathing, could see the bruising kiss on her lips.

"It seems I forgot," William said with a triumphant gleam in his eye, "to tell you I am taking Geoffrey back with me to the monastery. My messenger was quite taken with him and thinks a monastic life would suit him well."

"No!" Anya cried, bolting forward.

From the dais, Christian turned. "I'm afraid 'twill be impossible," he said smoothly. "I have already sent word to the king. Geoffrey is going to court to play his pipe and tabor."

William could not conceal his rage. "What right have you to choose the fate of a page in a noble's house?"

"None," Anya cut in, seizing the lie with relief. "I gave leave."

William gazed at one, then the other, then spun on his heel and left them.

Into the grim silence, Christian spoke first. "We have made a mortal enemy this day."

Staring after her brother, Anya felt a sense of dread. "Aye."

As the morning meal was served, Christian grabbed a hank of black bread and ducked out to the bailey, unable to yet confront the passion that had flared so fiercely between him and Anya this morning.

He found himself in the stables. The master and his boys were in the Great Hall with the rest, so he had the place to himself. At the dim cold within, and the smell of hay, a kind of peace flooded through him. Chewing the bread, he ambled through, eyeing the horses with a critical eye. One black gelding snorted and nodded as Christian approached, and he paused to let the beast snuffle at him, smoothing a hand down his flanks. Its eyes were clear, its coat gleaming and well tended.

"You're a fine mount," Christian said, stepping back. The horse danced a little, as if in anticipation of a hard ride. "But mayhap you have too much spirit for me just now."

From a corner came the sound of a pipe and Christian glanced over in surprise. "Geoffrey?" He peered into the shadows, spying the boy's slim feet on a pile of hay. "Why are you not within, eating?"

The child scooted forward to sit on the edge of the hay bale. Loosely he held his flute in his lap. A shaft of pale light fell from the window, highlighting the dark blond curls and the child's winsome features, now arranged in a guarded aspect. "I am not hungry," he said.

Christian nodded, sensing some disturbance here. "Mmm. Well, perhaps you might tell me of the horses, then. What is that spirited gelding's name, there?"

"Evered. He is my lady Anya's mount."

Smiling, Christian glanced back to the alert and restless creature, seeing Anya with her golden curls astride him. "'Tis no surprise."

He gestured to another, quietly munching hay. "And this one?"

"Juniper. He's very boring."

Christian chuckled. "Which is your favorite?"

The boy leapt nimbly down, but nearly lost his balance. He shook his head, and gestured for Christian to follow him into the deeper recesses of the stable.

In the last stall stood a gray with magnificent tail sweeping the ground. "This is Remus," Geoffrey said, his voice faint with the awe in which he held the horse.

It was a magnificent creature, fifteen hands, with none of the lumpish plodding aspect of a destrier or farm horse. It was nearly completely white, save a flash of black in the forelock, and the head was nobly held. "Aye," Christian said with a grin.

Remus only looked at them as if bored.

"My lady bought him—" Geoffrey paused, puzzled, and touched his head.

A queer, abrupt paleness bled all color from the child's face. "Geoffrey, are you ill?"

In answer, the boy sunk to a heap with a little sigh. Alarmed, Christian knelt. "Geoffrey!"

The boy fell back in a dead faint. With a curse, Christian scooped his slim body into his arms, feeling all at once the fever raging in the child, like a fire stoked for a festival. Cursing, he ignored the twinges in his arm and carried the boy into the Hall.

Anya picked over her food. Around her, the mood in the Hall was equally subdued. There was hardly a person in the room not in some way touched by the new fever—Erda's husband, Stephen's five-year-old, the bailiff's two daughters as well as his wife.

There were the predictable gaps in the work force, too. Tillie had not reappeared this morning, and her sister came around to say she was ill. Two of the stableboys and one of the guards had fallen to the fever.

And all had heard the death bells through the night, had seen the monk and his retinue ride away at first light.

Anya struggled with a nagging sense of guilt, of things left undone. She ought not to have kept them all on such slim rations this winter. Perhaps the feast had come too late. Perhaps the fever was a visitation from God, to send Anya back to the Church. Perhaps—

Perhaps 'twas a punishment for the sin of her new wantonness. She closed her eyes against the thought, for even letting a small memory of this morning into her mind sent a rush of renewed desire through her. Shamed, she bowed her head.

A stir arose from the tables and Anya looked up to see Christian come through the doorway with Geoffrey in his arms. Spying the still, slim body of the child, she thought he had been somehow killed.

Punishment. An agonized cry gathered in her chest as she slowly rose, stunned, watching Christian come closer.

"'Tis the fever, I think," Christian said, stopping before her.

She touched Geoffrey's slim chest, as if to assure herself he still breathed. Heat and the dampness of sweat met her questing touch. His breath rattled in his chest. "Bring him to the solar," she said, leading the way.

The first sorrow died away, only to be replaced with another worrisome wave as she saw the boy lie so still in her bed. The last fever had weakened him, and though he had seemed to recover well enough, his usual wild energy had been absent since. Why had she not seen that till now?

Swiftly, she removed his clothes and washed him with cool water. He shivered as she blotted the water from his skin.

Christian stood nearby, watching. "My lady, what might I do to help you?"

Anya carefully covered Geoffrey with the coverlets and brushed a lock of hair from the hot, damp forehead. Quietly, she turned to face Christian, her mind whirling with the things she had to do. All of them she must tend herself.

Except one. "Go you to the church," she said in a soft voice, "and there light a candle to Mary for the child."

Christian's clear gray eyes were all too knowing as he nodded. Anya bent her head to tuck the furs around Geoffrey more firmly. She began to sing a quiet lullaby, a hard ache deep in her chest.

But aching and singing accomplished nothing.

When Christian left to do her bidding, Anya went to the kitchen to prepare the herbs she needed—white willow and yarrow steeped in red wine with pinches of coltsfoot and pennyroyal. Her hands trembled as she made the familiar mixture, and once she had to pause to breathe deeply.

'Twas the faint that frightened her. Often when children fell in such faints, they never awakened again. Or if they did, they were simple, as if the fever had burned the reason from their brains. Her heart pinched.

Into a large, clean crock she poured the bulk of the wine and herbs, giving it to the women in the kitchen to disburse among the others in the manor who were ill. The rest she took in a cup to the solar, along with clean strips of linen. "Mary," she said, "make a pallet in the Hall if you wish. I will tend Geoffrey tonight and will need your freshness with the dawn."

Mary nodded. "Take a little of your potion yourself, my lady. I like not the weariness I see." Gently, she smoothed the circles under Anya's eyes. There was something else in the woman's knowing eye—pity. Pity at Anya's foolish lust for the knight who would so fleetingly be among them.

With a flush of shame, she bowed her head, thinking of the scene Mary had witnessed this dawn. What if it had been another?

Stinging a little with the knowledge of what sport they'd all make of her, she simply nodded. Into the solar she carried her supplies.

A hard wind battered the shutters, sending a chill through the room. Anya hurried over to fasten the latches more securely, but as she struggled with them, the wind won the battle, tearing the wood from her hands. The shutter slammed against the stone wall next to her. A massive gust of snow-laden wind swept in.

With a cry, Anya grabbed the shutter. It was much taller than she, reaching almost to the ceiling, and the wind buffeted her so unmercifully she felt like a feather torn free from the underwing of a bird. As she struggled, snow stung her eyes.

At last she managed to secure the latches, but turned back to near darkness. The wind had snuffed her candles and only the fire gave any light. Smoothing damp curls from her face, Anya rekindled the tallows, then bent over Geoffrey once more. As she had done with the knight, she urged small drops of wine through his lips, over and over until she was satisfied she had managed to get some of the medicine inside of him.

Then she dipped the cloths and squeezed them out and pressed them to his brow and chest.

It was all there was to be done.

And for two days, her routine varied little. The world beyond the solar narrowed to a dim flickering on the edges of her tunneled concern for the child who had come to mean so much to her. Vaguely she heard the bells for the hours, and the bells that were not the hours. A blizzard of new snow raged beyond the walls, but aside from sweeping away the fine residue that blew through cracks in the shutters before it could melt, Anya did not notice it.

Sometimes Geoffrey thrashed wildly in fevered dreams, his small body straining with the terror. Mostly he lay in a deep, unnatural sleep, his skin dry and hot as a rock in the summer sun.

Anya did not leave him.

*   *   *

Sitting by the hearth in the dark of a winter evening, Christian listened to the wind howl. He had planned to be well away from the manor by now, but even had not the storm come, he could not leave Anya at such a time. Never had her calm cracked, but he saw below her thin control to the terror that raged in her breast.

He could safely trust the weather would delay any message flying south to his father from William. Even so, a certain nagging sense of impending doom dogged him. As soon as the weather broke, he must leave Winterbourne.

He did not know what his father had planned, nor why he wished Christian dead again with such suddenness. Perhaps 'twas only that Etienne wished no lingering evidence of his early weakness roaming the earth.

But that did not quite ring true. Pope Clement himself had long had a mistress. He was discreet, but all knew and forgave his weakness. The sin Etienne had visited upon a young English girl, the love the pair had shared, was long ago. Surely none would hold such against him now?

Christian narrowed his eyes. There was something more—something perhaps only Christian knew.

In the early years, Christian and his mother had lived in Gascony, close to then-bishop Etienne. He came often to them, to share supper and wine and the nights. Christian's memories of the time were rich, happy, without shadow.

Even after Rowena died when Christian was nine, Etienne had seen to it that his son was well cared for. He was fostered in a great noble's house, but often spent time in the company of his father, who sent for him at regular intervals. In the abbeys had Christian learned to read and figure, absorbing eagerly his father's love of law and philosophy contained within the vast array of books on the shelves of such places.

He frowned. Through those years after Rowena died, there had come a deep and painful change in his relationship with Etienne. Or mayhap the change had been in Etienne himself. For all that he acknowledged his child, Christian often had the feeling his father could not bear to look on him. Gradually, Etienne ignored him more and more as his ambitions swelled, his ruthlessness grew, his greed exploded. By the time he'd reached his thirteenth year, Christian had held no more respect for his father.

When he was fourteen, Christian had overheard the plot to kill Clement. Enraged and devastated to learn just far his father would stoop, Christian had confronted Etienne just before the papal coronation, threatening to expose the plot if his father did not withdraw it.

His father had been furious. Well Christian remembered the apoplectic red of the archbishop's face, the vein pounding in his temple as he railed at his son's idiocy. Unrelenting, Christian cursed his father and stormed out.

To this day, Christian did not know whether it had been some advisor or his own father who ordered Christian to be killed.

Weary of the squirrels chasing their tails around in his head, he stretched and made for the solar to check on Anya. From the sideboard he took a tankard of ale and a loaf of bread. The range of movement in his arm was limited, but he expected it always would be now. The break had been a bad one, the setting poor.

Stepping over the sleeping bodies of manor inhabitants, he moved to the solar. Within, Ysengrin guarded the foot of the bed. He lifted his tail cheerfully. A low fire burned in the hearth, and the stub of a tallow candle filled the room with its distinctive odor. In the bed lay Geoffrey, his cheeks yet flushed, his body still. There was no sign of Anya at first.

Then he spied her, collapsed on her folded arms over the surface of a writing desk. At first he thought she, too, had fallen ill, but as he moved closer, saw that she was only sleeping. Her unbound hair spilled around her in cloaking warmth, tumbling nearly to the floor on one side. It was plain sleep had taken her unaware, for in her hand was a quill, the ink dried on her fingertips.

Quietly he watched her. The angles of her face were framed with wisps of curls, and he traced with his gaze the arch of her cheek and the slant of her uptilted eyes. Her mouth was soft.

A sudden snore rent the air, and Christian turned in surprise. In the bed, Geoffrey turned over, as if his snore had jolted him, and snuggled more deeply into the furs.

Christian crossed the room and touched the child, feeling the sweat and cool flesh of a broken fever. The child's breathing seemed more natural, too, his features arrayed in a light mask of sleep, not the unholy waxiness it had held before.

With a quick gesture, Christian crossed himself, murmuring thanks. Tomorrow, he would go to the church and make some offering to Mary.

Now he would tend to his poor, exhausted mistress. On the floor nearby the hearth was the pallet she had ignored these three days and nights. He brushed it clean and turned back the furs.

At Anya's side, he halted, overcome with tenderness. Each small detail that made her seemed freshly rendered for his appreciation—that wild tumble of dark gold hair, her slim waist and rounded breasts. Even the stain of ink on her long white fingers seemed poignantly dear.

Quietly, he bent over her, taking the quill from her fingers. So as not to awaken her, he eased his arms around her, slipping one beneath the crook of her knees, the other around her shoulders, and pulled her slowly into the cradle his body made. When her head stirred, she made a low noise of protest, but so deep was the exhaustion that she did not waken, even when he stood up with her.

She seemed so strong and fierce that the slight weight of her body surprised him. He lifted her almost as easily as he had Geoffrey, and would vow there was not much difference between them.

So deep was his pleasure in having regained his strength that he did not immediately settle her on the pallet. Instead, he stood in the orange light of the fire, holding her close to him, her hair spilling over her body and down the length of his own. Her head rested easily on his shoulder, as if it belonged there.

As he held her thus in the silence of a winter night, so far from any place he had ever known, his heart began to pound with a slow, deep thudding. He touched his chin to the crown of her head.

At last wearied by even her slim weight, he knelt and settled her gently on the pallet. Her hair spread over his knee and he touched it, watching orange light play over her face.

He wanted her. Painfully. Wanted to awaken her with carnal touches, raise her blood to the heat of his own. In his groin was the pointed weight of denial and interrupted pleasure. He longed to finish what they had begun a few days before in this very room.

But it was not the kind of urgent lust he'd known so often in his life for a woman, raging only in that one place. Instead, he felt a vast openness come on him, something wide and still. It filled his chest and belly and his limbs, dizzying and strange.

He touched her cheek with his thumb, lightly. Unable to resist, he pressed a gentle kiss to the center of her wide brow, and heard her sigh as she shifted.

'Twould pain him deeply to leave her. And now that Geoffrey was on the mend and the storm waned, he knew he would have to.

Because of that loss, he settled next to her on the pallet, careful not to disturb her, and pulled her close to him, promising himself he would hold her only. He settled his head against her hair, his arm around her slim form, and pressed a kiss to her shoulder.

Hold her. That was all he would do. Hold her close and smell her hair and revel in the exquisite agony of restrained desire.

11

At some point, warm and whole next to Anya, he dozed. And into that light sleep crept his familiar dream: the brace of candles flickering in the darkness, his mother kneeling, her veiled head bent over a sacrament. The dream spread its comfort through him like spiced wine.

Anya's stirring woke him. It was only a little movement of legs, a shift of arms, toward him, though, not away. In his loose embrace, she turned, pressing her face into his chest, curling her arms between them. In her hair he smelled a hint of rose petals.

God's blood. She roused him as no other.

He must have made some move, for she bolted awake suddenly, sitting straight up from her comfortable sprawl. "Geoffrey!" she said in an urgent whisper, blinking to clear her eyes.

He caught her arm before she could stand and stumble. "He rests well, my lady."

In the vulnerable place between full alertness and

her sound sleep, she blinked, her eyes owlishly round. "Christian? What—?"

"You fell asleep." He stroked her arm. "Geoffrey's fever broke while you rested. He'll waken in the morn much renewed."

She struggled to her feet and padded over the cold stones to the bed. Bending over the child, she touched his face. Her breath left her on a soft, whimpering sound of relief and she sank to her knees, burying her face in her hands.

Seared by her posture, Christian went to her. He thought she wept, but when she lifted her face, her eyes were dry. "He lives," she said.

"Aye." He smiled.

"Now we must send him to the king, else my brother will take him to Lichfield, and there make his life a living hell."

He'd forgotten the impulsive words to William, but saw what she said was true. "I'll see to it. Edward will not turn him away."

Her gaze went back to the boy, and Christian saw her fingers tighten on the furs nearby the child's arm. There was grief there, still, and he thought he understood it. When her own child had been taken, this one had filled her need to mother. Had not his own mother wept when he left her? "He will be well tended at Edward's court," Christian offered.

Anya nodded silently, and brushed a lock of Geoffrey's hair from his forehead. "'Tis dangerous to love a child," she said softly. "And yet I seem to have no voice in it. He came to us when he was but three, and I had need. . . ."

Still she did not weep, only stared with stricken face at the child. "At least he lives," she said at last.

"Aye," Christian said. He ached to hold her, but rigidly held himself where he was, kneeling next to her on the cold flags. "Come, lady, sleep now. Else you'll take the fever next."

With her head bent away, she asked quietly, "Will you hold me as you did before?" She paused. "I found much comfort in your arms."

Wordlessly, he reached for her, his hands trembling with the restraint he needed to be gentle. Close he drew her against his chest, pressing her head into the hollow of his shoulder. Her slim arms wrapped around him. A shudder of release passed through her. He tightened his hold.

And by the saints, it was a broad, deep thing, the feeling that filled him then! He closed his eyes to savor it, and it was as if he became as large as all the world, no longer bound by the mortal restraints of limbs and flesh and blood. He felt light as air and bigger than all the sky, and Anya with him, a presence sensed but not seen.

Awash in the holy feeling, he pressed a chaste kiss to her brow.

"Do you feel it, Christian?" Her tone was hushed with awe.

When he looked into her eyes, dark in the low light, he felt he could see through to her soul. He brushed her cheek and nodded, unable to speak.

Together they stretched out on the pallet, body to body, limb to limb, heart to heart. Christian felt an airless, thudding pain through his belly, not common arousal, but something almost fulfilled by itself. Afraid to disturb the vastness of it, he only held her, aching at the gentle swell of her breast against his ribs and the curve of her hip and the press of her soft belly.

He lifted his hand to her cheek. He allowed himself no more than that, only tracing the bones of her strong and winsome face. In the powerful, humming silence, their eyes locked.

Had he been asked to count the times he'd lain with a woman, he wouldn't have been able to tally them all. But never had there been this sense of making love without bodies, a feeling so rich it pulsed through him, endlessly, without the sharp rise and fall of sex, as if their souls were engaged in some business sacred and secret.

Without hurry, he lowered his lips and kissed her. The vastness trebled instantly. He touched her breast through her gown, just covered it with his palm, taking sweet pleasure in the fit of it to his palm, gauging the gentle weight against his fingers.

Anya shifted against him, and her tongue begged more of his mouth. Now the vastness was joined by restlessness and a certain urgent haste. As their mouths moved, explored, supped, he found he could not keep himself still. A vision of her body, naked in the low light of morning, passed over his vision and he unlaced her gown and skimmed the fabric from her body. She gasped when he touched her bared flesh with his hand, and Christian groaned with the furious need it kindled in him.

He lifted his head to look at her. The dark gold curls spilled all around them, tangling in his fingers. Leaping red light from the low fire touched her flesh, turning it rosy. Her shoulders were thin, the bones a little too prominent; she'd known hunger this year. He kissed the ridge, wishing he could put more flesh there, and pressed his jaw against her breast.

He kissed her throat. "This is dangerous," he whispered. "I have no choice but to leave you."

With strong hands, she grasped his head and pulled him up to look in his eyes. A sultry burning lay on her lips, full and wet from his kiss, and there was knowledge in her gaze. "Teach me, Christian," she whispered. "Show me what it is to lie with a man, so I do not spend the whole of my life wondering."

In answer, he kissed her. Pulling up her skirts, he stirred the already heated embers of her need, and took her hand and pressed it against his shaft, showing her how to move. He could not halt his groan of pleasure as she quickly found it to her liking. On her own, she unlaced his hose and let him free.

The pleasure of touching her, having her touch him, sent the odd vast sense of eternity spinning up another notch, until Christian feared they might die if they joined.

It would be worth the sacrifice.

He could not think, only feel, and wild roaring need in his loins now demanded all. He kissed her deeply, burying his hands in her hair, whispering her name as he shifted her legs and settled his between them in the dark, cold winter night.

With a single, fierce thrust, he joined them. Dimly, he heard himself cry, heard the sound mingle with the shocked, pleasured voice of Anya arching below him.

And aye, he'd surely die. His breath left him, his heart ceased.

He drove hard, grasping her shoulders, feeling her body convulse around him, and his own delirious vastness overtake him. At the last moment, he bent and kissed her, then tumbled into a small death, knowing himself forever changed.

*   *   *

Anya shuddered, filled with the fierce power that was Christian, in her and through her, around her. Against her breasts, she felt the rough texture of his chest. His broad thighs rested between her own, dense and strong.

Trembling, shattered, overwhelmed, she wept.

Christian broke away from her, cursing. The movement was so abrupt, Anya only curled into a ball to hold the warmth of his body, aching with his loss and unable to find the words to call him back.

He did not go far, only sat up and gathered her close, wrapping them both in the covers. His great muscled arms circled her, and she sat naked in his naked lap, enveloped in the sheltering size of him. He stroked her hair urgently. "Forgive me, Anya—'twas wrong. I let my cock think for me."

She closed her eyes and burrowed deeper, wishing they could stay thus for all of time. "I did—"

The words stuck and she lifted her head, swallowing. "I did not know 'twould be such . . ." She shook her head. "So much joy," she finally whispered.

His thumb stroked her cheek. "I did not hurt you?"

He thought her a virgin, then—no one had told him the story. "Nay."

"You are smaller than I expected. I thought since you had borne a babe, 'twould be easier for you. I should have gone more slowly."

She froze. "You know of the babe?"

"Aye," he said in a rough tone. "And the way it came to you, too. If it had not been so long a time, my sweet, I vow I'd track the whoreson down and cut that which he used away from him, and leave him to bleed."

A plethora of emotions raced through her, but his last comment stuck. "God's bones, Christian!" She laughed, more in relief that it seemed not to matter to him than anything else. "You've done more healing tonight than any vengeance ever could."

A purely male smile of pride touched his lips. "There is more, when you wish to learn it."

Again she chuckled. "Are men all so arrogant?"

"Only those with so much to be arrogant about."

"Ah." She became aware of the weight she must be for him, and shifted sideways, drawing him with her to lie on the pallet. He stretched out beside her, long and warm, and one great leg laced between hers. The furs cocooned them.

"You have bewitched me," he said and his expression was grave.

"No, Christian, 'tis you who have bewitched me. Never did I think I would love a man, not after—"

He pressed a finger to her lips. "Speak not of love, my lady, for there is no hope of that with us. I am a cardinal's bastard, with nothing to give you."

"And I am a woman who has borne the child of a rapist. What difference makes that to love?" Anya turned, earnest. "For love I do, dear knight, though well I know you must leave me."

He made a low, pained sound and buried his face in her shoulder. "Do not speak of it, Anya, I beg you. There is much wrong done in the name of love."

The words hurt her, and she pulled away from him. "Go then to find some camp whore, if love is such a sin."

His arms tightened, pinning her against him. When he lifted his head, his face was the warrior mask, dark and dangerous. "My father loved my mother," he said, "and he ruined her, and would murder her son. There is the love I have seen.

"Your brothers locked you in a room and stole your child—all for love of you. I will not love that way, nor let you." He kissed her, fiercely. "I will pray you bear no child from this, and thus our wrong will be lessened, and tomorrow, ask you of Mary what herbs keep babes at bay. To keep you safe, I will leave you when the storm breaks."

Tears came to Anya's eyes again, and she touched his face. "'Twas a great blessing to find you in the forest that day."

He sighed and pressed his lips to her neck. "I am a weak and intemperate man—"

"Thank the saints."

At last her irreverence jolted his sober humor and he chuckled. Wickedly, he traced her inner thigh with a tantalizing motion. "I believe I hear a purr."

"Aye," she said and sighed in contentment. Next to her, he was as big and warm as a bear. Idly, she traced a vein in the sleek flesh of his upper arm. "Your father is a cardinal?" she asked, a little in awe of one so highly placed.

Christian lifted his head to prop his head on one hand. "I did not know myself he'd risen so high until your brother came. Last news I heard, he was only archbishop."

"What knew my brother of your father?"

"I fear he knows all." His gaze drifted toward the fire. "All," he repeated grimly.

"But how? He has no ties to the papacy—and though his ambitions are greedy, not even he has aspired to that throne."

"We are very alike, my father and I. Your brother met

him once—and my father, he stands out."

Anya smiled a little, thinking of a man like Christian, older and more imposing, dressed in the glittering garb of the church. "Well I can imagine."

"William wishes to be rid of me anyway. All know my father aspires to the papacy and will not wish so flagrant an indiscretion as I represent flying in the wind."

Anya frowned. "It has been many years since your mother died. 'Tis not a mortal sin to father a bastard, or all the church would be damned. Surely he would not murder you for that?"

"Nay. Nor . . ." he shook his head. "He fears something, but I swear I know not what it is. Nor does your brother—but 'twould surprise me greatly if there was not a messenger on the road to Avignon as we speak."

"What will you do?"

For a long moment, he was silent. His hand moved on her ribs, back and forth, but she doubted he was aware of the restless gesture.

"That I do not know," he said at last. "I must leave here, that much is certain. I'm not without allies. 'Tis much now as it was the first time I fled my father in fear for my life—but God provided well then, and will again."

"I will pray for you, when you go," she said, aware of a plucking pain at the thought of him leaving.

"I thought you did not pray."

"I've no quarrel with God, as I told you—nor even the saints. And while 'tis true I face eternal burning for myself, while I yet live my prayers are as well crafted as any."

"Speak not of damnation," he said, hands tight in her hair. "I vow, Anya, that nary will I pass a church that I do not light a candle for your soul."

"Such fierceness," she said lightly.

"No woman so wise and kind and strong, one who cares for the lives in her care with such honor, will be allowed to be damned." He frowned. "Is it truly worth the price you pay in fear, Anya?"

She sighed. "When I've awakened from a dream of hell, it seems foolhardy, I must admit. But you cannot know—" She closed her eyes. "Aye, 'tis worth that and more."

He moved closer, and his nose touched her cheek. "Is there no one to champion you, Anya? Can someone not be sent to find your other brother?"

"John is on a pilgrimage to the Holy Land and has been gone now nigh on five years." She brushed her hand over the fur, thinking of the time of John's drunkenness. "He was not meant to be a soldier or a knight. He is too gentle for that life."

"So why did he not go into the Church?"

She shifted, giving him a sad smile. "The fief fell to him as eldest son."

"And William was not suited to that task?"

Anya laughed. "Nay! He is not graceful or clever on a horse. He drops his sword and misses targets . . . my father used to scream at him all the day and William could do nothing to please him."

"So you were your father's knight."

"Aye." She could not quell the pride in her tone. "He often mourned my sex."

Christian sighed, idly tracing the edge of her shoulder with one finger. "So it goes—a woman should be knight; a knight wishes to be troubadour; a troubadour wishes to be king; a king wishes to be a common laborer for the joy of using his hands."

"Is that what Edward wishes? To use his hands?"

"He is a common man and loves common things." He lifted up on his elbow again. "Just as your brothers wish for other things for their lives, so Edward wishes different things for his."

"And you, Christian? What things do you wish for your life?"

He did not answer immediately. Only stared toward the fire with a grave expression. The light danced over his extraordinary face and Anya felt a clutch of wonder that he had come to lie here with her on this cold winter night.

"I am weary of battle," he said at last. "My bones ache in the cold and long rides weary me." A quizzical frown touched his brow. "I would like now to be peaceful somehow, to live without strife in some quiet place."

"Surely there is some reward for you in Edward's service."

"No doubt there would be if I asked it. He too is a little weary with all the strife—and I am loath to ask of him anything until I . . ."

"Until?"

"I must go to my father," he said with a grim sigh. "Else I will be forever looking over my shoulder and will find no peace anywhere."

"Do you think your father was pleased with his choices? Did he want to be a priest?"

"His ambitions could be served only there." There was something both dangerous and sorrowful in his voice. "In the Church, a simple man can become king of all the world, no?"

At what price? Anya wondered. "You wish to hate him, but you do not."

He buried his face in her neck. "In all my wanderings, I've not met a woman like you." Slowly, his broad palm skimmed her flesh. Anya's breath caught high in her throat as he kissed her shoulder, his mouth rich and warm and moist.

"Without you, Anya," he said into the hollow of her throat, his lips moving with the words, "I would now be dead. I can ill express my gratitude—would that I could stay and help you fight your dragons."

Anya tensed at his words, for they made plain his reasons for lying here with her before the warm embers of the fire. In her eyes, in her words, she had told him what she wanted—to lie with him. And he, being male and not untouched by lust himself, had obliged her, since he could offer nothing else in thanks.

His hair, so coarse and cool in the night, trailed over her shoulder as he tenderly planted a row of kisses from neck to breast, and Anya felt a clutch of sorrow over the knowledge that he only came to her in gratitude.

And yet, what more had she hoped? That so grand a knight, so bold and sensual and strong a man might love her, a ruined maid with nothing but a small purse and middling manor to bring as dowry?

He was the sort of man who could command the heart of an earl's daughter, or a princess, for his virility and skills as a knight more than compensated for the things he saw as his lacks.

She should be grateful that his feelings for her, while not like her own, at least brought him here to her bed, where she might love him.

Blindly, she turned to him, pressing her mouth to his beautiful lips, accepting his well-meant caresses in the spirit he offered them. His wish had been to teach

her a man could be gentle, could give pleasure as well
as pain, and that he had done. In all her life, she
might have no more than this.

Before it had been Christian moving toward her,
giving to her a wild pleasure she had not expected.
This time, ignorant though she was, she would do her
best to return the favor.

Because his mouth on her neck gave so much pleasure, she touched her lips to his throat and experi-
mentally tasted the salt of his flesh there. His bristled
chin brushed her forehead. His hands shifted, pulling
her closer, teasing along her spine.

She resisted the languorous need she felt to accept
his ministrations and moved lower, tasting now his
nipples with her tongue and teeth, imitating his way
with her as well as she could, hoping 'twas the same
for a man. He made a soft noise of surprise, one that
deepened to a groan when her hand crept over the
flat of his belly to the velvety flesh of his manhood
and there coaxed it to a rigid post.

A trembling heat grew in her, and she knew not
what should be next. She shifted to a half-sitting posture, to ask guidance, sure he'd be willing to give it.

But as she sat up, he followed, and grasped her
waist in his palms, and swiftly lifted her into his lap.
With one arm, he braced her back and nudged her
gently backward, lowering his great head to her
breasts. She felt the brush of his beard singe the
aching points, then the heat of his mouth closing over
the place. Her fingers clutched at his arms at the
sharp jolt of sensation the combination wrought.
When he flickered his tongue over the place, and
moved ever so slightly against the aching juncture of
her thighs, though, she felt something else—a thrum-

ming that seemed to rise and build, fueled by his tongue and his movements below. All so gentle, so precise, as if he knew exactly—

An explosion centered low in her body suddenly ripped through her. In surprise, she went rigid, and fell against him, overwhelmed with the new feeling, so raw and uncontrollable.

With a powerful movement, Christian shifted and somehow impaled her, sending a new depth to the feeling. He grasped her hips and moved, showing her the way she should go. Eagerly, she responded, thrilling with the way it made her feel, the way it made him groan. She clutched his shoulders for balance and he suckled her neck. And just when Anya thought 'twas winding down, he made a low animal noise against her and she could feel a pulsing that echoed her own coming from him. His fingers dug into her buttocks.

Hearts racing, breath shuddering, they fell together to the furs, her legs locked around his waist so she would not be unjoined from him. Not yet.

He kissed her—her mouth and chin and mouth again, ungentle and unstudied. "Such passion is rare, Anya. 'Tis waste you have had no man these long years."

"'Twas different this time."

"Aye." The word was a growl, uttered into her breast. "Aye, 'twas the way it should be and what I was too hurried to give you before."

The first time had been holy, as much a sacrament as any she'd taken at the altar, but Anya did not say such aloud, for perhaps it was not the same for Christian.

"You will have to teach me, my lord, how to finish

as well as begin," she said with a low chuckle. "I fear I did not know how to go on."

"'Twill be my pleasure to teach you whatever you wish to know."

"Is there much?"

He lifted his head and a distinctly sensual expression glowed in his pale gray eyes. "Aye," he said, and the word was a delicious promise.

Toward dawn, he left her with a kiss. Anya lay in the dark room, replete, and slept well for the first time in weeks.

When she awakened, it was to see Mary towering over her. "Well, what have we here?" she said as Anya stirred. "If any in the house sees you this way, your secret will not long be secret."

Anya blushed. What did Mary see?

She remembered in a rush what Christian had told her to do, and tugged on the woman's skirts. "Come down here," she whispered.

The peasant sank to the floor, a gleam in her eye. "'Tis time I see that look on yer lips, milady."

"Stop it," Anya said, her face hot. She shifted uncomfortably. "There must be no babes. Methinks you know the secret to that magic."

Mary lifted her eyebrows, as if offended. "Me?"

Anya slapped her arm gently. "You. Will you tease me all or will you give me the answer I seek?"

Abruptly, Mary hugged her. "Ooooh, he is a plum, my lady. A great, big—oh, big!—plum!"

"Shhh!" Anya hissed, but giddiness overcame her and she leaned into the woman's shoulder. "Had I but known . . ."

From the bed came Geoffrey's voice. "Lady?" The sound was thin but true.

Yelping in happiness, Anya jumped up, wrapping her covers around her as she hobbled over to the bed. She bent and hugged the child in her joy. "Oh, sweet Geoffrey—what terror you struck through my heart!"

"How long have I lain here?"

"Days and days," she said, touching his cheek. "And more days will you stay until I think you well enough to rise. Mary, bring some food."

The peasant paused by the bed, and pressed a happy kiss to the boy's forehead. "Oh, young Geoffrey, 'tis good to see you so hale."

Anya caught her hand as she turned and gave a meaningful look toward the pallet on the floor. Mary winked. "Aye, milady. By evening."

With the cold thin light of morning, Christian made for the stables, taking with him an apple plucked from the winter stores. A guard on the walk lifted a hand and Christian nodded. In the air was the sharp, wet cold of clouds lifted, and his breath puffed visibly out before him, stirring the tiny flakes of snow glittering suspended in the air. His feet kicked through a foot of fresh snow—it piled high on the stable eaves and along the bailey wall.

It was beautiful. Christian breathed in the crisp, bracing air and smelled a hint of spring below the frost. The storm had carried with it the feeling of a last great stand of winter, furious, but fleeting. By evening, he'd wager there would be icicles hanging from the roofs and mud in every lane.

Which meant his time here was very short.

Ducking into the stables, he made for the stall of the gray, nodding to stable boys at work shoveling stalls and feeding horses. Anya's spirited black gelding danced up to the gate and lifted his head in greeting, sending his mane flying against the pale winter light. Christian smiled and wished for a second apple. Next time.

The gray ignored Christian when he came to the gate at his stall. The horse stared through the window toward the snowy forest as if enough thought might make the walls dissolve. "Remus, I have you an apple," Christian said, offering his hand over the gate.

A stableboy looked up curiously from his chores. "He won't have nothing to do with none of us, my lord. A bad-tempered beast." Lifting the edge of his sleeve, he displayed a bruised arch on his forearm. "Bit me two days ago, he did, when I tried to clean his stall."

Christian nodded sympathetically and turned back to the horse, patiently holding out the sweet. Remus swung his head around, eyed man and apple for a moment, and turned back to the window, heaving a sigh.

Christian did not go away, but stood admiring the beast, his arm propped patiently on the door, his hand extended. What a magnificent horse it was! Again he admired the graceful neck and head, the strength in the hindquarters, the proud arched tail, evidence of some Spanish blood.

Suddenly into the embrasure jumped the multicolored cat, Esmerelda. She meowed a cheerful greeting to Remus, arching her back and bumping her head against the horse's nose. Remus snuffled softly and nuzzled the cat, who rubbed back and forth against the great head. Their happy meeting accomplished, Remus shifted in the stall and the cat leapt nimbly to the horse's back. Remus stood very still while Esmerelda circled, round and round, and at last settled sleepily, her head cushioned in the mane.

With an insolent toss of his head, Remus glanced toward Christian. His disdain made Christian chuckle. "I see you need me not," he said, with a grin. Nonetheless, he let the apple drop gently to the earth inside the stall.

This was the horse Christian would take when he had to go. But even the thought of leaving sent his mood plummeting, and in that dark mood, he felt Anya all around him again, as she had been in the night.

He'd been wrong to bed her. Long before she knew if she would bear a child to their joining, he'd be on the road to Provence. Not for the world would he put her through more shame—and yet, to stay might put the entire village in peril.

A plucking guilt filled him and he knew not how to loose it. What had been done could not be undone—his sin had been committed. He hoped it would not cause her more suffering. It lay to him to see that there was no such play between them again.

God help him.

12

Upon reaching the abbey at Lichfield, William found the abbot in the infirmary, ill with the bitter fever that had befallen the manor at Winterbourne. The blizzard began to move in that same night, and within two more days, William himself was abed with the fever, which he'd no doubt drunk off the girl Tillie's lips.

So it was nearly a fortnight before the abbot called William, still weak but moving about freely, to his private chamber. The sun at last shone, illuminating the stained glass in the windows of the chapel and in the cathedral, giving light and air to the corridors linking infirmary, courtyard and offices of the church. Slowly William traversed them, vowing to take more care with the wenches he bedded in the future.

Nor had the abbot fared well. The straight figure was gaunt, and deep hollows marked his cheeks. In the corner with the window and its thick glass, the abbot sat absorbing the warmth of thin sun. "Welcome, Brother Simon," he said, gesturing for William to sit with him.

Even the short walk had wearied him, and William sank to a bench by the fire. "Thank you."

"So," said the abbot, "you saw him?"

"Aye. You were right—my sister has gained herself a champion."

The abbot nodded. "As I said. 'Twas worth going, was it not, to learn this morsel? Now we must plan how to rid ourselves of him."

In his exhuasted state, the elaborate plan William had concocted upon learning of the knight's father seemed to require more than he had in him to give. He nearly confessed that Christian de Morcerx was not some simple knight, but a friend to the king and the son of a cardinal. He closed his eyes, feeling dizzy. If it weren't for the messenger on the way to Avignon as of yesterday, he would have spilled all.

As it was, the abbot would be furious that William had acted alone. With a sigh, William said, "Abbot, even if we chase away the knight, I have little hope my sister will quit Winterbourne. Between that cursed child and her stubbornness, I have not yet thought of a way to dislodge her."

"The child?"

"Geoffrey. The boy my brother foolishly brought back to her before his pilgrimage. Naught I could say would halt his resolution she should have her son."

The abbot nodded slowly, pursing his lips in thought. "Is there not some way to part child and mother?"

"I'd planned to bring him back here." In truth, the

idea had only come to William as a method to spite his sister when she so infuriated him, but the abbot need not know all. "But it seems the knight is close to the king and has made arrangements for the boy to go to Edward's court."

"Ah." He coughed, the sound still deep in his chest. William waited as he spat into a cloth and sipped a draught of ale. "I expect something to be done, Brother Simon," he said finally. "'Tis for you to judge. By summer, I wish Winterbourne to be part of the cathedral's holdings. If the skies drown us all through the spring as they have done this winter, more will starve."

Grimly, William nodded. The unspoken threat hung in the room like a specter of his sister laughing. Either he delivered Winterbourne, or he'd find himself a long way gone—unless Cardinal d'Auch found it fit to reward one who had served him well. "I have in mind a plan."

Once he left the abbot, he sought out a trusted young monk. In a discreet voice, he said, "Carry a message to the Three Crowns to Harold Gramercy. Tell him there is gold for his task if he will do it now."

Anya scattered feed for the chickens about on the ground, taking deep pleasure in the sun on her head. The wind, shifting from the south, was warming, and all around her was the sound of melting snow. It dripped from the roofs and sent silvery rivulets down the manor walls. The bailey bustled with people scurrying about on their chores, whistling and singing, buoyed by the sudden appearance of spring.

The fever seemed spent—a single swing of the

reaper's scythe. Nine had been lost to it; four of them children. The rest were now recovered, though it seemed to take a good stretch of time, and none else had fallen ill.

A chicken clucked jealously and swirled under Anya's skirts. She frowned and shifted to shoo it away. Across the yard sat Geoffrey, bundled in a heavy woolen cloak. Only his face was exposed. Anya had insisted.

His eyes danced now as he watched Christian, splendidly handsome and powerful in his hauberk, playfully joust with a slender guard. He had borrowed a light sword of her father's to rebuild his strength, and by the clanking and laughter ringing through the afternoon air, it seemed it was quickly returning.

Still holding her apron and leading a trail of chickens, Anya drifted toward them. Christian's hair shone in the bright day, touching his broad shoulders. For so large a man, he moved lightly on his feet, quick and steady, the sword an extension of his arm. As she stared, he dodged the expert thrust of his partner and nearly stumbled. Laughing ruefully, he regained his balance with a single graceful turn.

Since the night Geoffrey had recovered, more than a week ago, Christian had not come to Anya again. In truth, he avoided her company at all turns. He slipped into the kitchen before meals to charm Erda into feeding him early, and retreated—often with Geoffrey— into the hearth room early in the evenings. She could hear them talking quietly, and knew Christian was telling the child a story of a saint each night. Every morning, Geoffrey came to regale her with the latest bloody chapter. This morning, he'd asked if she knew the story of Saint Thomas à Becket, who crowned the village church.

It was likely something Christian's own father had done for him, spun the legends of martyrs and confessors and extraordinary deeds done in the name of heaven. In all, not so different from the fairies and elves and witches of her own childhood.

A chicken pecked her toe, as if to remind her she'd forgotten her duty. Hastily, Anya dipped her hand into her apron.

When she glanced up again, she found Christian staring at her. He had finished his swordplay with the guard and now leaned on the stone wall, his breath coming heavily.

Boldly, she crossed the yard. "You need a talisman, my lord," she said, and pulled the string from her braid. "'Tis no fine silk ribbon, but it looks as if anything at all would be a help to you."

He grinned, and it was a devastating expression, dangerously male. With a quick lift of his brow, he said, "Mayhap 'twill bring me luck." He winked as he stood and readied himself for the next contest. He wrapped the string around his arm and held it out to her to tie.

"I cannot," she said, indicating the apron full of seed.

The gray eyes glittered. "You take one side. I'll manage the other."

She didn't wish to stand so close, but it was she who'd begun the game. Gathering her apron in one hand, she reached for the string with the other. Their fingers brushed. Even so small a thing sent a strange echo of their joining through her. Her cheeks felt hot.

What she would give to be over this silliness! All her life she'd done without it, and now when there was no possibility of fully exploring it, it came on her like this.

"Anya," he said quietly.

She kept her gaze lowered, working with him to tie the string. When it was knotted, he captured her fingers in his palm. "Anya, 'tis not—"

"Nay!" she said the word fiercely, to halt whatever apology he wished to tender. "Do not say it, my lord. Whatever it is, you have no need to make amends to me."

His voice was very quiet as he spoke again. "Walk with me."

"What of your sparring?"

"'Twill wait. This will not." He waved an end to the mock battle and took Anya's arm. "To the stables. I wish to ask you about a horse."

Ignoring the knowing smiles of those in the yard, Anya vented her panic and sorrow and hunger by flinging up her apron. Seed scattered in a mass, and an eager flock of chickens crowded around her feet. Blindly, she followed Christian to the stables. He wanted to speak of a horse! A horse!

And yet, what had she expected? Men did not spin songs of her beauty or weave ballads for love of her. She was only simple Anya, born in a simple manor, whose only life had been work.

Oh, but she had thought—

In the cold dimness of the stables, Christian shooed away a boy shoveling hay. "Go breathe the fresh air," he said, "put some color in your cheeks."

With a swift knowing smile toward Anya, the boy ran to do as he was told. Another one, thinking the knight and the long-dried-up lady of the manor were come to the private quiet of the stable to exchange kisses and illicit caresses! She might have borne their pleased little smiles if what they thought were true.

Tossing a lock of hair from her face, she said, "What horse?"

For a moment, he only stood there, looking at her with an unreadable and very sober expression. She braced herself for the excuses he would give, but even the thought of them humiliated her and she blurted out, "Do not shame me more by tendering apology, Christian. Just go and allow me to regain my peace."

"You know not of what you speak," he said in a low voice.

"Mayhap not. Show me the horse you wish to ride from here."

Abruptly, he turned and strode through the dimness to the far stall. By the door sat Esmerelda, fastidiously cleaning her face with her paw.

Christian stooped to pick her up. "Ah, just the creature I wanted to see." He stroked her, rubbing both hands over her body, even putting her on his face. The cat half closed her eyes, her purr roaring into the quiet, an expression of almost delirious pleasure on her face.

Anya knew just how the poor creature felt.

With a glance toward Anya, who did not see his purpose, Christian carried the cat to the door of the stall, and holding her close to him, reached into his pocket for an apple. "Remus," he said in a strong voice. "I have two treats for you today."

She should have guessed he'd pick Remus. "Christian," she said, "he is not well trained, and he's bitten every stable hand here. I will give you Evered, my own horse, who will serve you well. This one—"

He cut her a glance, a half smile on his lips. Remus came to the door, snuffling softly at Esmerelda. Christian held out the apple in the flat of his hand,

and the horse accepted it almost delicately. Still holding the cat, Christian reached up to stroke Remus's nose, making soft noises, nonsense chattering, really. The horse didn't move away, but allowed Christian to move his hand to his neck and forequarters, still talking quietly. When Esmerelda made a jealous move, he put her gently on the horse's back.

And still Remus didn't move away. With a pleased smile, Christian continued to touch the beast with both hands. Remus turned suddenly and put his nose right in Christian's face—she thought surely the horse would bite his nose—and snuffled at his hair.

Anya was unwillingly touched by the display. His talent for charming did not end at women, but extended to beasts as well. "And I suppose you can take wild honey from a tree without a single sting."

He chuckled quietly, glancing over his shoulder as he bent to let the horse nuzzle the crown of his head. "In truth, I can. My mother had the gift and showed me how 'tis done."

"There are those who would call such talents with beasts unholy."

His smile broadened. "Aye."

Remus, seemingly satisfied with his inspection, moved away. Christian straightened. He took a step toward her, and Anya took one backward, instinctively keeping her distance. She didn't trust herself with this man, and had more than completely made a fool of herself already.

His expression shifted with that telling step. "Anya," he said with a note of regret.

She held up a hand. "Do not speak of it."

Swiftly he closed the distance between them and captured her hand. Backed into the wall, Anya could find no escape. "You misread me," he said. "'Tis for your sake I have not come to you again."

Anya only looked at him, willing herself to at least pretend to be unmoved.

"Where did you learn to believe you are not beautiful, my lady? A woman at court with your charms would be vain and arrogant and might lie only with the highest placed men, perhaps only with the king himself."

"Christian, you need not tame me as you do the beasts and bees. I am a woman only."

"'Tis not so light a thing as that, Anya, and well you know it. I lie in that pallet alone and can think of naught but you." He scowled. "But I must leave—there is no hope for us. I'll not spread my seed and let it grow untended, not with you."

"What an honorable man," she said with tartness, and ducked away from him. Smoothing her apron down, she backed toward the door. "Remus is yours do with as you will. Soon the roads will be somewhat passable and you may go on your great quest. Your debt to me is paid, and I release you."

He laughed. The sound of it, rumbling with low seductive power from his chest, unnerved her. She froze.

"Come here," he said.

Anya shook her head.

He stepped toward her, a slowly graceful and powerful man. The teasing light fled his eyes. "What would you have me do, my lady?"

"I—" She stared at him, shaking her head at the visions that presented themselves. Foolish daydreams. "Nothing. There is naught you can do."

She walked to the door. At the threshold, she

paused to look back, marking his virile beauty well in
her mind. "For all the sadness I will feel at your going,
Christian, I cannot be sorry you came. For at least
once I've tasted that of which all the troubadours
sing."

He moved so suddenly she had no time to react.
One moment he stood there with the deep brooding
look in his face, the next he had captured her in his
arms. He swept her into his embrace, nearly lifting
her from her feet, his head buried against her neck.
"May God forgive me, but I cannot resist the lure of
your sweetness." With one enormous palm, he caught
her head and kissed her.

Anya nearly swooned at the unexpected feel of him
again, so close, the smell of his skin and the taste of
his mouth. And again like a blaze of light, the magical
thing flared between them, a dazzling flare. It shot
from the crown of her head through her body and left
her trembling violently, so violently it frightened her.
Panicked, she struggled against him, grasping his
arms for fear she would fall.

At her fluttering movements, his touch gentled.
His mouth softened. He supped of her lips as if he
were sampling some exquisite and rare dish, and his
fingers in her hair no longer felt bruising, but trailed
over her face, circled her neck.

The flare of brightness behind her eyes intensified.
Anya, wrapped in the weightless feeling, felt that her
body held no form, but dissolved and blended with
his, like flour in water.

Suddenly, the wild thought that he might be an
angel passed through her mind. An angel sent to protect her, protect Geoffrey—

With an urgent move, she pushed away from his

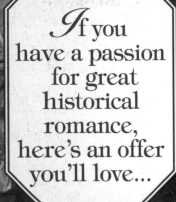

If you
have a passion
for great
historical
romance,
here's an offer
you'll love...

4 FREE NOVELS

SEE INSIDE.

Reader Service.

Yes! I want to join the Timeless Romance Reader Service. Please send me my 4 FREE HarperMonogram historical romances. Then each month send me 4 new historical romances to preview without obligation for 10 days. I'll pay the low subscription price of $4.00 for every book I choose to keep--a total savings of at least $2.00 each month--and home delivery is free! I understand that I may return any title within 10 days and receive a full credit. I may cancel this subscription at any time without obligation by simply writing "Canceled" on any invoice and mailing it to Timeless Romance. There is no minimum number of books to purchase.

NAME

ADDRESS

CITY   STATE   ZIP

TELEPHONE

SIGNATURE

(If under 18, parent or guardian must sign. Program, price, terms, and conditions subject to cancellation and change. Orders subject to acceptance by HarperMonogram.)

kiss to stare at him. If she were God, this is what angels would look like—so bold and full of life and yet so fair his eyes in this light almost seemed to hold no color at all. His eyes . . . like clouds.

If he were an angel, then would not seduction be a truly mortal sin? She dropped her hands and backed away. He was the son of a cardinal! And his name—oh, even his name!—was Christian.

She backed into the wall with a bump and grabbed behind her to the post, staring at him, wondering that she had not seen it before. "Forgive me, my lord," she whispered. "I do not mean to tempt you—it is only that there are so few things I've wanted. . . ."

"Anya, what is it? I truly didn't mean to frighten you."

She could only shake her head, her thoughts whirling—he tamed the beasts and had appeared from nowhere in the forest, out of the great strange storm. Oh, what had she done?

He threw up his hands and uttered a vile oath, whirling away from her in obvious frustration.

At the violent curse, Anya's breath left her on a sigh of relief. She pressed a trembling hand to her chest. "Oh, Christian," she said quietly, choking back an embarrassed laugh, "for a moment, I thought you might be an angel."

"What?"

"An angel, sent to protect me from my brother, to save Geoffrey from the fever . . ." She closed her eyes, cursing herself silently for the lunacy that overtook her in his company. "Before you came here, I was never given to these fits. You must think me mad."

"An angel!" He laughed, the sound rich and merry. He took her hand. "I have been thought many things,

my lady, but this is the first time any called me angel."
Still grinning, he cocked a brow, and in a low, rumbling voice, said, "If you knew what thoughts consumed me just now, you'd not think it either."

Mayhap he did not bed her for gratitude, but from real feeling. The hope made her bold. "What thoughts, my lord?"

He touched her lips with one long finger. "Thoughts of giving weight to the gossip flying all around," he said slowly. "Thoughts of showing you more of the sweetness that can be between a man and a woman." His finger dropped over her chin and drew little figures on her chest above her gown. "Do you wish that, Anya?"

Soberly, she nodded.

He sighed and inclined his head. His mouth looked severe. "I cannot tarry here long now, Anya. No matter how I wish to stay, I cannot."

"Aye, well I know."

Concern struck the gray eyes. "Do you? I wonder how you will fare when I go."

"No worse than before."

With exquisite tenderness, he cupped her face in his huge hands and planted upon her lips a kiss of promise and sweetness. "Tonight," he whispered and kissed her cheek, her nose. "Tonight, then."

Dizzy, Anya put her hands over his, closing her eyes to accept the kisses he pressed to her eyelids and brow. "Oh, yes," she said.

Suddenly she opened her eyes. "But where, my lord?"

"Leave that to me. Only be ready when Mary comes to you." He released her. "Go now," he said with a nod of his head. "Before your servants creep to the windows to spy on us."

13

When darkness fell and the manor grew sleepy, Christian crept through the Hall to find Mary dozing in the kitchen. "Is all prepared?" he asked.

Mary roused herself. "Aye, my lord. Just as you said."

"Fetch then your mistress."

As she scurried away, Christian ducked into the small room behind the kitchen. A pleasant scent of damp pine permeated the humid air, and a rushlight burned brightly from a sconce in the wall, its flame casting sharp shadows over the room. In a corner lay a straw pallet piled with furs, and as he had requested, water had been heated and poured. Broken light rippled over the surface.

Christian cast off his overtunic, eyeing it all with the practiced sharpness of many seductions. He liked better to have grapes or fresh peaches plucked from orchard trees, but tonight it was bread and butter and would suit well enough. He sat down on the stone bench set into the walls and took off his shoes.

"So I am to bathe you?" Anya said from the doorway, and her tone showed the displeasure with which she reagarded the notion.

He looked up. She came to him without artifice, without even letting down her hair, her only adornment a simple gold girdle he suspected she wore to hold her gown in place more than for vanity.

And yet, he had never seen a woman so beautiful. The bright flame made her hair shimmer. He stood up, his throat tight, and knew for all that he had planned it so, it was not Anya who was the seduced. He had vowed, over and over, to keep his distance from her, and yet here she stood, by his invitation, and he was the one who could not walk away.

He crossed the room and took her hand, drawing her inside so he might close the door. Her fingers trembled the smallest bit. Quietly, he swung the door closed. A blush stained her cheeks and he remembered her fear that she was wanton.

And yet, he, Christian de Morcerx, who had glibly talked his way into the hearts and bodies of more than one woman, could not think of a single word to ease her. Instead, he silently took up the end of her braid and untied the ribbon holding it. The hair began to unravel and he hastened its freedom with coaxing fingers, until the glorious untamed mass spilled all around her.

Then he rounded her as she stood frozen, and looked at her. "There is no woman more beautiful in all the kingdom tonight," he said quietly and caressed a curl. "Nor any I have seen in all my many travels."

Her slanted, almond eyes met his with suspicion

and disbelief, and he saw the wall of her defenses was firmly in place. So many times she had been wounded. He touched her throat, that throat that had been so savaged her voice was forever changed. He touched her mouth, that had cried out to be allowed to keep her child. He touched her hands, that had worked so hard.

"The water is for you, Anya."

She backed away, shaking her head, obviously embarrassed he would think of such a thing. Gently, he halted her, holding her shoulders and turning her around to untie the laces that held her gown. He kissed her neck thorugh the curtain of her hair.

"Please, Anya. Allow me to tend you as once you tended me."

Her voice was a whisper. "'Tis not seemly, my lord."

He lifted his mouth higher, to the lobe of her ear, and there suckled with a lingering persistence. "Think you this thought of mine is new? That never a man drew pleasure for himself in bathing the sweet flesh of his lady?"

"I do not—"

He touched her breasts, using his hands when his words would not coax her. She sighed and leaned into him, her body giving way to pliant softness.

Christian loosened the ties on her tunic and let it fall away to the floor, leaving her in the fine linen kirtle that hid so little of her fine form.

It too followed, and Christian could not halt the groan that escaped him. For days and nights unending he had thought of her like this, naked in his arms, and at last she was again. He knelt and kissed her breasts, small and tipped with rosy fruit that beaded in his mouth.

"Bathe with me," she whispered.

He lifted his head.

"There is room enough if we stand." She touched his shoulder. "In truth, I do not think I can bear to wait so long."

He stood up and shed his tunic, smiling as he pulled her close. "But you will see, my lady, how sweet the waiting can be." Their chests met and he nearly buckled into the need to bed her now, to hell with seductions and the gentleness she had not known. He carressed the smooth flesh of her buttocks and thighs, lifting her into him. Her legs wrapped around his waist, her arms around his neck, and she kissed him, long and deep and hungrily.

He could not bear it. Carrying her to the pallet, he gave in and took her in a wild rocking violence that had no relationship to the sweet gentleness he had imagined. But when she reached her height, crying out softly, her body convulsing around him, he thought she did not mind so much.

As they lay tangled, regaining their breath, he buried his face in the soft flesh of her breasts and laced his fingers in her hair. There was in his chest a pain of great depth, a pounding need that found only small expression in the bedding of her. Under his jaw, her heart raced and he took pleasure in the furious sound, content to lie there and listen to it as it slowed, his eyes closed. Her hands rested on his shoulders.

Slowly the creeping wonder stole back upon him. He kissed her breast and lifted his head. "You've seduced me again, my lady."

She gave him a rich and satisfied smile, sloe-eyed with passion, her hair in a glorious spill around them. "So I have. Do you mind?"

He inclined his head and said with mock resignation, "Well, 'tis difficult to satisfy the roving hordes, but a knight must do what he is able."

An unmistakable expression of hurt crossed her features before she shuttered her eyes quickly. "Like a stallion among the mares, I suppose."

"Oh, sweet lady," he said, touching her face. "'Twas only a tease, not serious."

The deep blue gaze met his and he cursed himself for the lack of trust he saw. "I wanted to seduce you slowly, but my passion overtook me. Think you that is the action of a man who plays stud?"

"I know little of such things." She swallowed. "And perhaps you think 'tis a kindness to give me what I asked in return for saving your life."

"Is that what you think?" he said, beginning to see how her logic had led her. "That I bed you in gratitude?"

She did not answer, but only stared over his shoulder at something he could not see, her mouth tight.

"Anya," he said quietly, "truly—I have not slept for wanting you these last days. Since I first awakened to find myself in your care, I've longed to touch you this way."

To show her he meant what he said, he shifted to one elbow and tossed back the furs to expose her torso. He touched her. "I wanted you," he murmured and bent his head to kiss her belly. "I want you still. I cannot think for it sometimes."

And this time he took her slowly, remembering to do all he had planned when she first came to the chamber tonight. He stirred the embers of her satisfaction until again she moaned and clutched him. Ah—slow, reverent, he thought, tasting her thighs, the crook of her elbow. She giggled when he touched the tender undercurve of her breast, and wiggled when he brushed the soles of her feet. And when he felt it time again to join with her, that too, was slow and right, a gentle, wide tumble into exquisite pleasure.

Anya savored each moment of the night, knowing there were few hours left to them. She reveled in his kisses, and the skillful play of his hands, but more she loved the way his face changed here in this isolated corner of the manor. His guard dropped and he was no longer the fierce and terrible knight, nor charming rogue, but only a man—a beautiful, intelligent man—who longed for peace.

Peace, she thought as they lay tangled on a pallet of straw that smelled of dust and harvest. His great head rested on her breast and she ran her fingers idly over his well-muscled back, over and over.

A broad sense of freedom touched her. Here in his arms, she was something new. Not John and William's sister, nor Anya the ruined, nor mistress of Winterbourne. Only Anya who had learned to be a lover this night, and felt the deep, rippling satisfaction it gave her body. She chuckled softly.

Christian raised his head. "What is that for?"

She smiled. "Well I understand now the wish for all to couple this way. I vow I feel better than I have in all my days."

"Aye." He laughed with her, pressing a fleeting kiss to her lips. "'Twas a great kindness of God to give his minions something so fine to ease their plight."

Beyond, a bird called—the winsome, wistful song

of a blackbird. They both turned their heads to the sound. "Dawn is not far distant," she commented quietly. "Soon 'twill be the sparrow joining that song."

His hand tightened infinitesimally around her waist, and Anya saw true regret in his eyes. "All too soon our idyll ends."

"When will you go?"

His voice was soft. "As soon as I'm able to mount Remus. A day or two—no more. Geoffrey is well enough to ride to Edward, and I will deliver him there before I travel to France."

A sudden, searing realization of all she would lose ripped through her. Not only this brave and kind and handsome knight who'd awakened her to pleasure—but Geoffrey, too. Thick grief filled her throat, and to her horror and astonishment, there were sudden tears in her eyes. In an unsteady voice she said, "He is my son, you know."

"I guessed as much."

Anya felt hot tears leak from her eyes, and run in trails over her temples into her hair. "My brother John stayed drunk three years after the attack. I don't know what made him sober, but he left the manor one morning, and brought Geoffrey to me two days later."

In memory she saw the day, John dressed all in black as was his wont, returning on his great black horse, with a small blond child in the saddle before him. *I could not bear to see you grieve so long,* he told her, and put the child in her arms. *'Tis your son, Geoffrey.*

"Does Geoffrey know you are his mother?"

"No. Only my brothers, though Mary guesses."

"So that is the extortion William uses."

Anya nodded grimly. With a quick gesture, she brushed away her tears. "You must think me mad for wishing to hold the child given me in that brutal time."

His clear gray eyes met hers with compassion. "I think you brave and strong. And he is a fine child who will one day take care of his mother well."

Her tears burst fresh through the walls of her defenses and she buried her face against his bare shoulder. "Oh, Christian, I will miss you both so desperately!"

And she wept, as she had not since she was twelve. Wept away the long-held scars and sorrows, wept away the false fronts and brave smiles she'd given so often.

Christian held her tightly, stroking her hair and her back, kissing her forehead, not urging her to stop as so many men might have done. She was grateful, for once begun, the rain of cleansing tears became a flood, sweeping away all the past sorrows, making her new.

When at last they trickled to nothing, she lay spent against his warm chest. She had always thought tears a weakness that gave no help, but in their aftermath, she felt braver, able to face the future, whatever it held.

A little pale light seeped into the room. "Day breaks," Christian said with regret.

Together, silently, they stood. There was no passion left in them, nor shame, either. Together they bent over the water in the tub and splashed it over their faces, and washed away the smell of their lovemaking. Still damp, still bare, they embraced.

Anya let go of a shuddering little sigh as she leaned

against the crisp hair of his chest. "Always I will remember this night, my lord."

His embrace tightened so fiercely she could scarce breathe. She felt his lips on the crown of her head. "Anya, I vow—"

She lifted her head. "Nay!" she cried softly. "Make no promise, no vow."

With a serious expression, he nodded and let her go. He bent to lift her kirtle from the floor. "Let me help you."

It was as the fabric settled over her body that she heard the first faint scream from beyond. And in the same instant, she became aware of the subtle scent she'd been smelling on the wind.

"Fire!" Christian shouted.

For a long moment, Anya stared at him as he dressed in a rush, without understanding his word. And even in that short time, the smell of smoke gathered power, and slight tendrils curled through the shutters.

And now she heard the shouts of the men at arms, and the new bustle of activity beyond the small room. *Fire.*

Grabbing her tunic, she tossed it over her head and raced out of the room with Christian. They met the scullery maids coming out, but Anya could not find it in her to care.

Now there were real screams and shouts of confusion. Anya ran to the doors to the bailey. "Oh, God!" she cried. "The village!"

Huge black plumes of smoke filled the graying, predawn sky. On the walls clustered hoards of hastily dressed men-at-arms, and a line formed from well to wall to douse the roof of the manor to keep it safe.

Christian, buckling his belt, ran down the steps toward the stable, and emerged with the stable boys and her own horse. He reeled a moment, barking orders to several guards yet standing in a stunned, not yet awakened state, and they ran with him as he rode through the gates. To the village.

A sharp, biting terror licked Anya's heart, but Christian's ability to take charge moved her. Lifting her skirts, she ran into the manor and shouted for all to come to her. Dispensing orders to even the youngest pages, she dispatched some to the village, some to the wall to keep watch on the manor roof and outbuildings and held back a few to begin baking bread. Only God knew when the flames would be under control, but those fighting the blaze would be hungry.

And then she gathered her skirts again and went to the bailey. She knew what she had to do, but it gave her no pleasure. Smoke filled the air, thick and noxious. She blinked against its sting, moving alongside the line of men, smoothly passing buckets hand to hand.

Now she could hear the roar of the flames themselves, devouring all in their path. With a sick feeling in the pit of her stomach, she forced herself to climb a ladder to the top of the wall to get a better look.

Stephen, seeing her, ran lightly toward her. "My lady," he said, knowing well her aversion to heights, "take my hand. I will lead you to a safe place."

Anya accepted his help with gratitude, fighting waves of dizziness as she mounted the walk. She didn't dare look around until she had something solid to which she might anchor herself, and kept her gaze trained carefully to Stephen's sleeve until she entered the small guard house at one corner of the wall. Here, in spite of the openness that allowed a wide view, the roof gave her a sense of safety.

Letting go of his arm, she gripped the edge of the embrasure and stared in horror at the scene before her.

Through the forest, it was impossible to see all, but it was plain the entire village was engulfed. With a small moan, Anya swayed. "There will be nothing left."

"Nothing," Stephen agreed in a grim voice. "'Tis odd how all is burning so fast, with all the rain. You cannot see it from here, my lady, but from the tower 'tis plain it burns from the outside toward the middle."

Stricken, she looked at him. "Show me."

"But—"

"Show me," she said more firmly, gripping his arm.

He nodded and led her again along the walk. From the corner of her eye she saw far, far below the tiny figures of the men, now wet with sloshed water, and wearying, passing bucket after bucket after bucket. She lifted her head toward the roof to see if it was yet safe, and the sudden motion sent her balance askew. She swayed dangerously. With a little cry, she grasped Stephen's arm with both hands, her heart skittering in a wild pattern.

He paused to allow her to recover, and Anya stood very still, gazing at the gold stone of the manor wall until the sickening dizziness passed. "Go on," she said. "I only looked away too quickly. Tell me, is the roof afire?"

"Nay. It yet holds."

The tower required another bit of climbing, but the stairs were stone and enclosed, and the small respite gave her a chance to regain her nerve. At the top, she moved to put her back against the wall before looking out, and she kept an eagle's grip upon Stephen's arm for balance.

He pointed. "Look."

Anya raised her eyes. From this vantage point—so high!—she could see through and over many of the trees and into the small hollow where the village stood.

"You see how it burns from every quarter?" Stephen said. "North, south, east, and west."

Only the center of the village was yet untouched, the square where the fine church stood. And there the villagers gathered at the well, insect-size from this height, fighting to save their beloved church while their homes collapsed around them. A contingent of women led restless goats and sheep from the flames to the south of the fire, where already the blaze had done its work and a handful of burned piles smoldered with only tiny flickers remaining.

As she stared at it, Anya knew the first stirrings of defeat. For she did not see how the villagers could weather this last disaster. Illness and hunger and grim weather had wearied them all too much. Now they would be forced to crowd into the manor, as many as she could house, and the rest would throw up shacks in the baileys. Come spring, rebuilding could begin, but for now . . .

With weariness she said, "It seems at last my brother has won."

14

By *evening, the village* lay in smouldering ruins. Anya walked among the charred timbers and singed trees, feeling ill. A damp, rotted scent of devastation permeated the landscape. Only the church remained whole, and soot streaked its whitewashed walls.

Around her moved the displaced villagers, poking through the ruins in the dimming light of day to see what might be salvaged. They were eerily silent, their only sounds the scrape of shoe and the rustling of clothing, the occasional soft cry of loss or relief.

As stunned as the rest, Anya wandered through the square, staring at the remains of the alehouse and the half-standing cottages. Sheep and cows, rounded up in the north pasture, made plaintive cries.

Christian guided a wagon through the ruins, loading it with retrieved salvage. From mud puddles he plucked wooden cups and a tankard, scraps of unburned clothing, harnesses and saddles. Anya watched him without feeling. From head to toe he was stained with soot and ashes, and if not for the fine clothing, he would have been indistinguishable from any of the peasants.

As if this misery were not enough, the sky had begun to cloud toward the end of the afternoon. Heavy dark clouds, laden with snow or rain. By the smell of the wind, Anya thought it would be rain this time.

Wearily, she lifted her mud-heavy skirts and picked her way through the broken lane to Christian's side. "We must return to the manor before the weather drowns us. I have yet no thought on how we will arrange all for sleeping, but it must be done soon."

He wiped a forearm over his blackened face. "Aye." He straightened with effort, and she saw the hard work had renewed the pain in his shoulder. "Like as not, a meal will ease the sorrows here."

She nodded. "Erda has made a feast fit for kings. At least all will have full bellies."

"How many will you need to house?"

"Three score, perhaps less." She tried to remember how many had been lost to the fever and could not. "Most can sleep in the Hall, the rest can spill into the church and stables."

With a grim expression, Christian surveyed the burned village. "I have not seen a fire so vehement in many years, nor one that took a whole village so quickly." His eyes narrowed. "It seemed to burn from all quarters all at once."

"I saw." She would not think on this yet. Not yet. "Come, let us lead the way back to the manor, where all might find comfort in a good meal."

She turned without waiting for his reply and headed

toward the path to the manor, gesturing toward a knot of villagers to follow. "Come," she called. "Tomorrow is soon enough to see what you've lost. Tonight, let us eat and drink and forget our troubles."

"*Our* troubles, my lady?" snarled one man, grizzled and thin. "Your house is not burned to the ground. You are not starving, as we are. You will still have all you need, while we face the new year with nothing."

Assorted grumbling agreement met his bold words. Anya straightened, feeling the first raindrops fall to her bare head. "I did not light your fire, John Carpenter, nor trample the crops. If you choose, you may stand in the rain and complain, but I am going to my supper and will hear anything else in the warmth of the Hall. Those who wish to join me are free to do so."

"She's right," cried a woman's voice. "I made the very gown she wears now, and it fit her then. She starves with the rest of us."

Vindicated, Anya lifted her sodden skirts once more, and bent her head against the rain, but a voice from the vestibule of the church stopped her. "Nay! You lit no fire, 'tis true," said Father Gerent, his voice booming and strong without the slurring of drink. "But well we know your sin! This fire was punishment upon us from the Lord on high for your unbelief!"

She spun around. "Do not begin your petty grievance here, Father!" With a furious gesture, she flung dampened curls from her brow. "For once can you not leave us all in peace? Who knows why a fever rages or a fire begins or a harvest fails? Why are there good years and bad, no matter who rules or—"

"You have deepened your sin with fornication,

Anya of Winterbourne!" the priest roared. "God forgave until you repeated your sin!"

"Aye," called out a woman's voice. Tillie, standing
in a black rage at the edge of the gathering villagers.
"We have all seen how ye threw yerself at the knight,
until he did what any man would do—taking even the
dried-up spinster of Winterbourne for his pleasure!"

"I warned you—" Anya began.

The priest had finally gained the villagers' attention
and would not let so ripe a chance slip by. "We had
fevers and little food, but we managed," he cried out
in his booming voice, seemingly unconcerned about
the rain plopping all around them in ever-increasing
strength. "When did the fever steal so many of our
young? When she brought the knight from the forest!"

An uneasy rippling of agreement met his words, as
even those who might have been inclined to support
her remembered the way things had happened.

"All saw her sneak into the stables yesterday, forni-
cating in front of God himself with no shame at all!"
Tillie put in. "And now God has punished us for your
sin!"

"Repent, ye fallen woman!" cried the priest. The
villagers surged toward her, their voices a grumbling
roar. With the first knife-sharp trill of fear, Anya
stepped back.

"Enough!"

The voice was loud and deep and cut through the
mutterings and dangerous growling like a blaze of
sunlight through rain. Christian strode forward, shoving the priest from his perch. "I will hear no more
slander here today, or all will sleep in the mud of the
burned houses. You fight and point fingers, but who
among you is without sin to cast the first stone?"

He cast an accusatory eye among them, daring any to come forward. With sharpness, he pinned Tillie where she stood.

Anya, heart pounding in fear and rage and a certain guilt, stared at him. Once more, she was transfixed by the change in him. In spite of the soot and the grime, in spite of the ragged mass of his damp, dirty hair on his shoulders and the streaks of black on his face, he commanded their attention utterly.

He pointed a finger toward them. "Who has not gained from some kindness offered you by your mistress? Who has not benefited in some way from what she gives? Who among you did not feast at the manor not a fortnight ago, and who did not awaken with a heavy head from all the wine?

"Sleep here in the wet and stink if you will, but none will slander Anya of Winterbourne while I yet have breath."

With a quiet rumbling, they all filed slowly toward the manor. Anya did not move. Rain fell on her face, soaked her hair and cloak, but she simply watched them part around her, their heads lowered against the weather, shoulders slumped.

An ache filled her. Christian joined her, and took her arm gently. "Come, Anya. Food will ease you."

Still she didn't move. "Nay, Christian, I have lost. Tomorrow, I ride to Lichfield to see my brother."

"They are only distraught. All will be less grim on the morrow."

A part of her wanted to lean into him, to rest once more against his broad chest and feel the gentle power of him envelop her.

And yet, she could not. For all that she rejected the priest's words publicly, she knew she had sinned. "I have indulged a selfish wish for you, my lord," she said quietly, staring at a heap of blackened timbers still smouldering in the gloaming. "And well I know what my penance will be. I am to lose Geoffrey and Winterbourne—and perhaps the abbey will care for the villeins in ways I have not been able to do."

"Anya—"

"Say no more," she said wearily. "I have chosen."

"I ride with you, then," he said.

Anya only nodded.

In the crowded Hall, Christian took a tankard of ale and settled in a corner nearby the hearth. Around him, the villagers ate with the appetite of exhaustion, their faces and clothes stained with the fire's mark. A ghostly stench of smoke hung in the air, overriding the rich scent of the roasted pig Erda had prepared.

Christian himself had feasted well, catching a glimpse of what meals had been like in the days before the poor harvest. The pig had been cooked whole and stuffed with apples and onions and herbs. Fine flour had been mixed into the rougher grains to make a light wholesome bread that had been braided and brushed thickly with butter. Capon pasties and trout and fritters loaded the sideboards. There was even, to his delight, a thick frumenty, a pudding made with almond milk—one of the few dishes for which he had a weakness.

For all the feasting, he could not help but compare the mood of this grim night with the winter feast a few weeks before. That night, laughter had been by far the brightest noise, joined with happy chatter and bawdy jokes. Music had filled the room with a joyous noise, and all had danced until they could dance no more. And then the steward, known near and far for his stories, had spun ballads for them.

Tonight, only Geoffrey's lonely pipe played, and it carried a wistful note. No light chatter competed with the sound, only the dull thunk of knives on the wooden tables and the low buzz of worry.

It was no wonder, if they were as tired as he, Christian thought. His very bones ached with the labor of the day, and his lungs burned with the smoke he'd breathed. In his shoulder, which had been feeling well, there was a dull pain, made sharp when he moved. Riding would be a trial.

A girl joined Geoffrey in his corner and began to sing. Her voice was clear and sweet as she gave them a sad ballad of a husband come home to find his love abed with another. Geoffrey joined her in the refrain, his tenor taking the harmony as the girl's voice rose with almost unbearable poignancy to the murder all knew was coming.

Around Christian, the weary lot shifted, taking their cups and turning to face the sound. Nearby, he heard a man humming along, and a woman in a soiled and worn gray gown wiped away a tear as she rocked her toddler.

From somewhere, a psaltery was produced and given to the hands of a fat old man. Geoffrey bent and picked up a tambourine to give the girl.

The songs they sang were ancient, the verses that cooks hummed as they stirred a fire, that a farmer whistled as he plowed, that children enacted in the stillness of summer evenings. Each told a tale; a knight gone off to battle, leaving behind his ladylove to waste away in her tower; a brokenhearted father begging his daughter to marry the butcher to save her honor.

All were tales of love gone awry or faith broken or sorrows borne. Their melodies were haunting and deceptively simple.

There were others, Christian knew. Bawdy, loud songs of women outsmarting foolish men or the weak defeating the mean and strong. But this group tonight wished no stories of triumph. They did not wish to laugh or dance or clap their hands. They wanted to sing along with quiet, tragic ballads and grieve.

As he listened, Christian watched Anya moving among the gathered villagers. She, too, was grimy and weary. She had washed her face, but there were smears of black on the worn green gown that seemed to be her favorite work dress, and the hem was muddy. Around her face and along her neck, unruly curls had sprung free of the mussed braid.

He could see fatigue in the rigid way she held her shoulders and the darkness below her eyes. And yet she moved among the peasants in the Hall relentlessly, pausing here and again to comfort a newly wed maid who wept over the fine wedding gifts now lost to the blaze; took a mewling babe from the weary arms of another; hunched in discussion with her bailiff and the captain of the guards. A discussion, he guessed, about how to shelter so many—for only God himself knew how long.

Studiously, she avoided Christian. After the ugliness in the village, he understood it and kept himself distant.

But watching her now lift a hand to her temple and close her eyes, he could not quell his need to somehow comfort her. Getting to his feet, he went to the kitchens and asked Erda, there laboring still, to brew a potion for the headache. When she made it, he carried the cup carefully into the Hall, but Anya was nowhere to be seen.

Spying Mary, Christian asked, "Where has your lady gone?"

The woman lifted a jaundiced brow. "Have you not done enough, my lord? Can you not leave her in peace now?"

"What peace, Mary? Where"— he gestured with an angry hand to the crowd in the Hall—"will she find rest in this?"

"You will go on your way and leave her to manage all, as she has always done. To bear the weight of the gossip swelling even now. The priest speaks ill of her, and will convince the rest that she is the source of their troubles." Her cheeks were bright red. "Had you honor at all, you'd marry the girl."

"Marry." The word felt odd on his tongue. "Marry so she might grieve as widow when those who want me dead succeed? Marry so she must take my burdens atop all those she carries now? Marry so none who might offer true protection and hope for her will find her?"

"Pah! Excuses all."

He gripped her arm. "Nay, Mary, you do me grievous insult. 'Tis Anya I think of, not myself."

"'Tis not *think* you do at all, my lord," she returned. "She saved your life. You might at least save her honor."

"And I, upon my honor, vow to save her life—and this place she loves, and that son she cannot claim." Fiercely, he bent forward. "You know not of what you speak."

"Aye, my lord, I do ye grievous injury and ask ye forgive me." Her tone was mocking.

Christian dropped her arm. "I say again, you know not of what you speak."

She gestured toward the solar. "She went there, only a moment ago."

"I vow, Mary, to do what I might to see her brother suffers for the pain he has caused her these many years."

"Go to her."

He found her where he knew he would, sitting in the window seat of the solar, the shutters open to the brisk, rain-peppered wind. Her arms were folded over her chest, and only a single candle gave any light. "My lady," he said quietly, "I have brought you a tisane for your head."

"You should not be here, Christian," she said without turning.

He held the cup out. "Drink it and I will go."

Slowly she turned. "If any saw you follow me, 'twill only heat the gossip the more. I beg of you, go now."

He did not reply, only stood holding the cup out. At last she sighed and accepted his offering. "I cannot even think for the pounding in my head."

Climbing the steps to the dais, he settled next to her on the stone bench. "You mustn't take it so much to heart, Anya."

She sipped the tea and regarded him with something verging on pity. "What must I do to make you go?" she asked.

"There is naught you can do. A friend you need this night."

"Is that what you are, Christian? My friend?"

He reached for her hand, holding her gaze steadily.

"Aye," he said in a low voice. "Whatever else there is or will be or has been, you may count me friend."

The stricken expression in her dark blue eyes made him ache to comfort her all the more. "Then leave me now, friend. I must somehow make myself ready to leave this place."

"Anya!" he said, gripping her fingers more tightly. "You needn't leave."

Her eyes narrowed. "You heard them. No more do they wish for me to be their mistress, so no more shall I be."

"They are only frightened, and lashed out at you in grief. All know you are a fair and kind mistress, who works side by side with them. All know your brother will not care for their troubles, only what he can claim from their fields."

She stared into the darkness beyond the embrasure, her lips tight. "Since you know all, Christian, tell me how the manor will survive without my brother now? 'Tis a month or less till the fields dry for planting, and the men will be needed there, not building the ruined village. And where am I to find the money to help them? They cannot live here long, so crowded and unhappy." She shook her head. "Nay, there is no help for it. To my brother I will go."

He stared at her, feeling helpless and frustrated. She had saved his life, given him shelter, and how had he returned the favor? By casting more shame upon her and helping her lose Winterbourne.

With regret, he let her hand go and rose. "In the morning we ride. Do not stare long into the night, my lady. To spar with your brother, you will need to be fresh."

She shrugged listlessly. "There is no sparring ahead. He has won."

He has won. Christian scowled, thinking of the village this morning, the way the flames seemed to come from all directions all at once, burning in a wild inferno.

Surely not even William would stoop so low as to burn the villagers to gain his prize. Or would he?

Christian turned back to her abruptly. "Will you give in so easily? I thought you more a warrior than that."

Her chin lifted. Life-giving anger replaced the defeat in her eyes. "So easily spoken, my lord! Have you not listened?"

"Aye, I listened," he said, grabbing her shoulders, forcing her to look at him. "I hear the fretting of some silly noble maid worried for her soul and the good opinion of ungrateful villagers. Already you are condemned for all eternity, my lady. What difference will defiance make to that?"

"'Tis not defiance!" she shouted, flinging his arms from her. "What they said was true. I have sinned most grievously! Not only in lying with you, but in the foolish pride I have displayed in this matter. The abbey will feed the village as I cannot. It will see them housed and cared for. I will go and do my penance as William wishes."

"You cannot!"

Her mouth thinned to the stubborn line he so recognized. "I must and I will."

The words tumbled from his mouth without his help. "Marry me, Anya."

Stunned to silence, she only stared. Then she laughed outright. "Marry, is it? Pray you, how do you plan to win the agreement of my brother in your suit?"

He straightened, surprised he had not considered it

before. "Though the king. Your brother cannot deny what the king has granted."

She pushed away, agitated, and poked the fire. "No," she said finally. "It will give no help, for you have no more than I."

"I can protect you and help you. Please, my lady," he said with outstretched hand. "Will you let me be your champion?"

"Save your pity!" She whirled to face him, fury plain on her flushed cheeks. "Leave me at least my dignity, my lord. Of my free will I choose to go to my brother and trade him the village for a nunnery. I should have done it long ago."

"Anya—"

"Leave me! I do not wish to look upon you just now."

For one long moment, he stared at her, aware of a hollowness in his chest. From behind her, the fire leapt to an orange glow, lighting the edges of her hair. Her eyes blazed.

A thread of powerful desire wound through him. The night they had spent in the room behind the kitchen—only last night?—tumbled into his mind and he knew she could be no more sated by their passion than he.

For a moment, he wondered what a kiss, planted on her slender white shoulder, might accomplish. Surely he could melt that anger, or rather turn it to passion.

But warily, he considered the sharp poker in her hand, the poker she used to stab at the fire. To cross the room toward her was to risk injury just now. He chose to keep his limbs this night.

"So be it," he said, and left her.

15

William bent over an illuminated text, taking pleasure in the fine hand of the monk who'd copied it and the bright, sharp colors of the illustrations. His mood this morning was good. The illness had passed finally, and beyond this small chamber fell rain, sweet and clean, smelling of spring.

So when his messenger, dispatched to Provence so many weeks before, appeared in the courtyard, William smiled broadly. The youth was clearly worn, but he'd made good time. Giving his horse over to a stable hand, he brushed rain from his cloak and hurried toward the abbey.

William went out to greet him. "Ho, young Renault! What news have you?"

From a leather pouch, the youth took two letters. William raised a brow in surprise. He turned them over to check the seals.

"The first was given me in Carpentras," the youth said. "As I rode out, a page gave me the other to deliver to you."

William smiled. "Well done, boy." He clapped him on the shoulder and took the letters to his cell.

The first was, as he expected, from Cardinal d'Auch. It struck no coy tone, and respected William's intelligence. The cardinal asked that William keep his knowledge to himself. One paragraph particularly caught his attention.

> You say my son has taken up your sister's cause. He is a noble sort, and will not shirk his duties. Do what you might to get them both to Carpentras on whatever errand you might manufacture. From there, I will manage all.

William folded the parchment thoughtfully, gazing through the small window in his wall to the restful view of the courtyard beyond. Perhaps the brigands he'd sent to the village had not been necessary after all, if he could rid himself of his sister another way.

No help for it now. The men had reported back to him last eve. The village was cinders.

With considerable curiosity, he broke the seal on the second letter. From another cardinal, John Duise, no doubt a competitor for the papal throne to which d'Auch aspired.

Interesting.

This letter detailed the pope's gruesome illness and the certainty of his death.

> It seems to all a fulfillment of the curse of the last grand master of the Templars, Jacques de Molay,

who cursed pope and king with his dying breath. And now 'tis urgent the right man is chosen.

William frowned, trying to think if he'd ever met the man, and could not place him. The superstition of a curse annoyed him no small bit, but he was intrigued at the request that followed:

D'Auch is an evil man, with great hidden sins in his past, and I would see him thwarted. A handsome reward is in it for you if you send Christian de Morcerx to me, in secret, so I might lend my protection.

Pursing his lips, William carefully hid both letters. What sin lay in d'Auch's past? Was it great enough to bring down his chance at the papacy if uncovered?

Linking his hands behind his back, William stared out to the rainy courtyard, his eyes narrowed. If the sin were not of magnitude, why then would he wish his son so urgently, when the man had obviously kept to himself, well out of his father's way, these many years?

If d'Auch were exposed and William had allied himself with him, any gain he hoped to achieve would be lost. On the other hand, all believed d'Auch would be pope, and William had never heard of this Duise. Which meant little, since he lived so far from the loop of gossip.

Was there a way to appease both? He would think on it. One way or another, he meant to win this skirmish.

Well pleased with all that had transpired, he settled back to wait. For Anya, he knew, would soon appear.

*   *   *

Thick fog laced through the gates and clung in streamers to the treetops above the courtyard. Anya eyed it grimly, worried that it would muffle the sound of outlaws in the forest until they were too quickly upon them. It had been in such a fog that her parents had been murdered.

Impulsively, she called to Stephen. "Order three more guards to ride with us," she said.

He inclined his head. "'Twill leave the manor walls weakly defended."

"Make swordsmen of some of the villagers, then," she said and thought a moment. "John Carpenter has a sharp eye, and perhaps 'twill ease his bad temper to walk the walls with soldiers."

Stephen smiled. "Wise choice."

"For a mere woman."

He laughed. "I bid you good journey, my lady, and quick return."

Anya lowered her head to hide the swift grief his words gave. She had told none but Christian of her plans to give the manor to the abbey. "Thank you."

The yard was filled with peasants roused from their sleep in the stable loft, as well as horses and men-at-arms. Geoffrey, his color high at the adventure ahead, sat astride his pony. Anya touched his leg and smiled up at him. His hair gleamed with a good brushing, curling around his ears and the collar of his fine cloak. "Handsome you are this morn," she said.

He cocked his head, and she saw in the gesture a shadow of Christian's male arrogance. "One does not greet one's king as a ruffian."

She wanted to chuckle, but restrained herself.

"True enough, young Geoffrey." Shifting, she lifted her skirts, ready to check the rest of the party.

A slim hand on her shoulder restrained her. "Will I please, do you think?"

"Oh, yes, Geoffrey. And this way, you may choose the life you were meant to have—that of a musician—instead of knight out in battle. I can think of no better path for you."

He gave her a tremulous smile. "Aye. The saints were kind to bring us the knight."

Anya glanced over her shoulder to where Christian stood, gentling Remus as if he might really plan to ride the beast. Tucked into a basket, her head popping over the edge, was Esmerelda the cat, perfectly at ease. Anya shook her head. Patting Geoffrey's leg, she strode across the yard.

"Surely you do not mean to ride him," she said.

Remus lifted his head and whickered, as if in agreement. Fog swirled in the currents stirred by his restless feet.

Christian gave her an impish smile. "Nay. For now he will only come with us. I ride the chestnut gelding today, but will lead Remus as we go." Absently, he stroked Esmerelda's ears.

"I am rather fond of the cat," Anya said with annoyance. "And you will carry her away to France?"

He gave her a stricken glance. "I had not thought . . . forgive me."

When he made a move to take Esmerelda from her place, Anya stopped him. "Remus will not go without her."

He lifted a brow.

"Leave me Ysengrin in her stead, and we will call ourselves even."

The dog, recovered from his bruises, ran around the perimeters of the traveling party, herding the rest of the hounds away from the horses' hooves. Anya whistled for him. Eagerly, he bounded over and licked her hand. "'Twould be a fair trade."

Christian measured her soberly. "I thought you were to surrender yourself to a nunnery, my lady. What need have you of a pet there?"

She met his gaze, feeling anew the lump of home-sickness already filling her. "True enough."

"I say again it need not be so, my lady."

Anya clutched her skirts in her fists. So easily he offered her heart's desire, as if it were no more than paying a slightly troublesome debt. A simple matter, easily disposed of.

For him, no doubt it was. Men took such things lightly, and she could not blame him for the habits of his kind. But neither would she humiliate herself by accepting so casual a solution to her problems. Better the dry life of a nunnery than one spent in a constant struggle to hold to her dignity in the face of her desire for him. Oh, no—she could not bear even the thought of it. Daily in his company, attempting to hold to some semblance of control? Nay, she'd be mad in a matter of weeks.

She did not answer, but only made for Evered and mounted. "Are we ready?" she called to the numbers. "Let us be on our way!"

The journey to Lichfield was not long, only a few hours by horse. But the fog made riding treacherous, and the road was thick with muddy slime. It was with relief they saw the walls of Lichfield come into view.

The ride had been more difficult for Christian than he'd originally imagined. This morning, after the work in the village yesterday, his body had been weary and aching, old battle wounds flaring in his hip and legs, his shoulder throbbing. The break had been unclean and would likely always give him pain in damp weather, so he bore it as well as he was able.

But as their small party rode into the town, he cursed the thought of the long journey that lay yet ahead, first to London to speak with the king, then on to Provence.

God's bones, but he was weary of a knight's life. Midsummer would mark his twenty-sixth year—deep he longed to turn his life from the labors of the battlefield to the labors of the land. It seemed, in this bleak mood, as if he never would.

Anya rode up beside him. "We'll take rooms at the Three Crowns, ahead there."

"An inn, my lady? But the monastery—"

"Soon enough I'll be cloistered. For tonight, I would be free yet."

"As you wish."

She frowned. "I like not your color, Christian. Are you taking a fever?"

"Nay," he said firmly. "Only weary from the work of these two days after so long an idle time."

She shrugged, and Christian found he missed her solicitous concern of the past. A weakness; one he'd do well to overcome.

Inside the inn, he secured one room for Anya and her maid, a young girl from the village, not Mary, who'd been left behind to help manage the flood of villagers now housed under the manor roof, and one for Christian and Geoffrey. The men-at-arms would sleep in the stables.

As the horses were led around, Christian ordered meat pasties and ale from the mistress. Anya and Geoffrey disappeared up the stairs. Christian settled at a broad, scarred table in a corner, thereby to hear what he might of local gossip.

By the time he'd consumed his third pasty and second tankard of ale, he'd begun to think he'd hear no gossip of import. But two clerks dropped into the table nearby him and his eavesdropping proved notable.

Over their ale, obviously thinking themselves safe in such rough surroundings, the clerks gossiped in Latin about the Church and the king, then spread their net and wandered into gossip of France, where King Philip had put the last of the Templars to death. Jacques de Molay had cursed both pope and king from the flames. "And now the pope lies ill with a most loathsome disease," said the clerk relating the story, voice soft with horror. "What will happen to the king?"

The pope was dying.

Christian leaned back with narrowed eyes and lifted his cup, listening as the two speculated over which of the reigning cardinals might next take the throne. One thought it would be Etienne d'Auch; the other cast his bet upon John Duise.

Hearing the news, Christian felt a bitter smile curl his lips. At least his father's motives for trying to kill him so long after the original attempt became clear. Etienne sat so close to that crown he'd sought all his life that he could nearly taste it—and he would take no risk his self-righteous son would snatch it from him.

There was curious satisfaction in knowing his father worried over it; probably twisted and turned at night while he sweated over the possibility Christian would descend upon him at the last moment.

With a mean and small part of his heart, Christian took pleasure in the thought of the satisfaction such an act would bring to him. Especially if he might reproduce the "accident" that had befallen Pope Clement at Etienne's order. He smiled at the thought.

But the emotion was deeply rooted in bile, and Christian knew 'twould be himself poisoned by embracing such ignoble motives. He'd make himself no better than his father.

"I doubt I've seen so acrimonious an expression on your face before, Christian."

He looked up as Anya swept into a chair opposite. He lifted his hand for the mistress to bring another cup, but Anya forestalled him. "I need naught. I go to see my brother now, while Geoffrey rests. Before you take him to the king, I would know where I am to be living."

Christian stared at her a long moment. There was grief in the lines around her mouth, a certain air of defeat, yet well he recognized the familiar straight determination in her shoulders. "You will go through with this madness?"

"Aye," she said, lifting her chin. "We need not broach the matter again."

Christian lifted a brow sardonically. "Ah! Afraid you'll give in?"

"To what?"

"My offer stands, Anya. I would protect you against your brother if you so choose."

"You have nothing, Christian! You might well save *me,* but what of the villagers who suffer for what I've done?"

The words seared his pride. "Truer words were

never spoken, my lady." Tightly, he stood. "Come, I'll walk with you to the abbey and there you may lay your sacrifice at your brother's feet."

"Christian, I'm sorry. I didn't mean—"

"You only spoke the truth," he said, unable to look at her. "Let's be done with this."

The day was still damp and overcast, and even the simple exertion of walking tired Christian, a fact he would not reveal in even grimmest torture. 'Twas only that the wound was not fully healed, he told himself, the jolting of riding all the day when he was unused to it.

Anya, too, seemed weary—or perhaps only reluctant—for she did not fall into her usual striding gait. Indeed, she walked slowly in the cool, overcast afternoon, her braid swinging gently side to side. He saw men casting looks over her slim figure, speculative, lustful glances that annoyed him deeply.

Anya seemed not to notice them. He sighed, feeling his irritation at her crumble, for he knew the reason. She thought herself soiled and plain. She did not expect lust, so did not see it.

Across the lane from the abbey, she suddenly halted. The steps to the cathedral were bustling, and clerks and monks in their rough habits swirled around the place like busy birds. Anya stood at the edge of the street, her face pale, her eyes painfully blue in their tilted frames. Christian saw her press a hand to her stomach, as if for courage.

Silently, he cursed her foolish, stubborn pride. "Anya, do not do this thing. If 'tis so distasteful to take me to husband, let me appeal to the king for another for you, one who will have what you need to save your villagers."

She lifted her eyes and stared at him for a long moment, bleak emotion bared there. At last she forced a smile. "You've been a great help and comfort to me these weeks, Christian. In that you have fulfilled your debt."

He sighed, shaking his head. "'Tis not to pay a debt I wish to help you. 'Tis that you have no other."

"Nor have I ever," she replied with a toss of her head, looking back to the abbey. "Well enough I've done."

"Well enough," he repeated, taking her arm. "Look at me, Anya of Winterbourne."

Her jaw set, but at last she lifted her eyes to his face.

"Will you never seek something for yourself?" he asked.

"Aye," she said softly. "I asked the saints to save my child, and they did. I asked to be taught the secrets of that which transpires between men and women—and you gave me your knowledge." She took a breath. "I ask now for the village to be saved, which I am wise enough to see I cannot do."

He stared at her, his heart filled with a plucking pain. The clouds overhead gave an almost translucent beauty to her smooth white skin, and set off the tenderness of her lips, the gentle flush of health in her cheeks. He thought of her wasting away, unloved and unfulfilled in a nunnery, and he wanted to drag her into the nearest doorway, and there show her once more what she would miss.

That face, those lips, that responsive body and passionate heart were made for the earthy love of men, the lusty pleasure of children.

Yes, he'd like to take her, to fill her again with his seed. Instead, knowing he had nothing, he took her arm and led the way into the abbey.

*   *   *

A novice led them to a small cubicle of an office to wait for William, who left them waiting a long time. Anya paced the small chamber restlessly, touching the small luxuries the canon was permitted. From the nave came the sound of monks chanting in liquid harmony, lending the room with its careful neatness a sense of elegant quiet, unbroken by the passions and turmoil of life beyond.

Anya felt her resentment fade. This was the life she would face now, one of silence and prayer and the comfortable companionship of other women. There was a certain solace in the thought, in the clean simplicity of such a life. No more to worry over the peasants or the stores or that the guards would get drunk and fight over some kitchen maid.

Nearby the thick glass of the window, Christian sighed heavily, drawing her attention. Obviously lost in his own thoughts, he leaned against the embrasure, his expression taut. Light caressed him, catching the waves of his long, loose hair, washed over his sharp jaw and broad, intelligent brow.

A pain twisted her heart—a longing to know again the heat and teasing of him against her, a wish to bathe his long, scarred and muscled back, a need to lie with him and bear for him a babe who might own those ghostly eyes.

More—oh, more, too, she wished. She disliked the wariness in his face now, the worry, the grimness. All had disappeared at Winterbourne as he played at swords with the guards and told Geoffrey stories of the saints in the evenings and even as he took charge during the fire. Winterbourne fit him.

Perhaps it was selfish of her to deny his bid for her hand. Perhaps he did not do it only to help her, but out of some need of his own.

And yet, this very need she felt to give him all gave her pause. How could she bear his unrelenting kindness forever more, even when the gratitude and lust faded in his eyes? How could she bear it when he tired of her and found some willing village wench to bed?

Aching, she turned to pace anew. On William's desk lay an open manuscript, turned to an illuminated page of angels singing. She touched the gold with a fingertip, wishing life were as clear and beautiful as the reds and blues on that page.

Peeking from between two sheaves of the manuscript was a letter with a seal she recognized—Father Gerent's. Amid the strangeness in the room, Anya felt a shock at the striking familiarity of the seal. Without thinking, she plucked the letter from its place. It was only a litany of complaint and tattling about Anya. She rolled her eyes. At the end, there was a warning about the knight, who was becoming troublesome and might prove more of a stumbling stone than they had anticipated.

"Christian!" she said in a whisper. "Look!"

He turned and made to move toward her, but a footfall beyond the door stopped him. Anya hid the letter in her girdle, shifting her cloak so it was hidden in the folds.

Her heart raced with suspicion. Hitherto, she'd thought her brother only lacking in compassion, not actively evil. But if he'd paid the priest—and it seemed he had—to tell tales of her, what else might he have done?

When he stepped into the chamber, he seemed unsurprised at their presence. "Greetings, sister," he said smoothly, as if she often stopped by the abbey for a moment's conversation.

Quite the reverse was true. She stared at him, thinking of the village burned from all quarters at once, as if—

As if the fire had been deliberately set. Surely not even William would stoop so low, would he? Her mind whirled. She must find a way to trip him. That he seemed to expect her was damning, but not proof.

With a warning glance to Christian, she said, "I have come to appeal to you once again, William. Speak on behalf of Winterbourne to your abbot so the villagers whom you loved as a child do not starve."

A flicker of surprise crossed his face, so fleeting she could not be sure she'd seen it. He shrugged. "Unless you've come to say you will deed the land to the abbey as I've wished these many months, my answer has not changed."

"There was a fire," she said abruptly. "The village is no more."

He straightened, lifting one unsympathetic brow. "A pity."

Rage began to flicker behind her eyes, and she carefully controlled her urge to strike him with the fists now balled at her sides. Dignity demanded she remain still. "You seem unsurprised, brother," she said quietly.

The smallest gleam of triumph shone in his eyes. "'Tis not an uncommon occurence—villages often burn."

"In weather such as this? When one can barely keep a hearth fire alight for the dampness? And I suppose 'tis common for a whole village to burn from all directions at once."

He looked at her. "Everything, hmmm?"

"All but the church," she spat out, "which all saved as their homes burned."

"As it should be."

She looked at Christian, who stared at William with a virulent expression, his eyes ablaze with hatred. His burly arms were crossed over his chest and his sword in its scabbard gave off a dull glow.

As if he sensed her gaze, he looked at her. The smallest uptilt of his jaw, the slightest cock of his brow, were enough to relay his challenge: Would she cave into this brother, do as he wished? Or would she fight?

For a long moment, Anya was torn. The peace of the nunnery after so many years of struggle would not be unpleasant. Her primary reason for avoiding one before had been Geoffrey, and she was to lose him now anyway. She could take Mary with her, and make herself a comfortable place among the women there. A world of women without men—now there was a thought!

And yet, it meant henceforth she would never see Winterbourne. Not hear the shouts of children playing in the smoky light of an autumn afternoon, nor dance with the household on Martinmas, nor hear again the ballads of restless troubadours, only holy music for all of time.

To change it, she had only to humble herself enough to accept the hand of a knight, whose only flaw was that he did not love her.

But how then would she save Winterbourne? See the peasants fed and the village rebuilt?

With a blaze of insight, she whirled. "To tell you of the village was not my only quest here today," she said. "I have come to ask for my dowry."

16

"Your dowry?" William echoed.

"Aye, William, that which my brother left to me and put in your safekeeping."

"'Tis only when you marry that you may claim it, and only under my guidance. I have not given approval for a marriage."

"I will marry Christian de Morcerx, there standing in your doorway."

"The bastard son of a cardinal with naught to his name?" William laughed. "I think not, sister mine."

"'Tis not your choosing," she said. "The king is my overlord, and to him I will answer."

William dropped forward, his palms landing flat on the surface of the desk. "Go then—ask the king's blessing on this unholy alliance. If you can gain his favor, you'll be welcome to your pitiful dowry. But even it will not save your peasants!"

"It shall," she promised. "And I'll build Winterbourne

into a thriving town, if only to see you mourn it the more!"

William straightened, his eyes very still. "Sir knight, know you of the bastard son she bore to a brigand in the forest? That Geoffrey for whom you've found a place with the king is the bastard of a common thief and rapist."

"As I am a common bastard, born to a woman outcast by her own," Christian said in a low and dangerous voice, "I have sympathy."

"You're both fools."

"Mayhap that is so," Christian returned. "But no greater fool than you."

Together, Anya and Christian left him.

William strode through the abbey in a fury. The bitch had outsmarted him again. All his life, at every turn, Anya stood in his way, gloating, her damned eyes laughing at him when he overbalanced at the tilts and fell in the mud, when he had been so painfully smitten by a neighboring girl and been so humiliated by her at fourteen—! Always.

And here he'd thought her neatly trapped from all sides and she pulled a champion from her purse.

He burst into the abbot's office. The abbot, still weary and gray, turned with a scowl. "Brother Simon—"

"Father Abbot, my sister intends to marry. Not even the burned village has daunted her—she will take her dowry and rebuild."

"But you hold the dowry. Simply withhold it."

"She rides to the king to ask his blessing."

The abbot waved a hand. "Ah, well, then 'tis not to worry. He will not grant it if we ask his help."

William slammed his hand on the desk. "You know not the whole of this story! Her knight is well thought of at court, and the king is indebted to him in some strange way. He will grant their petition, I'll wager, and Winterbourne will be lost to the abbey forever."

The abbot pursed his lips. "There is no quandary without answer," he said calmly.

William frowned, wondering how to best balance his interests with the abbot and the cardinals in France. But as he pondered, the abbot said, "Have not I heard a tale of her quarrel with the Church? How can she marry without confession and repentance?"

Realization dawned slowly, and William flushed at the plainness of his solution. "She cannot."

The abbot smiled, but was abruptly overtaken by a fit of coughing. Clapping William on the shoulder, he said, "'Tis a sin to indulge anger, Brother Simon. But 'tis not the damage of body that is the greatest trouble, but the damage to the mind. One cannot think in anger, only react."

"Aye, Father," William said, bowing his head. "And 'tis a great weakness of mine."

"So I have seen." He moved away dismissively. "There are texts to help you."

William bowed his head respectfully. "I will meditate upon it."

"See that you do."

Not until they were out of sight of the oppressive abbey did it sink in what Anya had done. She stopped abruptly outside a jeweler's shop, closing her eyes. "Christian," she said. "I do not want you to think you are in some way required to—"

"Required?" he echoed.

She took a breath and looked at him. "To do more than you have done already. Once we are wed and I have my dowry, I'll not hold you to vows."

He did not answer for a moment, and Anya saw his jaw draw tight. "There are many hurdles yet ahead, Anya. You see your quarrel with your brother, and in your temper, you won a point over him." The gray eyes held a grim light. "'Tis not finished."

Anya pressed her lips together for a moment. "I know. I only meant to tell you—"

"That my obligation is finished once you have your dowry." There was a harshness in his words.

She nodded.

Without speaking, he turned and strode onward, his steps long in the lowering light of early evening. Anya hurried along beside him, catching her skirts in one hand so she would not trip. His anger bewildered her.

"What have I done, Christian? You offered—I only took what you gave."

Beneath the spreading bare branches of an ancient oak, he stopped abruptly. With a sound of frustration, he took her face in his hands and kissed her.

Anya grasped his wrists, swept instantly into the painful pleasure his touch gave. She tasted frustration and desire on his mouth.

He lifted his head. "Think you that is the way all men and women feel when they kiss?" he said fiercely.

She looked at him, touched his hand on her face. A finger of sunlight broke through the scattering clouds and caressed his jaw, showing the blond bristles of beard around his beautiful mouth. "When good things come to me, there is always some terrible cost I must pay to have them, Christian. Till now you've only been help and joy—and I fear the price of that joy."

"Oh, I've no doubt you'll be asked to pay dearly, my lady." He pressed a kiss to her brow. "But it shall not be me. I promise, Anya, true husband I will be to you."

She smiled indulgently, knowing what men promised in the heat of lust was often not true in practice. Soon or late the day would come when his eye snagged on the swinging hips of some young beauty. She was not young now, but his gratitude did not let him see it. But she would not quarrel. "All right."

He shook his head. "You will see, Anya of Winterbourne." Glancing over her shoulder to the street, he tugged her behind the wide body of the tree and kissed her more intently. "We will be parted on the morrow," he said. "Send your woman to sleep with Geoffrey and let me come to you tonight."

His mouth moved to her throat and Anya struggled against the dangerous heat he roused in her. "Nay, my lord," she whispered, willing herself to ignore the length of his hard thighs against her own, the surety of his fingers slipping up to mold her breast. "I will not lie with you again until we are safely wed."

"Till we are wed?" he said, lifting his head. "To what purpose would you deny us this pleasure?" As if to illustrate, he bent and captured her lower lip between his own. "To what purpose, Anya?"

She pushed at him, and heard her breath coming in embarrassing little gasps. "I do not wish to displease the saints. I wish to be a virtuous woman, so the heavens will not see fit to punish me."

"'Tis not heaven that's punished you, but man."

"Perhaps then, I'd ask protection of those saints against those men." There was a hint of bitterness in her words. "'Twould be a comfort to feel that shelter."

He lifted his head with reluctance, and tenderly brushed a curl from her cheek. "I wish you might see your true worth, sweet Anya. So many things—"

With a sigh, he straightened. "So be it. 'Tis not such a far distant day that I cannot wait." A slow, seductive smile touched his lips. "But the burden of virtue lies with you. I cannot promise to resist you always. 'Tis not in the nature of a man."

"Pah!" she said, but cocked her head in acceptance of his challenge. "The burden always rests with the woman, does it not?"

He let her go. "Come, we must return before dark falls."

As they neared the inn, he said, "Anya, you know I must go yet to Carpentras. We will be wed, and you may return to Winterbourne to begin the rebuilding. When my business in Provence is finished, I'll return to you."

"When you have killed your father?"

He said nothing for a moment. Then soberly, he said, "I heard gossip that the pope lies near death in France. 'Tis that which led my father to seek me out again. Until I put this mystery to rest, I will always be hunted."

So, in truth, not much would change at all in her life. Anya nodded. "On the morrow, I will return to Winterbourne. When you have seen the king, send word and I will return to Lichfield, where we will meet again with my brother."

"That I will do." Outside the door to the inn, he paused and leaned close, as if whispering to her. But his lips touched her neck in a seductive caress. "Since you will not send your woman away, will you at least consent to sharing a tankard of ale with me?"

"Aye—if Geoffrey might come, too." A pang touched her. "I would spend this last night with him."

"Done."

At dawn, Geoffrey crept into Anya's chamber. She awakened to his palm on her cheek. "Geoffrey, what is it? Are you ill?"

He slowly shook his head. "I am frightened."

"Oh, sweet!" She shifted, scooting close to Gertie, who slept on obliviously, to make room for him. She patted the place next to her. "Tell me about it."

He crawled beneath the covers and rested his head on her shoulder. "I remember naught before Winterbourne. What if I do not like the court?"

Anya smoothed his hair, drawing comfort from the lean warmth of his small body next to hers. "You'll like it, child. 'Tis gay and rich. There you'll taste of sweets like you've never seen and see the most beautiful ladies and play your music for the most powerful men in the land."

"Can you not come, too?"

A pain stabbed her. "If only I could," she whispered, closing her eyes. He smelled of horse and child and innocence, and she breathed it deep against the day she would no longer scent it.

And yet for all the grief the parting caused her, it was good for Geoffrey. She did not like to think of him wounded in battle, wielding a sword to cut down soldiers, riding too long and too far for too little gain. As bastard, he had nothing coming to him upon maturity, so would have to become knight-errant at the mercy of mean-sprited lords, or take up a monk's life. Naught could give him the joy his music could.

"Go and make me proud of you, young Geoffrey."

He wept a little then, though she saw it pained him to be so weak. "I do not wish to leave you, my lady! Cannot I make a place in your Hall?"

"Aye, Geoffrey. If you find the court unsuited to you, I will make a place for you in my Hall." She planted a kiss to his head. "Always you have a place with me. Always, do you hear?"

He nodded, his fingers clutching her sides almost painfully.

'Twas time to move him from grief to action. "My lord will not abandon you there if he sees 'tis not best for you. He's fond, you know. And he will bring you back to me if needs be."

"Aye."

"In truth, sweet, 'tis a far better chance he grants than what I could give. Brother Simon threatened to take you away to the monastery. Did you know that?"

Geoffrey looked up in horror. "Nay!"

"'Tis true. The knight spoke for you then, with this plan. So 'twas to save you the life of a monk we send you to the king." She chuckled. "Go now and make yourself ready. I will meet you in the yard."

He rose and paused, then leaned over and kissed her cheek. "You've ever been good to me, my lady."

Anya held to her emotions rigidly. "Go, child."

When he left her, she buried her face in the mattress and let the tears come. Gertie wakened and eased close, putting a gentle arm around her mistress, murmuring quiet condolences.

She could not go down to the yard looking so bleak, so after a little she dried her tears and splashed cold water on her eyes. Gertie dressed her in the fine gown embroidered with paisleys, with gold at cuffs and hem. At the girl's insistence, Anya let her hair be woven into a clever arrangement of braids, so when she went down, she felt a noble sort of lady.

Christian greeted her with a cocked head. "What manner of woman is this?" he said with a teasing smile. "One would think 'twas you going to court."

Anya touched the arrangement of braids beneath her veil and rolled her eyes. "'Twas Gertie's doing. She scorns my workaday look."

"Well done, Gertie!" Christian said with a wink.

A young monk ducked into the tavern. "Be you Anya of Winterbourne?" he asked.

She nodded and he gave her a letter—a summons from William for Christian and Anya to attend him at the abbey at the hour of Tierce. "Thank you," she said to the young monk, who bowed and left.

"What can he want?" Anya said.

"Perhaps he regrets his hasty anger and wishes to make amends," Christian said, tongue-in-cheek.

Even Geoffrey snorted over that. "Brother Simon is never sorry."

"True enough," Anya said.

There was naught to do but go to him to find out, so again she and Christian traversed the streets of Lichfield to the abbey. William met them. He didn't make them wait, and even offered freshly baked bread, which both declined.

"I would know your business, brother," Anya said briskly. "There is much to be done and already we have lost good hours."

William straightened, folding his hands before him. Anya saw suddenly how the place suited him—there was the same liquid quiet about him as about the room, a prim order in his neat robes and the careful combing of his hair. "I have conferred with the abbot and the bishop and given much thought to your petition."

Anya shot a glance toward Christian, who stood without expression beside her.

William looked from one to the other. "I have decided to grant your petition to marry, Anya."

She lifted her eyebrows in surprise.

"There is, of course, a condition."

"Of course," she said ironically.

"You must make your full confession to Father Gerent and perform what penance he requires to atone for your sins. The betrothal may be made formal today, but until you have repented, you cannot marry."

Knotty dread filled Anya. For so long she had resisted, it would be no simple task to humble herself to confess to the priest who held nothing but ill-will toward her. "Must it be given Father Gerent?" she asked quietly. "Is there none here who would grant me confession and penance?"

"You know it is against Church law, Anya. How can you even ask it?"

"He will humiliate me," she whispered. "I know it."

"Then you must choose which is more important to you: the marriage and your dowry to save the village, or your precious pride."

"I am not the only child of my father to be thus afflicted," she said sharply. "'Tis only—"

Christian's hand on her arm stopped her. Taking a long breath, she reined her temper. "Very well. I will make my confession and accept whatever humiliation the priest hands to me."

"Then may I wish you my best, sister?"

She narrowed her eyes. Too easy. "What of my dowry? I would have it given over now."

"'Tis already done. This morning I've sent to Winterbourne to have the priest read the banns on Sunday and accept your confession. When you have given it, he will give you the dowry, which is in his keeping till then."

Anya stared at him for long moments, feeling deep ripples of warning in her limbs. She trusted this not at all, but could see nothing to do but agree—for the moment, at least. "Thank you, William," she said. "I am ever in your debt."

He allowed the smallest smile to touch his lips. "Aye."

17

As they left the monastery, Christian strode so quickly away that Anya caught his arm. "I cannot walk so fast, my lord!"

He willed himself to her pace and tried to calm his worry. "I dislike the ease of this," he said. "There is some trick here."

"Aye," Anya said grimly. "And I'll wager the trick will be revealed when my penance is named."

There was dread in her words. Christian paused, frowning. "What think you they will do?"

She lifted her eyes, and he saw there the first true fear he'd ever seen in her face. "I know not." Her gaze left him, to stare unseeing toward some distant point. "But I have been the target of their punishments before."

Christian remembered what Mary had told him of her travails. "I will journey back with you now to Winterbourne, then, and—"

"No! Geoffrey must be far from their reach before my penance is told. I would have him out of their clutches." She fingered the edges of her sleeve. "I will go alone to Winterbourne."

Guilt twisted within him. Perhaps, without his bullying the day before, she might have made a less costly deal with her brother. He gazed at her hands, careworn and yet so slim and elegant, and took them into his palms. "Fear not. You're braver by half than both of them. Their petty minds will seek to humiliate, but you are stronger than they, and will conquer them in the end."

The dread did not entirely flee her eyes, but he saw her shoulders straighten. Abruptly, she stood on her toes and pressed a kiss to his lips. "I am forever in your debt, my lord. I have longed sorely for a friend."

He caught her neck and kissed her hard. "Friend I am no longer, Anya. Lover and husband henceforth."

Her smile was sad. "Husbands and lovers are often cruel and inconstant. A friend I can count on."

"You will see," he promised. "I vow you will see, my lady."

Then came the moment Anya had been dreading for several weeks.

Geoffrey stood nearby his pony, his face pinched and white. His cloak and blouse were neatly brushed, and his hair combed with water to make it lie down.

Anya smiled, hiding the sharp squeeze of her heart. "You've the chance to learn all the ballads in the land," she said with forced brightness. "Will you come play them for me at harvest?"

He nodded. Anya saw he meant to be brave now,

and squeezed his hand. "Send word to me if needs be."

"Aye." He shifted, foot to foot, and could not meet her gaze. Anya saw a shimmer of tears in his eyes. With a pang, she realized she only made the parting all the worse.

She bent and brushed a kiss to his cheek. "Go with God," she whispered, and rushed away blindly, desperately trying to keep her emotions in check.

Around her, men began to mount, some of them going with the party riding to the king, the rest with Anya back to Winterbourne. Christian, in mail and well armed, gave sharp instruction to the guard who was to ride with her. The man nodded seriously.

Standing there in sunlight at last carrying hints of spring, with the rattle of harnesses and murmurings of men, with the sound of a city coming to full movement around her, Anya realized that Christian, too, was riding away.

She was struck with a sudden fear that she would never see him again, that something would befall him on the road. Or—more likely—he'd see the ladies of the court, arrayed in their finery, and wonder what value he'd seen in a rough country woman who worked like a peasant and was years beyond her best beauty.

As if her gaze pricked him, he glanced up. Dressed in his warrior garb, with horses milling behind, and his great size unbowed by the weariness of weeks past, he looked forbidding and strange.

Then a gentleness came in his eyes, and he dismissed the man with him. He crossed over to her and lifted her hand to his lips. "Lady Anya, be well. Heal your village and make it sing again."

She gave a small, bemused laugh. "That I can do."

He bent over her hand, holding it tightly in his own and pressed a fervent kiss to her fingers, his eyes closed. "Godspeed," he said gruffly, and just as Anya had done moments before, hastily turned away, shouting for the men to mount.

As they began to ride out, he spared one glance over his shoulder and lifted a hand in farewell. Geoffrey, too, waved, and she could see the tears he couldn't stop falling on his cheeks.

Mutely, Anya prayed for protection for them both, watching until long after they'd been swallowed by the bustle in the Lichfield streets.

The sunlight lasted. As Anya rode over the rise nearby the manor, that cold spring light showed all too clearly the ruin of the village. Blackened timbers and scorched trees stood in haunting reminder of the tragedy that had struck them. At the center of the dismal scene was the church, washed clean of soot by a recent rain.

As her small party rode through the manor gates, Anya spied Father Gerent, hands folded over his sow's belly, his tonsured pate shining. A slug of dread punched her anew as she stared at him. He met her gaze impassively, and only lifted his chin, then brought it down in a nod. He knew. He would be ready for her.

Even in two days were there a thousand details all begging her attention as soon as she dismounted. Her feet no more than touched the ground before Stephen and the stable master and a dozen others crowded around her in a clamor.

"My lady, you must speak to—"

"Lady Anya, Erda will not listen—"

"Mistress, my babe lacks—"

"The noise of the peasants disturbs the horses—"

Anya raised a hand. "Enough!" she cried. "I will tend all, but give a woman a breath of air!"

Pushing through them, she made for the Hall. Everyone trailed behind her like an untidy army of ants.

"Milady!"

"Lady Anya!"

"We must—"

"You are needed—"

Anya lifted her skirts to climb the stairs, ignoring them—only to be greeted by a new chorus in the hall. Villeins and servants raised their voices in protest, complaint, quarrel. Anya blinked at the onslaught, her head pounding. "Leave me be!"

Fiercely, she elbowed through, aiming for the solar. At the threshold to her sanctuary, she said as calmly as she was able, "Give me an hour to collect myself and I will hear all, but one at a time, as suits civilized folk, for I vow I cannot sort this noise."

With cold fingers she touched her temples, and snagged a page by the shoulder. "Go to the kitchen for my headache tonic. Erda will know what to do. Wait for it and bring some bread and wine, too."

The boy bobbed and raced off to do her bidding. Anya shut the door. With a weary sigh, she sank onto the trunk nearby the door and numbly sat there, staring at the wall. With a distant portion of her brain, she saw the painted border of violets and ferns had faded. It needed touching up. Below the border, the latticework pattern painted in gold and brown still looked crisp enough except where Geoffrey's hands had smudged dirt at a child's height nearby the door and again by the raised dais by the window.

Those smudges of child hands would stay.

She felt utterly empty, a cup drained and left to be tossed around in the rushes by curious dogs. There was nothing left in her to give to the hungry, clawing group beyond her door.

The feeling frightened her. Always there had been at least a drop of courage left in her cup, and one drop, gathered carefully, seemed to always grow to more. Now she could not even gather that single precious drop.

The boy came in bearing her tincture and the a tankard of watered wine. "The cook bade me bring this, too," he said holding a crock of soft white cheese and a hunk of black bread.

"Thank you." As he departed, Anya at last gathered herself enough to shed her cloak.

Mary scratched at the door and poked in her head. "Milady?"

"What is it?" Anya said with exasperation.

Mary came in, her round rosy face beaming. Glancing over her shoulder, she whispered, "Is it true?"

"What true?"

"That you are betrothed!"

Anya avoided her gaze. "Aye."

"Ooooh!" Mary squealed and grabbed Anya's face, planting a great, sloppy kiss upon her cheek. "You snagged the knight, milady! That big stallion for your bed!"

Grabbing Anya's hands, Mary laughed and yanked Anya to her feet, spinning her in a dancing circle. "Think of the babes you'll bear! Oh, and the getting of the babes!" She let go of a bawdy laugh. "'Tis grand news."

Anya pushed her away. "Stop it."

"Milady, surely you are not displeased."

"Nay," she said with dignity, turning to drink the tincture for her aching head. "'Tis only you make it sound like the happy end of some silly ballad."

"It is!"

Anya turned. "No. 'Tis only business, that he may claim a bit of land and I may have my dowry from my brother to rebuild the burned village." Shuddering at the bitterness of the herbs, she gulped a sip of wine to chase the taste away. "You go about like a happy nurse and all will laugh at me. Only you are fool enough to see romance where lies none."

"So are all noble marriages business," Mary replied. "But not all knights stir the blood as our fair Lord Christian. Can you find no little joy in that?"

Anya bent her head, smearing cheese on black bread. "A little. But once we are wed, he flies directly to France, while I stay to rebuild the village. I expect my life will change little."

"Ah, so there's the truth of it!"

"What?"

"Never mind, lass. Never mind." She came forward. "Sit. Let me brush this tangle for you while you sup. The lot of them won't be patient long."

Anya gratefully complied. The cheese settled well, and the wine began to ease the pounding army feet in her temples. As Mary loosened the thick braid and ran a pig bristle brush over her scalp, the pain eased even more.

Licking her fingers, she asked, "How long has the priest been hovering?"

"Since Sext, when a messenger brought him news from Lichfield."

"Did he make public the betrothal then?"

"Nay. I overheard the guards that overheard the messenger."

"So by now 'tis common knowledge."

Mary laughed. "In so bored a group, all were grateful for happy news."

"No doubt."

Mary brushed firmly over Anya's scalp and Anya closed her eyes at the pleasure. After a silent moment, Mary said cautiously, "There is more on the gossip's tongues."

"Pray thee, tell all."

"They take bets on what the priest will give as penance. And gamble over what the time will be when you kneel for that confession."

"And?"

"Tomorrow at dawn so you'll rouse the priest from his sleep."

In spite of herself, Anya chuckled. "Clever. I had not thought of it."

"The penance is divided."

Anya looked at the windows.

"Some say you'll be on the road as pilgrim before the week is out. The rest say you'll be forced to take a beating in the public square, given by your brother's hand."

The food in her belly turned to stones. "Holy mother of God!" It would give William great satisfaction to so humiliate her in public.

"So be it," she said, finding after all a drop of courage left in her cup. "At least it's quickly won. Give me my veil. I would end this torment of wonder now. Go tell the priest to make ready for me."

If it was to be a beating, William would not be here to give it today, that much she could ascertain. But she left her hair free to give modesty if she were stripped to the waist.

Then she settled the veil and fillet over her head and from a drawer took her rosary beads. Holding them close to her heart, she knelt before the altar of Saint Anthony in a wordless, nameless plea for help. Heart pounding, she kissed the beads and turned toward the door.

Christian tended Remus carefully. The creature grew more alert with each hour, as if he had only needed the freedom of the open road to make him live again. He appeared to have made peace with Christian, for as he curried his coat and shoveled his oats, Remus only stood there, whickering softly as if in conversation.

Esme circled around Christian's ankles, purring. He made a mental note to bring her scraps as soon as he was able. To tide her over, he knelt and scooped her up, scratching her ears. "Will you ride all the way to France, little cat? See the world with me?"

From behind him in the stables came a stir of voices. Before Christian could straighten, the king appeared on the threshold. A sturdy, muscular man with golden hair and alert, boyish eyes, the king was covered with grime. His boots were thick with mud.

"Christian! They told us it was you and we thought it a trick!"

Christian knelt, smiling, his head lowered. "Hale and whole, my liege, as you see."

The king waved him up. His eye sharpened. "Was it the Scots? We were asked no ransom."

"Nay, my lord." Wincing a little at the stir of fire his abrupt movement gave, he shook his head. God's teeth, two days of riding and he was a whipped pup. "'Twas French brigands on some errand of my father's."

Edward lifted a heavy brow. "The pope is dead. Word came only this morn."

Christian sighed.

"Walk with us," Edward said, gesturing. Men-at-arms dropped back to a discreet distance. "We are glad to see you well, old friend." Edward said. "Think you the journey to Provence would be overtaxing? We seek a man to smell the way the wind blows in Carpentras."

"Old and weary I grow, my lord," Christian returned with a wry grin, "but ever I am your servant."

The king chuckled. "Such humility sits ill on those shoulders, Christian. Well we remember the battles we shared over chess in our youth."

"'Tis truly meant," Christian said seriously. "In my honor you may trust."

Weariness like nightfall suddenly deepened the lines in Edward's face, gave age to his eyes. "Few enough have spoken thus."

From the edge of the stable wall emerged Geoffrey, white-faced and pinched. In his slim hands he carried his pipe and tabor. "My lord?" he said quietly.

Christian held out an arm to draw the child forward. "My liege, I've brought you Geoffrey of Winterbourne, to please you with his flute and drum."

Edward straightened, the lines of strain easing as Geoffrey nearly overtipped in his bow. "Let us hear it."

Geoffrey scrambled to lift the instrument to his lips. He blew forth a lilting ballad meant for dancing.

Christian smiled as the king's face lost its look of strain. The boyish ease returned. He cheered loudly when Geoffrey finished, bowing with a flourish.

"Can you make a place for such a boy?" Christian asked, knowing the answer. "He needs shelter."

"Aye," he said with a happy smile. "As you well know. Boy, go you to the steward and he will find you a bed. Each night at my supper you will play until you choose to play no more!"

A blaze of joy crossed the elfin features. "Oh, thank you, Your Majesty! Thank you!"

As he rushed off, Edward asked, "What is he to you?"

"The bastard of a noblewoman who saved my life."

Edward's smile grew inquisitive. "And who might she be?"

"Anya of Winterbourne."

"I know Winterbourne—a plump fief."

Christian watched a trio of women sail through the bailey, gowns glinting with gold, their fingers and wrists adorned with jewels. One smiled coquettishly at him, and he allowed himself a small appreciative smile in return. He was glad, suddenly, that he had not brought Anya here with him. In her simple dress, with that singular braid, she would have felt alien and out of place. And yet, to his eye, she was by far the most alluring of these.

To the king he said, "'Tis that Anya I've come to speak of."

The king lifted a brow.

"I'd take her to wife."

"A wife, Christian?" There was bitterness in his tone, for all knew his own wife pleased him little. "The Great Lion of Gascony is going to fall at last?"

"Aye. Soon or late, a man must beget children and settle his lands, no?"

"If it's lands you seek, there are better plots than Winterbourne."

Christian bowed his head. "'Tis a generous offer, my liege, and I'm grateful." He paused to let the king enter the passageway, and followed behind. In the torchlit gloom, he said, "But 'tis the mistress of Winterbourne only I will take to wife."

"She saved your life, you say?"

"She and the boy dragged me half dead from the forest."

The king wrinkled his nose. "She must be past twenty to have a child so tall. And no husband?"

Christian found himself reluctant to tell the king all. The story was long and tangled and he wished only to settle this business so he might take some supper and rest, then ride early away. "She would not be to your taste, my liege, but I find her a calm and easy companion, and she needs a champion."

The king peered sharply into Christian's face another long moment. At last he nodded. "So be it then. She shall be your wife."

Christian bowed, relief winging through his breast. Now any child she bore from their union in his absence would at least be blessed by vows and no bastard. "Thank you, my liege."

The king gestured for Christian to follow him into a well-appointed chamber. "Enough business. We'd enjoy an evening of drink and dice with our old friend."

Christian nodded. "'Twould be my pleasure, my lord."

18

A trail of villagers swarmed through the gates and down the road into the burned village, dancing behind Anya as if she were the pied piper. She carried herself straight and without shame, trying not to mind their curiosity, but she longed to be able to do this thing in private.

The scent of burned timbers and charred feathers hung in the cool, late afternoon, and a wren hopped along the trees, as if to see what the excitement was about. Anya clutched her rosary beads so tightly her knuckles felt bruised. A thready pulse beat in her throat. She could feel it skittering.

Before the solid white church, she stopped. The gay crowd following swarmed into a new arrangement around her and abruptly settled into silence. Anya's terror leapt another notch. She thought she might vomit on the porch before she could go in the doors.

A woman came forward and pressed Anya's hand, bright blue eyes full of sympathy. Another came then, and another. Then a man, and one more. Each steadied her, whispered a kind word.

Father Gerent opened the great door, releasing a waft of incense into the gathering twilight. Behind him, Anya saw the wink of candles against darkness and the gentle shine of gold threads in the altar cloth.

He made no move, only stood waiting. His robes were brushed, his face clean, his eyes sober. As Anya stared at him, her feet stuck fast to the ground, she saw a flicker of sympathy—even kindness—in his round face.

It unstuck her feet. With trembling hands she lifted the heavy skirts of the good embroidered tunic she'd donned this morning.

"Come in, child," the priest said, and stepped aside to let her pass. Her hem caught on his shoes, pulling her up short. Her shaking hands lost their grip on the rosary and the beads fell to the floor with a clatter.

Anya froze once more, overwhelmed with the holy odor of incense wafting out to mix with the clean smell of wax tapers burning. An ache bloomed in her heart at the unexpected pleasure of the once-beloved smell of church. Deeply she breathed it, tasting the sweaty bodies of village men who came fresh from the fields, a flavor of mildew, a wash of wood and beeswax.

And with a painful, swelling pinch, she felt her mother all around her, for well had she loved her church, her God. Poignantly, she remembered the feeling of her mother next to her as she prayed, heard the soft sound of her breath, smelled the oil of cloves in her hair.

It had been so long.

Above the altar hung a great wooden crucifix that gleamed in sadness against the candles. Some of the dying day illuminated the deep hues of the precious tiny circle of stained glass in the nave.

Anya turned, gripping her beads. "I am ready."

Into the confessional she moved, and knelt. "Forgive me, Father, for I have sinned," she said. "It has been nine years since my last confession."

Nine years. It seemed, all at once, too many years, too many days to put right.

But until she made some attempt, no dowry could heal the broken village, so she began where she could. "I have been willful and prideful. I have bowed only to my own desires." Her throat felt tight. "I refused to be cleansed after the birth of my child . . ." she faltered ". . . but only because the pain in my heart was too fierce."

A tear struck her hand, hot and wet. She drew a breath, worrying the beads between her fingers. "I have allowed my heart to overrule my head at every turn. I have lain with a man not my husband and have borne a bastard child without shame."

"Do you repent and grieve these sins, daughter?"

She squeezed her eyes closed against the vision of Christian moving over her in the room behind the kitchen. Against the sweet, hot mouth of her newly born babe suckling her breast, of that same child running, dancing, laughing.

Her chest ached. How could she say them nay? Deny them as if they were not the best moments in a life otherwise burdened with only work?

And yet, those moments of painful love were not all. In her mind she saw spring at Winterbourne and tasted the richness on her tongue. She remembered the blackened sticks of the village and the faces of the hungry children.

Winterbourne. For Winterbourne, she could pretend she grieved and repented.

"I repent my sins," she said clearly.

Beyond the linen, she heard the priest sigh. In relief, she thought—till he spoke. "Child, acted I alone your penance would be light, for well I've seen the price you paid for your sins of pride and willfulness. I have seen you don the mantle of service with rare joy, working in the fields and birthing calves. 'Twould be hard to find another mistress of such kindness in all of England."

Anya waited as he hesitated, fear growing in burning leaps in her stomach.

"'Twas your anger I sought to break these many years, and that has vanished like a mist."

Her mouth was dry. She could not swallow for the dryness.

"But I act not alone," the priest said at last. "The Church wishes to spear your heresy for all to see, for a tiny seed of ferment grows to mighty revolution. The Church wishes to see you make public penance, for all to see."

A beating. Anya pressed the cross to her lips and squeezed her eyes closed.

"I am given leave to read the banns at Mass tomorrow and give unto your keeping the dowry your brother left," Father Gerent said, "but you cannot marry till a pilgrimage you make."

A gush of relief washed through her. "To Canterbury?" It was a common site. Even if they bade her walk, she could return in time for spring planting.

"Nay." The priest's voice was so grim, Anya froze once more. "To the tomb of Saint Mary Magdalene."

She frowned. "But where is that?"

"In Provence, my lady."

The news of the pope's death lent urgency to Christian's quest. The day after his talk with the king, he rode to Winterbourne. This time he rode Remus, and though the horse balked a little, within an hour he was content and clopping brightly along the road.

They made Winterbourne near dark. The last of the shepherds were letting sheep into their pens, the bells of ewes close to birthing ringing quietly in the still air. Stragglers brought hares and new greens for supper. And in the bailey there was an almost festive air.

A cheer went up as Christian and his party rode in, a general welcoming that drew the attention of others, who took up the happy greeting. He smiled in bemusement—obviously the banns had been read— and lifted a hand in greeting.

He dismounted and strode through the milling group, his eye alert for Anya. He found himself hungry for the sight of her, and anxious to spend as many of the next few hours in her company as possible. At first light, he would ride to Carpentras, on both his errand and that of the king.

As if called by his wish, she appeared at the top of the stairs to the kitchen, dressed in her worn work dress, a rumpled apron tied over it. Steam-loosened curls sprung around her face, and her cheeks were red with heat. His heart lifted, and he climbed toward her eagerly.

She didn't smile, and he felt a sharp sense of worry. Surely the penance could not be so bad as that? She looked whole and well. "Greetings, my lord," she said.

And even the sound of her voice was welcome, that husky ruined voice, so lyrical and sweet to his ear. All the women at court, in their jewels and velvets, paled before the simple beauty of strong Anya in her work-stained gown.

Devilishly, knowing the villagers were on his side, he leapt nimbly up the last two steps and snagged her hands. Laughing, he kissed her. Whoops came from the villagers below, and bawdy calls.

Blushing, Anya pulled away. "My lord, you'll make a fool of me."

"No more fool than me."

She lifted her eyes and he saw again the darkness of worry there. "What is it?"

"Come to the solar. I will explain all."

As they passed by the kitchen, she shed her apron, tossing it on a three-legged stool. "Tillie, take my place."

The Hall was bustling, the edges littered all around with rolled furs and crude pallets, scattered treasures in small piles. All had been shoved aside to make room for the trestle tables now being readied for the evening meal.

For all the crowding, there was a sense of calm in the room that had been missing when they left four days ago. "All seems well in hand," he commented.

She made a rueful sound. "'Twas not so last eve, I can tell you." She motioned for him to follow her into the solar, which he gladly did.

As he turned to close the door, he pressed a secretive finger to his lips, winking at the page beside the door. The boy, about twelve, grinned and nodded.

Christian closed the door firmly. Anya turned at the sound. Swiftly, before she could protest, he caught her up in his arms, lifting her as easily as a child, and sat with her in his lap on the bed.

With a flustered flurry of movements, she pushed away. "I cannot think with you holding me thus," she protested.

He restrained her easily. "Good," he said, and kissed her properly, taking her mouth with an almost savage pleasure. She tasted the way he remembered, of work and light and a drugging, unnamed flavor that belonged to her alone.

She resisted a little, but with a little cry gave into him, her mouth softening, her hands buried in his hair. He touched her breast, just to weigh again the fullness in relation to his palm. She made a soft, longing noise.

Encouraged, he tumbled backward, bringing her with him, and swiftly put her on her back so he might feel her against the length of him. He kissed her neck and jaw and stroked the narrow length of her waist. "Anya, I am half mad for want of you."

He bent his head over her loose gown, pressed his mouth to the inviting swell of her breast, trailed his tongue in circles over the flesh. "Tell me you do not long for this, my sweet. Tell me you wish me to stop now."

Her fingers tightened in his hair and he felt the tension all through her body. He lifted his head and supped again of her lips. "Tell me."

She arched a little, yearning, and returned his kiss. With a soft sigh of hunger, he kissed her deeply and stroked the point of her breast the way he'd learned she most liked, slow and sharp. She moved urgently, pulling his head close, her teeth against his lips, biting and—

He felt dampness, and lifted his head in surprise. Down her cheeks washed a great, silent torrent of tears. Instant shame struck him, and he sat up. "Oh, Anya, forgive me." He gathered her close, pressing her head into his shoulder. "Forgive me."

She made no sound, but he felt the strain of the silence in her rigid shoulders, in the painful clutch of her fingers on his arms.

He stroked her hair. "God, I'm a selfish beast," he whispered. "Anya, I swear I'll not tempt you again till the vows have been said. I swear it. Shhh."

When the tension began to ease from her back, she said quietly, "I seem not to be such a virtuous woman."

Chastened, Christian lifted her chin with his fingers and place a gentle kiss on her mouth. "'Tis not you, Anya, but the beast in me. Forgive me."

She wiped her cheeks and pulled away. This time he let her go.

"Made you your confession?" he asked.

"I did."

"And your penance?"

She turned. "To make a pilgrimage."

He let go of a breath of relief, nodding. "Canterbury?"

Her smile was bitter. "Nay. The tomb of Saint Mary Magdalene. Fitting, is it not?"

"But 'tis a journey of weeks and weeks! Farther even than Carpentras!" He jumped to his feet. "Those bastards. They only wish to remove you so the church can seize Winterbourne. They think you'll not return at all."

"As my brother John did not."

Christian cursed again, pacing, trying to think of some overlooked clue to end the mess.

"I cannot marry till I return," Anya said, "but even there, I played into my brother's hands, for the dowry is freed for his use in my absence."

He looked at her, understanding now the weight of worry in her eyes. "Anya . . ."

"If there lives a fool greater than I," she said, "I do not know her name."

"You are no fool, my lady, only the pawn of greedy men." He put his hand on the hilt of his sword. "I vow they will not win, for you have now a true champion in me."

The brittle lines of her face softened. "As I have since I found you in the forest, my lord."

"Together, then, we travel." He smiled. "There is some joy in that, no?"

"But your business is urgent!"

"None so urgent I cannot ride with you, my lady."

Anya stared at him for long moments. "And what of your quest?"

"If I am to be the instrument of his death, as it seems I am, then 'tis only a mercy to grant his life a few more days."

"Do not speak of killing him, my lord. Murder is a grievous sin."

He chuckled. "Now that you have confessed, you intend to uphold the Church?"

She shook her head with a frown. "I wonder if you can kill him, Christian. You are no ogre, and once you loved him."

"So now I am a coward?"

"No. I hate my brother, but I could not kill him. Nor live with my guilt if I did."

"But you have not killed," he said in a low voice. "I have. For duty, and in battle, and by mistake. 'Tis the way of the knight."

"Well I know the ways of knights, but also I see the way of you. Mayhap there is some way besides killing. That is all I ask you to see."

"Mayhap," he repeated, and shrugged. There was no other way, but he would not say it now. She did not know Etienne d'Auch.

A scratch sounded at the door. The boy put to guard peeked in. "The priest seeks an audience with you both."

"Send him in," Anya said.

Christian glanced at her in surprise. She gave no explanation, but only welcomed the priest in and saw him settled in her chair with a cup of ale.

"You read the banns?" Christian asked.

"Aye, at morning mass." His old face smiled. "And a cheering there was in that full church, too."

Anya gave Christian a half smile. "Glad they are to know a man will lead them again."

"And glad for you, too, my lady," the priest said.

"Perhaps." She shrugged. "What brings you to my solar, Father Gerent? Did I forget some instruction this morn?"

Grimly the priest shook his head. "Nay, 'tis more than that." From his girdle, he drew a letter. "The steward used to read for me the letters your brother sent. And wrote the ones I sent in return." He shifted uncomfortably. "For three months, the monk who brought them also read them, and waited to hear my reply."

"What is it?" Christian prodded, impatient.

"He plots to kill you both," the priest said heavily. "With Etienne d'Auch."

At Anya's dismayed cry, Christian smiled bitterly. "You see, Lady Anya, there are times one must do what one must."

That sharply bitter smile haunted Anya through the evening and into the night.

She, Christian, and Father Gerent spoke at length on the plot. Father Gerent knew little. Nor did Anya entirely trust him—though she couldn't think what purpose it would serve to bring news of a plot, she thought it best to take all with a grain of salt.

As they sat before the hearth in the solar, she said as much. "Why should I trust a single word from your lips?"

He leaned on his knees, and Anya saw again that he was growing old. The hair circling his tonsure was nearly all white. "Mayhap you should not," he said. "I could understand well if you did not."

She opened her mouth to answer, but Christian held up a hand. "Let him speak."

"The day of the fire, I saw the villagers would kill you on my word alone. If it had not been for your knight, the frenzy might have—they might have burned you at the stake."

He paused for a long moment. "And for what would it have been? My own pride that a girl should defy my word. *My* word."

"What do you know of the fire?" Christian asked, leaning forward. "Was it William?"

"Oh, I suspect so. . . . but he said naught to me."

An overpowering sense of nausea swept over Anya suddenly, as vile and deep as if she'd scented the carcass of an overrripe deer. She stood up, grasping her stomach, and ran to the embrasure. Flinging open a shutter, she breathed deeply of the cold night air. It calmed her.

From behind, the priest said, "I have overtired you, my lady, and you must leave with the dawn. Go with God's grace."

She nodded. Grasping the shutter in her weakness, she turned. "Thank you, Father."

Soberly he nodded and shuffled out.

Christian's expression was knowing. "Betrayal is a wretched thing."

"Aye." She sank to a cold stone bench, staring at the sky, bright with stars. "How long will we travel?"

He stepped up to the dais and settled on the bench beside her. "You'll not see Winterbourne again until Assumption. At best."

At best. If no thieves cut their throats. If they did not become too entangled in the plots of cardinals. If Christian vanquished his father before the cardinal killed him. If the assassins who'd tried once to kill Christian did not try again—and succeed.

"I wonder what plot my brother's laid for us," she said quietly. "He sends us both south, so far. And in your case, I can see the wisdom of it. If your father becomes pope, William stands to gain much."

"Then we shall see to it d'Auch does not ascend that throne."

Lost in her thoughts, Anya barely heard him. "Will he send an assassin to the tomb? Lie in wait at Carpentras?" She looked at Christian. "I am afraid."

He took her hand. "That way lies madness, Anya. Together we will face all. I will not leave you alone to fight."

"Nor did my parents," she said, "not of their own will."

"Is it death you fear?"

She clutched his hand, drawing strength from the broad warmth. "I know not." Then she shook her head. "Not death. I fear for Geoffrey, alone with no protector. I fear for the people of Winterbourne." She watched the ominous circling of a bat above the trees. "I fear you will die protecting me. Most of all, I fear my brother will win."

Wordlessly, Christian held her hand, as if he knew there were not words enough in the world to ease her. After a time, he said, "Think only of tomorrow, my lady."

His smile was gentle as he pressed a kiss to her brow. "Sleep, now. In the morning, we will go."

He left her, but Anya did not stir—for frozen in place she was by her cowardice. 'Twas a thick coldness in her gut, shameful and sickening, but she could not deny it.

She was sore afraid. In the morning they would leave for France. For places she had not seen, nor barely heard tale of. All her days had been spent within a few hours' ride of Winterbourne. At Winterbourne, she was known. At Winterbourne, there was safety and familiarity. She knew just how the light would break at all hours of the day, whether it was Martinmas or Good Friday. Here she knew the sounds and the smells and the things that grew.

With a soft cry, she buried her face. So afraid.

She feared she'd not walk the soil here again, nor look upon Geoffrey's face, nor hear Mary's bawdy laugh ring into a misty morning, bright and alive.

She did not fear death—only death so far from where she was known. If death caught her on the road to France, who would be there to say, "Here lies

Anya of Winterbourne who loved a manor in the thick woods of Leicester, who bore a son and tried to be kind and at last ended her war with the Church"? Who would know?

Tonight she thought of her brother John, so long now on the road he must have learned the taste of the air in a thousand villages. Tonight she wondered if he were dead. Or if he had at last walked the streets upon which Christ had trod. She found she missed him the more now that Geoffrey was gone. John and Geoffrey and their music . . .

Her fear should have been tempered by the presence of her champion, by Christian. But it was not! When he rode this eve into the yard, her heart hurt with the love she bore him—and what woman would fault her? 'Twas a rare man who was fair and strong together, could be gentle or raging as need demanded. 'Twas what women dreamed a knight could be.

But she feared the love she bore him, feared the sorrow it might bring. Already she was much in years. Already her breasts were not so high as once they were, and her skin not so bright. How could he think he would love her when she had lost her teeth and her breasts flapped?

He did not love. There was the rub. He thought to do her a kindness, and for the moment his lust was sated by her newness. But 'twould not be long . . .

Oh, she was sore afraid!

19

The day was cold and rainy as they set out, and the weather did not ease through the day. By the time they reached the monastery where pilgrims were housed, Anya was soaked to the skin and had passed a mood of ill temperedness some miles back. All day, she'd ridden without complaint, without speaking her fears, without expressing anything at all except a grim determination to be done with this thing and return to Winterbourne.

The villeins had seen them off, trailing behind for nearly a mile until they had at last left them in the mist.

For the past mile, the daylight had been fading, giving even greater chill to the air. "I vow I will kill my brother," Anya said as the monastery came into view. They were the first words she had spoken in hours.

Christian gave her a halfhearted smile, and Anya saw his face was white with exhuastion, his shoulders rigid with the double-stepping gait of the beautiful and transformed Remus. "The first day is the worst, my lady. You will grow used to the riding. By the time we return to Winterbourne, you'll be as seasoned as a young knight."

Liking not the pinched look of his mouth, she said, "And you, my lord? Will you be crippled by the end of our journey?"

A flicker darkened the gray irises for a moment, then was replaced with a forced smile. "Nay. I'm only feeling the twinges of my months of leisure. You spoiled me and now I must suffer the pangs of rebuilding my fortitude."

Anya nodded, but noted as he dismounted that he could not quite hide the rigid way he held his shoulder and left arm. Stiffly he rounded Evered and lifted his arms above his head to help her, too, dismount.

She lifted a brow. "Move away, lord knight, or I'll kick that aching place. You'll not lift me when you are so weary."

A thunderous expression filled his face. "You mother me all to Provence like this, and I'll leave you to take your pilgrimage alone."

"'Tis no mothering. Move back, I say."

He stood where he was. Just as stubbornly, Anya refused to dismount. Immovable, they glared at each other through the relentless rain. "You may well be obstinate, Christian," Anya said at last, hungry and ready for a place to sleep, "but I have had to outlast two brothers and all the men in the Church."

"Get yourself down then," he said with annoyance, and strode away.

Giving a grunt of satisfaction, Anya did just that, and gave the horse to the stableboy who'd watched all. "Who be the apothecary here?" she asked him.

"Brother Hubert," he said. "You'll know him by his red hair."

A small stream of travelers were gathered inside, getting ready to take the meal about to be served. As Anya joined them, a sharp, sweaty odor struck her—a food smell she couldn't quite identify. With a quick frown, she covered her nose.

Christian waited just inside the door, aloof but unable to hide the pasty tone of his skin. As she neared him, a waft of air from the kitchen hit her face, and she nearly gagged.

"Ugh!" she whispered at his side. "What is that smell?"

He didn't even deign to look at her. "I smell only good mutton, my lady."

No, not mutton. Like sweat or—"I cannot bear to stand here and scent it."

"Then you'll go hungry tonight."

Another gagging wave of the odor washed over her. "Better starvation than eating whatever it is I smell." She backed away. "Bring me bread, if you might?"

He nodded without looking at her. As she backed out of the hall, she saw him discreetly cradle his left elbow in the palm of his right hand. The infirmary monk would know what to give. She had coin enough to make an offering.

Once she found the monk she sought and asked him to take a tisane of willow and black mullein to Christian, Anya found she cared little for bread or anything else. Her exhaustion suddenly caught her. Wearily she found the women's quarters and claimed a pallet on the floor nearby a woman with a small child in her arms. Soaked, hungry, stiff from riding all, she didn't care. In minutes she was asleep.

*   *   *

'Twas not such a simple matter for Christian, who ached all the more once his body was still. The cold, damp weather, coupled with such hard riding, had jolted alive the bees in his shoulder. He cursed the weakness, but he dreaded climbing astride Remus again.

If only he could keep the place warm, 'twould not be so excruciating. Perhaps in the morn, he'd somehow wrap it with wool, to protect it from the cold.

And slowly, the tisane a novice had brought him eased the worst of it. Anya's doing yet again, he'd wager.

He shifted carefully, thinking of her stoic endurance of the day's miserable journey. Through the rain and over muddy roads they'd ridden, and the woman had not uttered a single word of complaint.

How would he ever gain her true respect after all the tending she'd given him? Once again, she had seen through his ruse of bravery and tended him. Once again, she'd treated him like a child or a brother, not a man with whom she had shared passion.

At the manor, he'd seemed to gain her respect, had indeed felt more man with her than ever he had with a woman. He'd fought to save the village, had been able to repay his debt to her by saving her child from the monastery.

And yet, in Lichfield, when she had scorned his ability to help her with the manor, his pride had been again wounded. It still smarted a bit. Whatever he did, he would not let her tend him again. No more debt upon his pride. He couldn't bear it.

At his side, a man snored abruptly, as if making a

derisive comment on Christian's thoughts. It startled him. As his bad temper faded more and more with the comfort of lying down, the good mutton in his belly, the tisane easing his pain, he realized he was being merely churlish.

'Twas a woman's way to tend the sick, to cluck over injuries and pains, to see that a man had enough food in his belly, and good linens on his bed. Just as men swaggered to show their strength, women went about tending quietly their frail sides.

Thank God. The tisane had eased him so much he thought he might even sleep.

Wasn't much of his posturing and bad temper the result of his own fear? His fear that he might not be able to protect her? That because of the injury that stiffened him so he might not wield a sword well enough or quick enough if there arose a need?

More than once he'd seen such an injury be the death of a knight when he grew too sure of his prowess, or would not be humble enough to admit it weakened his ability. Many a knight willingly chose such a death over the quiet of retreating to the countryside to tend sheep.

Christian much prefered the latter. Aye, at Winterbourne, with Anya, he could be happy.

And there lay the source of his fear. Never had he asked the saints for happiness. He'd taken what he could find and made the best of it. Not since early youth, while still with his mother, had he dared to dream of peace or love or happiness. Now it was so near—and to achieve it, he had to face the greatest challenge of his life, one that might have killed him at his best.

If he were slain, what then would happen to Anya?

Darkly, he wondered if he might teach her to use a sword. If ever he'd known a woman equal to the challenge, 'twas Anya.

Finally sleep overtook him, and Christian dreamed of a brace of candles in a shadowy church. He smelled incense and saw his mother kneeling nearby a man.

In his dream, he was happy.

Christian's prediction proved to be true: in a few days, Anya's strength increased and she did not mind the long days of riding so much. She still felt overwhelmed at moments with an almost drugged somnolence. The rhythm of the horse, the smell of the wind as they approached the Channel, the warming sunshine, all combined at moments to cloak her in waves of sleepiness. Once or twice, she nearly drifted off. Christian teased her about it.

His good humor seemed restored once the wet weather cleared. Anya had arranged to take a bottle of the willow tisane with her when they left the monastery—and it cost her deep—but it was well worth the price for the help it lent Christian. The teasing, cheerful man who'd told Geoffrey stories and sparred with guards in the bailey returned.

As they rode, she noted a curious habit. Playfully, but with serious intent, he stabbed at the air with his sword as they rode. Or simply took it out and lifted it up over his head, or out in front, holding it a long, long time. The look in his eyes at such moments frightened her.

Only the crossing of the Channel nearly undid Anya. She'd never seen so large a body of water, and it terrified her to be unable to see land on the other side of it. It churned and moved, too, in ways lakes only moved in terrible storms.

Manage it she did, however. Christian worried that she'd be seasick, but the movement of the ship seemed not to bother her once she grew accustomed to it, even when a squall whipped in and sent most of the passengers below with green faces.

It was something of an accomplishment, she thought, and stood with Christian on deck, watching him with a hungry pleasure when she thought he wasn't looking. His face had grown brown over the past few days, his cheekbones highlighted with a wash of sunburn that made the lines in his face even more beautiful. His hair, grown much too long now, tossed in the wind as he stared toward France, and his father.

Sensing a little of his turmoil, she stepped close and leaned on the rail next to him. "All will be well, Christian," she said.

Distractedly, he nodded. "I have not been on French soil since I was fifteen. 'Tis beautiful in the spring. You'll like it."

"Ah, but I'm an Englishwoman, with long, deep roots," she said with a smile. "'Tis bred in us to hate our southern neighbors for their invasion so long ago."

Her jest did not have the desired effect. His sober expression only deepened. "My mother was English," he said.

"And did she miss her homeland?"

Christian looked at her, his eyes capturing the color of the sea. "No. She loved my father. He was her home."

When he was in this dark mood, Anya realized how little she knew of the man who'd stolen her heart. She longed to smooth those shadows from his face forever, and knew she could not. She could only listen. "And you, my lord? Do you miss your homeland?"

He didn't answer, only leaned on the rail with one elbow and looked at her soberly. "Nay," he said at last. "I hate my father."

If only that were true, Anya thought. If he truly hated, she would not worry so that he would be killed.

But Christian did not hate. Only a glimpse through the shroud of his male armour let her know it, only the most fleeting wisp of pain in the cloud color of his eyes. Mixed with his hate were betrayal, hurt, mayhap even a hint of bewilderment, that of a boy badly wounded without reason.

She swayed forward and allowed the first intimacy she had let pass between them: she put her head against his arm. "Ah, Christian, I would that I could kill him for you."

At last the smile returned to his face. "Spoken like the true warrior you are, my lady." He lifted her hand and kissed the palm, but then moved away.

"Forgive me," he said, "but if we are to wait until our wedding day to make love again, you mustn't tempt me so, Anya."

Just for a moment, she thought of tossing away the silly vow she'd made to herself and the saints: *Just let us live to see Winterbourne again and I will not lie with him till we marry.*

Then she thought of the dangers yet ahead, the things each faced before they could return safely home, and she tucked her hand into her skirts and turned away.

*   *   *

As they reached Burgundy, it became plain the stakes were even higher than Anya thought.

Chased from the road by a violent thunderstorm, she and Christian found shelter with a handful of other pilgrims huddled in a mean hovel. Though it was only midafternoon, Anya was starving and looked forward to the bread she carried in her pouch.

As they ducked into the little hut, she was struck in with a scent of roasting mutton mixed with the dampness, and the grime of unwashed pilgrims. Her appetite fled.

Feeling a little ill, she settled against the wall in a corner and huddled in her cloak. In the gloom, she could make out little but that the group was a rough one, and she was thankful for Christian's great presence as he settled next to her in a rattle of spurs and scabbard. He wore no mail, only his leather hauberk, for the weight pained him. In his arms, he carried Esmerelda, who snuggled into the folds of Anya's cloak comfortably and began to purr. With a smile, she said, "What a good traveler she's proven to be."

"Aye."

Ysengrin, too, trotted in and settled by them, bringing with him a smell of wet dog. That single note, added to the others in the room, made Anya's stomach roil. 'Twould wound the creature to send him away, but she nudged him with her toe. "Go to your master, Ysengrin. I like not the smell of you."

Agreeably, the dog slumped at Christian's side.

Anya closed her eyes. Outside, rain poured in torrents and thunder crashed in the trees. Against her belly, the cat purred with a comforting noise. Next to her, Anya could feel Christian's warmth along the side of her body, and she felt oddly dizzy with the sense of his size.

Anya buried her nose in her woolen cloak to shut out the smell of the meat. Suddenly, she scrambled to her feet and bolted for the door, running out into the pouring rain. She made it as far as a sheltering pine before she rid herself of the bitterness in her belly.

She felt better at once. The wet air smelled only of spicy pines and leaf mold and clean, clean rain. Trembling, she breathed in the cool scent, feeling her belly settle.

With a single deep breath, she straightened. And the furtive truth came home.

She was with child.

Standing beneath that great old pine, Anya was stricken with equal measures of joy and dismay. First she laughed—how could she have been so blind? The twisted way things smelled, the odd nausea, and her touchiness all pointed that direction. But most of all, Anya, who never slept, should have realized how out of character her sleepiness was.

She pressed a palm to her belly in joy, thinking of the babe there. "Oh, little one," she whispered, "welcome to you!"

Christian's child. A babe with his cloud-colored eyes, with his beautiful smile. She'd once borne a son and would not mind a daughter to giggle with—boys didn't giggle as girls did. And girls were not sent off to be fostered—

"Anya." Christian touched her shoulder. "Are you ill, my lady?"

She turned with a leaping sense of joy. And right there beneath the dripping branches, she nearly spilled her discovery, nearly clutched his hand and pressed it to that magical place.

But she did not. There was enough to worry him

now. 'Twould be unfair to burden him further. And while she was joyful, perhaps he would not feel thus.

"I'm fine," she said. "Ate something that disagreed with me, I suppose."

A flicker of a frown crossed his brow. She had the sense he was going to say something, but shook his head. "Come back inside."

At the thought of the mutton smell, her stomach roiled dangerously again. "I—"

"You wish to sleep in the rain tonight?"

"No." She gathered her skirts and drew the hood of her cloak over her face. She'd do her best, sit close to the door, keep her eyes averted.

It served well enough, though she did not eat the meat. After the rest had had their supper, a man began to tell the tales of his travels, for he was on his way home from the Holy Land. His hat was festooned with palm leaves and shells.

Anya listened eagerly, imagining John making just such a trip. She couldn't resist asking, "Saw you many pilgrims from England?"

"Aye, milady."

"My brother left five years ago, and we know not if he died. A very tall man, with blackest hair and eyes blue as the sky. John of Winterbourne?"

Another man answered. "I met John of Winterbourne at Jerusalem. He was well."

Anya leaned foward eagerly. "How long has it been?"

The man shrugged. "A year, perhaps less." He wiggled his nose. "Ye needn't worry, lady. He was hale as a pair of oxen."

"Oh, aye!" the first man cut in. "I remember him. The one who married the—"

The second man cut him off. "Aye, he's well."

"Married?" Anya echoed. Why would he send no word of such news? "Who?"

"He's mistaken," said the second man. "'Twas not John of Winterbourne."

Anya could tell he lied. Her brother had married, but the pilgrim chose not to tell her more, and she couldn't very well pry it from him.

"Did he say if he planned to return to England? Ever?"

"I'm sorry, milady. He didn't say."

Disappointed, Anya nodded and pulled her cloak around her again, retreating to her own world. Christian nudged her.

She looked up. "Let me hold you," he said quietly, so only she could hear. "I swear I will ask no more than that."

Anya hesitated only a moment. She nodded mutely. He opened his arms and she settled against his broad chest, sighing as his arms enveloped her in warmth and comfort. A soft, light kiss fell upon her hair, and Anya closed her eyes.

Again she thought of the babe—a babe! The first quick rush of dismay was gone, and only joy filled her. As she listened to Christian's heart beart, to the sound of his breath moving below her ear, she snuggled closer to him, curling like a kitten into the curve of his body. Her head filled with happy visions, she fell into the vast, yearning sleepiness of the past month.

Christian held her close, smelling her hair and the damp wool of her cloak. Her slim, small body always surprised him, for her presence was very large and energetic, not at all fitting to the actual size of her.

He felt it when she slipped from rest into deepest slumber. Her hands went lax, her head slumped into the cradle of his shoulder, all tension fled her limbs. Odd to see her sleep so often, she who had told him herself that she'd never slept more than Matins to Prime since childhood. The journey must be more wearying to her than she let on.

It worried him. She tried to hide it. Chattered all the more when it came on her, but he worried that she was taking one of the creeping diseases that struck travelers sometimes.

His arms tightened another jot as a pain filled his chest. By the saints, he had not planned this—had never planned to love. Even now, slumped ungracefully in the deepest of sleeps, she was uncommonly beautiful, that tendril of gold hair curling around her neck, the slanted sweep of lashes on her cheeks, the relaxed lushness of her lips. He watched her breathe, allowed himself to press his mouth lightly to her smooth brow.

Nearly a month they had been together every moment of every day. He chose monasteries for their sleeping arrangements as often as he could, trying to prevent what he felt tonight.

Through the day, he watched her ride that spirited black gelding, watched her laugh at some antic of Remus or Ysengrin or Esmerelda, watched her lean forward eagerly to listen to some traveler's tale, her eyes bright, her mind eager for the filling, and he was enchanted, betwitched.

Besotted.

Never in his life had his attention been snagged so thoroughly by any woman. Never had he been so acutely aware of her every movement and gesture, so alert to the subtle nuance of tone and pitch in her voice or laughter. Never had he spent endless days with his cock at near full-alert for so long a time.

Nor had he ever foregone the pleasure of bedding a willing wench in favor of one who would not give him what he wanted—needed. Three times on this journey, he'd had opportunity, and three times turned them away. One last night, a tavern wench nearby the monastery, had been more than eager. She followed him from the tavern and grabbed him from behind, and when he simply disentangled himself, ran in front of him to yank at her bodice. Like Tillie at Winterbourne, she'd likely made it her business to know how best to please a man, taking the only option open to her to rise above her station.

Once, he would have taken her without a second thought, relieved his bodily needs and forgotten her the next day. Last night, he'd only turned wearily away, mounted Remus, and flung a coin at her. "Find another," he said, gruffly. And went back to the monastery to sleep among men.

In his arms, Anya shifted. Her breast now lay only a fingernail's length from his draped hand—and he knew well how glorious it would feel in his palm, how much that flesh would welcome his touch. He need only shift the smallest bit to brush that tip into arousal.

But he had promised. Rigidly, he lay there, willing his manhood to ease its grip on him. He moved his hands from temptation, lower on her arms, and forced himself to close his eyes.

The room was silent. The pilgrims all slept like the dead. Christian breathed to ease his arousal, and was well pleased at his self-control.

Into the silence crept his doubts once more. 'Twould not be long now till they rode into Carpentras and Christian would confront his father—and he still had no plan, had not found any way to make the task palatable. As they neared the city, he worried that Anya might be somehow put at terrible risk.

Pilgrims on the roads had told them of the harshness of the Church in southern France. Christian knew a biting worry each time he thought on it—worry that Anya's war with the Church would be enough to cause her to come under suspicion. Though Father Gerent had made plain that William and Etienne were in consort, it hadn't been plain just how. Perhaps this was the tool Etienne would use.

He frowned in the darkness, and rested his cheek on her hair. The slim weight of her against him was more precious than anything he'd known. He would die to protect her. And perhaps that was the cardinal's wish. Etienne would not care for the fate of an unknown woman, and would use any tool at his hand to rid himself of Christian.

The worries chased themselves in his mind. Etienne, William, Anya, the city and the possibility of lurking assassins in alleyways. He clenched his eyes closed. He still could not wield a sword as well as he liked. Though his strength was much improved, his shoulder would never be as strong as it once had been, and his arm tired easily. He'd not be able to lift a sword in true danger for more than a little while. If he were swift and his aim true, that would be no worry, but even a simple band of brigands could unhand him quickly.

It was too dangerous to take her into Carpentras. He would disguise her as a peasant and send her with a group of pilgrims to the tomb. And warn her how to survive if his business in Carpentras left him dead.

Thus settled, he slept with Anya cradled close against him.

20

Christian did not tell Anya of his plan to dress her as a peasant and send her on when they reached Carpentras. He knew if he gave her much time to think on it, that sharp thrust of her jaw would appear and she'd find some way to thwart him.

As they rode now toward Donzère, a little village near his boyhood home, his mind was not on the familiarity of what was around him, but upon Anya, sitting astride her horse, her hair flying out behind her. This morning she had seemed a little peaked, and disappeared into the woods for a time. Now, however, her cheeks were flushed with the bright sunshine and she'd shed her cloak.

Since he'd held her through the night, he'd found them monasteries and safe quarters again, where they could not lie together. He could not bear another night such as that one. His temper had not been the most even since then.

Oblivious to his discomfort, Anya admired the flower-dusted fields and the rich beauty of the Rhône. The sway of her spine, the length of her thigh outlined below her skirt, the curve of her cheek—all made him long to grab her violently from the horse and take her wildly amid those tender flowers.

He knew he could coax a response. For all her pretense of aloofness, he caught her sometimes looking at him with a darkly hungry expression.

Ah, by the saints—he could no longer bear it. He opened his mouth to call to her and suggest a small break to eat before they traveled on. But just then, a church spire came into view, indicating a town.

He cursed violently. Esmerelda, asleep in her basket, opened one yellow eye as if in censure.

"My lord knight, will you tarry a little here? Perhaps there's a tavern where we might have a draught of ale. I'm very thirsty."

He only nodded, sure he'd growl if he so much as spoke a word.

They rode around the bend in the road and there lay the village—only a smattering of dwellings and a few shops. In the distance, blurred by the morning haze, was a manor built of stone.

It was the church that seized Christian's attention. "Halt, Lady Anya!"

She turned, curiosity written on her face.

In the churchyard, an elderly priest bent over the stones, tugging out weeds. As the pair reined their horses, the old man straightened expectantly.

Christian looked from priest to church. It was a simple place, built of light stone and carefully whitewashed. His heart pounded fiercely.

It was the church in his dream, or one very like it.

He looked at the oaks growing alongside the road, bending to shade the walls, and narrowed his eyes. Yes, the trees in his dream were smaller, as might be expected.

"What is it?" Anya asked.

He lifted a hand, unwilling to explain if he were wrong. "Wait here."

Dismounting, he swiveled his glance again toward the manor shrouded in haze. It jarred his memory not at all. Perhaps this church was only like the one in his dream, then.

Inside. He would know inside.

The priest, seeming to sense his intent, made his way to the side door, and as Christian entered through the main doors, the priest stood before the altar.

He was old, with a slump in his frail shoulders, and only thin gray wisps of hair sticking out over his ears. As Christian paused to let his eyes adjust to the darkness inside, the priest simply waited, folding his hands before him.

And now, laid over the scene, Christian saw his dream. His mother, veiled and beautiful with jewels sparkling at her waist and around her wrists, her great fall of hair tumbling down her back. Candles winked and incense filled the air. Nearby, in the shadows—

No, no shadows.

Christian strode forward, his spurs clanging against the stone floor, the sound sharp in the expectant silence. In his gut, anticipation swooped like rooks.

Nearby where the priest stood, Christian paused, narrowing his eyes as if to see. He took another step, and when the scene still did not quite match the angle in his dream, abruptly knelt where he stood.

All swung into place. The shadows of the dream that had so long haunted him cleared away and he saw what had been hidden.

His father, kneeling in sacrament next to his mother. The priest over them, reciting words Christian's boyhood mind could not comprehend, but he'd heard often enough since.

They had *married*.

Stunned, Christian stared at the priest, who said at last, "You are the very image of him."

Christian nodded. "Why did you do it?"

"He was my bishop—and I was a young priest, with no prospects if he chose them to be gone."

"And all these years, you've said naught?"

The priest bowed his head.

Christian leapt to his feet. "He wants to become pope!" he shouted into the dim silence. "Will you stand by and let a married man lead all the world?"

"He is married no longer, but a widower," the priest returned sadly, spreading his hands.

"It matters not—he broke his vows abominably," Christian said. Behind him, he heard the door swing open and someone come in. Anya, no doubt. "He tried to kill Clement when I was fourteen. He's tried to kill me twice."

The priest slowly nodded. "All sins may be forgiven by our Lord. 'Tis not for me to make judgments on the ways of God. He has not seen fit to tumble him yet— perhaps 'tis His will your father is our next pope."

"All can be forgiven but a married priest!" Christian shouted. "Not even the pope himself can erase such a parody of vows."

The priest only continued to stare at him sadly, shaking his head. "God does what God will, my son."

Furious, Christian drew his sword and felt himself well pleased when the priest showed the first glimmers of alarm. "And God uses the hands of man for his tasks," he said in a low voice. "You will come with me."

"To what purpose? Who will believe the word of a humble village priest?"

From the back of the church came a strong, youthful voice. "I will."

"Jean-Luc, return to your tasks at once. I gave no leave for you to come to me."

Not Anya, Christian realized, but someone else. Careless of him to not have glanced back at least to see. Still holding his sword, he shifted to see who walked toward them on padding feet.

A youth, no more than seventeen, strapping tall and rawboned, approached. With a fleeting sense of shock, Christian recognized one of the brigands who had attacked him on the Scots border. "You!"

The youth, dark and plain, knelt at Christian's feet. "My lord, I am your eternal servant and will do as you bid forevermore."

The priest made a noise of resignation. "The boy thinks you're Christ, man. He dreamed the church when he was fleeing England and came to me asking for a place."

"You dreamed it?" Christian asked. "What did you dream?"

"That a lady with golden hair would ride here on a black horse, bearing a child. And that you would be with her."

The boy still knelt at his feet and Christian said irritably, "Get up. I'm no more Christ than you. And my Lady Anya sits beyond on her black horse, so how can I know if you lie or not?"

The boy got to his feet, but kept his eyes lowered. "I have no proof, my lord, but that I am here when I was not before." He lifted his head now, proudly. "I asked God to let me serve you and he led me here."

Christian sighed. From the rear of the church, he heard a smothered giggle and realized Anya had come in with the youth. He sent her a look he hoped would quell her, but it only seemed to give her more trouble.

"Lady Anya," he commanded. "Come forward."

Her nostrils quivering with repressed laughter, she did as he asked. To his surprise, she paused by the boy and whispered dramatically, "I thought him an angel, so you are not alone."

Confused, still shocked by the revelations here and the absurd aspect of a bandit praying to serve him and being led here, by God, to do it, Christian scowled at both of them for a moment. Then the brigand's words struck home. "Bearing a child?"

"Aye," the bandit said. "I set you free in the Great Darkness and 'twas that that led to the child."

"Great Darkness?"

Anya answered. "Two days before I found you in the forest, there was a terrible storm. It seemed for a little as if the sun had been blown out by the wind. All the animals went mad, yipping and lowing and yanking at their tethers." She shrugged. "Then the darkness cleared again and didn't come back."

He'd heard of such things. He also recognized a hurried dodge. Her voice was too rushed, too breathless. He thought on her fleeting illness of a morn, her avoidance of mutton, her sleepiness, her inability the night they slept with the peasants to keep down her food. "Are you bearing a child, my lady?" he asked with dangerous softness.

She lifted her chin. "Will you believe the fantastic dream of some child?"

"It seems so far 'twas a dream of some weight," he said drily. "Will you tell the truth to me, my lady?"

She swallowed. "Aye, my lord, a babe grows in me."

For a moment, he only stared at her, his sword loose at his side. Stared at her slanted blue eyes and round breasts and tangle of golden curls. Very slowly, he smiled. "Well it might have been better timed, but happy I am you'll bear me a babe, Anya of Winterbourne."

Tears, so rare in her, filled the blue eyes.

Christian stared at her a moment longer, seeing now what should have been plain—her breasts growing fuller, her skin taking the clear radiance of motherhood.

At once, a tangle of fierce protectiveness came on him. "This one you shall bear in peace and honor, my lady." He stepped close to take her hand. "And suckle all the day and night if you choose."

The rare tears spilled silver on her radiant cheeks. "Mayhap you are an angel, Christian. There are two of us now who think it."

Christian glanced at the youth, standing alongside Anya with a wide-eyed expression, then back to Anya. He gave her a wicked smile and touched her belly boldly, caring not for the eyes of the other two. "Remember I have disproved your notion before."

Her smile was tremulous, joyful, and Christian was suddenly reminded of what lay yet ahead of them. He would not let his child be born as bastard, nor let Anya carry the weight of it again.

"Father," he said, "I will free you if you will now marry me to the Lady Anya, with this youth here as witness."

"Nay!" Anya cried, catching his arm. "'Twill bring more disaster, my lord."

He couldn't believe it. "What disaster?"

That chin swung upward. "I have made a promise to fulfill my penance before we marry, my lord."

"To men who long only to bring you to a bad end!"

"Nay." She shook her head soberly. "'Twas the saints I promised."

He grabbed her arms. "Anya, there is no promise I will yet have mortal form by the time you finish your penance! Miracles there have been this day, but I think it rare a dead man makes a good husband."

"If we marry, you or I—or both—will die."

"If we do not marry now, you will again bear a bastard!"

The priest spoke. "Have faith, my son."

"Faith!" Christian spun around. "Faith that God chooses best and well? That God who let my father try to kill Clement and then his own son?"

The priest gave him a beatific smile. "Nay," he said quietly. "The God who brought you to a woman who adores you, the God who saved you twice from death, who sent you a devoted servant by giving him a dream. Look at them, Christian. A fallen woman and a thief—willing to follow you to death."

Christian stared at the priest. "She is not fallen," he said fiercely.

The priest did not reply, but only seemed to wait.

Christian turned and pointed his sword at the raw-boned youth. "You."

He stepped forward. "My lord?"

"You will come with us, and protect my lady at risk of all. Can you wield a sword?"

"Aye," he said and bowed his head. "'Twas I that felled you at the borderlands."

Christian sighed. "Very well. You'll come with us."

He glanced toward the priest. "You are free. I'll not compound my father's sin by kidnapping an old man against his will."

"Bless you."

"Let's be on this journey, then," Christian said, gesturing toward the doors. "I'd be done with it."

He felt Anya's gaze on him, but did not look at her. A child—*his* child—his love, his life. And she would not wed him. Would not sleep with him.

Irritably, he strode outside. The thought of the babe made him wish to touch her all the more, to see what changes it wrought in her slim, beautiful form. To see—

He'd go mad with want afore 'twas all done. Death would be relief, at least.

With a glower at the wooden statue of Mary nearby the door, he muttered, "Couldn't you help a man once in awhile?"

The roads grew more congested as they neared the busier, warmer cities to the south. Darkness fell before they reached Carpentras, and Christian called a halt outside a weatherbeaten inn already crowded.

Anya didn't care where it was. She wanted only sleep and peace. The ride had been hard and long beyond all the rest that had transpired. She felt weepy and emotional and exhausted. Not to mention starved.

To her enormous relief, there was no mutton for supper, only a thin soup and bread with no butter and poor ale. Nonetheless sated, Anya claimed a place on the floor. At least the rushes were clean.

"Wait, my lady," Christian said, and spread his horse blanket over the rushes. "'Twill help a little."

Nodding wearily, Anya settled again. To her surprise, he settled next to her in the shadowy light. "Come here," he said. "I am exhausted and would have you at my side so I may sleep without worry. You lie against the wall. I'll lie outside."

It was merely a practical arrangement, Anya knew, but it surprised her anyway. He'd spoken barely three words after they left the church, and never met her gaze. He'd also seemed to go to some pains that they were never forced to lie together.

Which was as well. When she was close to him, she forgot her vow, forgot she must please the saints—forgot all. And now it was no different. He smelled of horse and ale and leather, and there was in his hair a hint of sunny wind. "Christian," she said softly, "do not be angry with me."

"I am not angry. 'Tis a foolish emotion." But he spoke with his eyes closed.

Anya sighed. There was no arguing with that wounded male pride and no way to make him see reason till he overcame it. "Very well."

She covered herself with her cloak and curled up. Beside her, Christian shifted. "Why did you not tell me, Anya?"

"I wished to save you from more worry." They both spoke in low tones, for around them the room was settling and sighing as the occupants fell to sleep.

"You'll go with Jean-Luc to Saint Maximin on the morrow. Alone I will face my father."

Anya lifted her brows. "No, I think not."

"You have no say." He'd lifted himself to one elbow, but now fell back on the blanket and closed his eyes. And damn him, but he was so beautiful she could scarce breathe for it. Travel-worn and unshaven, his cheekbones sunburned from the long days, he moved her to a level of lust she'd not known existed.

And yet, his words annoyed her. "So I am, after all, mere woman with no thought in my mind."

He frowned, but the comment pried his eyes open at least. "You're foolhardy when it comes to your own safety. 'Tis the babe I protect."

"Think you I'd risk the safety of my own child?"

"You think little at times, my lady."

Stung, she slapped his arm. "That is a lie! 'Tis your lion's pride that is wounded tonight because I would not marry you this afternoon." With a little noise, she flung herself back.

Stiffly they lay side by side. Anya closed her eyes, trying to shut out the feel of his long male warmth next to her. With a grunt, he shifted. All alike, she thought, all of them. Did God make not one man who could see a woman as she was?

Soon the room was silent with only breath and the rustling of clothing, but Anya found sleep had fled. She stared into the dark, wondering what lay ahead on the morrow in Carpentras. Would Christian vanquish his father? Or would he falter at the end and die himself?

Christian shifted again, and she felt the irritability in it. Good, she thought with a tinge of meanness—he didn't sleep either.

From some corner of the room came a soft, barely audible sigh. A woman's sigh, rich with anticipation, then right after it, a little louder, more emphatic cry.

Anya stiffened, for she knew the sound. Oh, yes, she'd heard it on her own lips at Christian's coaxing. An awareness of her limbs, curled only inches from his gold-dusted body, filled her.

A shivery cry, soft but distinct, wound into the

sleeping air. Christian shifted mightily, flopping from one side to the other, and she felt his knee barely touch her thigh. She closed her eyes at the bright shock of such a small contact.

Now the woman's lover made a deep, low, groaning sound and it lasted a long, long time. Anya fought the picture the sound conjured in her mind, but it blazed over her imagination: Christian bathed in flickering yellow torchlight, his weight braced on his hard muscled arms, sliding home. . . .

Only a fool could mistake the sounds that came next, the earthy grunts and urgent rustling—oh, they tried to be silent, but the pleasure was too great, and small gasps of approval rent the air.

At the same moment Anya clapped her hands over her ears, Christian shifted again. And now it didn't matter that she couldn't hear the lovers, for she could feel her own, hard against the length of her back. His hand lit on her hip and only rested there, but it was a broad, warm palm and burned her.

His mouth fell against the curve of her neck. She squeezed her eyes closed and kept her hands clamped over her ears, willing herself not to feel the seeping, swirling need that rose in her, curling from her stomach into her breasts, like a flower climbing a wall.

Christian shifted closer, and his mouth moved relentlessly, touching each tiny rise of bone in her neck in turn, edging along her hairline and down again to her shoulder, suckling and teasing, nipping as if he would eat her.

His hand moved from her hip and she thought he was going to leave her alone, that he was taking the hint from her refusal to respond and would turn away. His mouth left her neck, and the places he had kissed grew cold.

He plucked her hands from her ears and leaned closer to trace that edge with his tongue. And suddenly, his hand cupped her breast. "Do nothing," he said against her ear, nearly inaudible even an inch away, and she thought fleetingly he knew more about silence than those others had. "Do nothing," he repeated, "then the saints cannot punish you."

Her breath caught, and she nearly spoke, but he touched her lips.

He drew her cloak over their heads, covering them completely. Anya still lay on her side, her back pressed into his chest, and he seemed content at that. Reaching for the laces of her tunic, he untied them, kissing the skin he exposed, making Anya shudder. His hair brushed her skin as the gown loosened. He skimmed it from her arms, brushed his fingers over the curve of her breasts, kissed her slowly—a shoulder blade, her spine, her neck, her arm.

All so deliberate, careful, slow, so there would be no sudden noise, no hint of sound for those beyond. His lips suckled, but made no sound when they moved.

Aye, she wanted him! Wanted to kiss and touch him, the way he was, and in urgent hunger, she started to turn.

He stopped her, his hands holding her where she was. "Remember the saints," he breathed into her ear.

He touched her naked breasts, slowly rubbing and plucking and stirring the painful heat down low. Against her hip, she felt his fierce arousal.

What a luxury a sigh now seemed! She trembled almost uncontrollably, shaking like a quivering leaf on an autumn wind. He skimmed her skirts up her thighs, so her gown was bunched all in a lump around her waist. She caught the blanket and buried her face in it as his long, skilled fingers stroked the quivering flesh of her thighs, touching that oddly crawling feeling there.

He moved and suddenly his flesh was against her, nudging her hip until he shifted her with his hands. Still not a sound from him, not even his breath. Anya could not have helped him if she'd tried; the effort of holding back the hungry cries took what strength her desire left, and she could not halt the quivering limbs.

He shifted her hips and nudged gently at the center of her in warning. Slow, slow, slow he filled her, only a tiny bit at a time so there would be no sudden thrust that would cause a cry.

And oh, it was what she wanted. Fisting her hands, she bit the blanket fiercely to contain her sounds. As he began to rock them, together, his mouth landed on her neck and she felt then his effort to hold his own sound as he suckled harder and harder, matching his thrusts. One hand slipped between her legs and sent her spiraling from this place and into him, out of the world and into the place where only she and Christian could go, alone together. His mouth was almost painful on her shoulder as he tumbled into release, and his body, too, seemed to tremble.

At last, they swooped and circled and returned to earth, but not to the crowded inn. Anya didn't move away as he pulled her gown over her shoulders and laced again the ties. His hand fell again over her breast, gently stroking, then slid to her belly and stayed there, soft and protective over his babe.

Nestled and sated, they slept.

21

Etienne d'Auch stood by the wide embrasure of his apartments in Carpentras. His hands were linked behind his back. Below, washed in bright warm sunlight, lay the bustling streets of the city. And about to walk those very streets, according to the man now giving Etienne his report, was Christian.

"Is the girl with him?"

"Aye, and a servant of some sort, by the look of him."

Etienne nodded. "Watch them. Soon or late, my son will attend some business. When he is gone, bring me the girl."

The brigand bowed his head. "Aye, milord."

Etienne turned. "If you do not carry this out correctly this time, I will kill you myself."

The man's head bobbed eagerly, like a chicken gobbling. "No, no. I will not fail."

Etienne waved a hand and stared back at the streets.

Ah, Christian. His son. He smiled in anticipation. Of all his enemies, his own blood had proved to be the most worthy opponent, and that pleased him. Not enough to let him win, of course, but enough.

Restlessly, he rubbed his temples. In his age, he was loosing his edge—it was well there was only one more great battle to wage. Had Clement lived another two or three years, Etienne would not have had the mettle left in him to win the crown he'd been fighting toward since early youth.

As he sat so close to that pinnacle, he knew a vaguely depressing sense of futility. What, after all, would it bring him? Would it be worth the price he had paid?

Overlaying the scene of bustling pilgrims and peasants and merchants that filled the street below, Etienne saw an ethereal vision of Rowena.

Rowena.

Even after twenty years, the sorrow of her death had not left him. And there were those who said the loss of his mistress had changed him. Oh, ever had he been an ambitious and driven man. Ever had he dreamed of the papal crown and worked toward it with the single-mindedness of one who had no other dream. His career had been brilliant before he'd stumbled over the shining Rowena in an English nunnery, there hidden to be protected. And she had bewitched him.

For ten years, his life had been magical. The worries of the Church did not concern him overmuch, and he was able to advance quickly thanks to the balance she gave him. She'd borne him a son, fed him, pleased him.

He had loved her more than all of God's world, all the heavens. And she had died.

More often than he wished, he wondered if his

refusal to leave the priesthood had hastened her passing. In a moment of weakness, he'd allowed her to talk him into marrying her in the obscure little village church, and had even, perhaps, believed he would give up his career for her. Perhaps he might have done it.

But he had not. And Rowena died, taking with her all the light in his world, leaving behind her son to stare at him with Rowena's accusatory eyes for the rest of his life.

He lifted his eyes to the heavens, wishing he'd at least had the courage to end his life when he'd found her dead. All he had left was the papacy to make it all make sense.

To take that crown, he had only to close forever Rowena's eyes in the face of her son. At last.

Christian could not convince Anya to let him go into Carpentras alone. She fought him with all the wiles in a woman's arsenal—tears and pleading and the babe in her belly. Finally she simply stood her ground and quietly said, "If I let you go without me, I fear I will never see you again."

He had capitulated. Now they rode toward the place amid a thick crowd of travelers. It was hot. Below his hauberk, Christian felt rivulets of sweat soaking his shirt. His hair stuck to his neck.

But he'd known this heat all his early life and reveled in the depth of it. It was hard on Anya with her thick English blood. She rode beside him without complaint, her head covered with linen to block the sun, but below the veil he saw the beads of sweat on her lip and the stern way she kept her jaw tilted. When they had begun their journey, spring had only begun in England, and that after a long cold winter. With the various delays and bad weather of their journey, it had taken nearly six weeks to come to Carpentras in the south of France, but not even that was enough to prepare her for the heat of a southern locale. In the city, where the stones held heat long past dark, it would be worse.

Christian knew he would have to finish his business here quickly if she were to remain in good health. He rode close to her. "Once we find a place to sleep, I will find a woman to attend you today, my lady. You need one of your own sex at this time."

She didn't protest, as he expected, but only nodded. "'Twould be a comfort. I am weary already of the—" she stopped.

He raised his brows. "What?"

She heaved a sigh. "Men never know what it is to feel so much. Honestly, I ache for Geoffrey, for news of him. I ache for my own home and the way it smells and the familiar sights I've always known. I dislike your France. 'Tis too hot and it smells odd and I know not a single face in any crowd."

He took her hand. "My lady, you are weary. All will be well."

She stared at him with lake-blue eyes. "Will it, Christian? I am beset with dread now we are nearly here."

"Anya, I ask again for you to hide yourself as a peasant and go on to Saint Baume to the shrine, and I will meet you there when my business is finished."

"Can you not leave him to his fate and come with me? If he gains the papacy, what difference will it make to us?"

Christian narrowed his eyes. "The task has been

given me, Anya. Alone I know the secrets of his life. He is a murderer and adulterer and should not lead the world. How can you ask it?"

"Because I care not for the politics of Church and king, only the peace of my home, with you in it!"

"Is honor, then, only valid when a woman chooses the stakes? In your honor, you promised to make your pilgrimage to the tomb before we were wed, and even with a babe growing bigger each day in that belly, you will not wed me! And yet you say 'tis better for me to ignore the hidden evil of my father?"

She lowered her head. "Forgive me," she whispered, and touched his hand. "Well I know your honor, Christian. And well I know you will not rest till it is done."

He clasped her hand, slim and graceful against his own. "Soon it will be."

She raised her gaze and he saw the doubt there. "Make it quickly."

"Aye," he said grimly. "That I will."

At the gates, he saw the crowd slowed to a milling knot. The sun was high and it would mean a long wait here to get through—and he wondered with a quick stab of foreboding what caused the delay. "Jean-Luc," he said, "ride up ahead and see if you can see what causes the delay."

"I can tell you, my lord. 'Tis a fair." He pointed to the peasants and merchants dragging their wagons of goods behind them. "Shall we wait till dark? I may be known here."

Christian shook his head. There was more danger in bandits than in guards. "None will know you as a young novice." Jean-Luc had bought this morning, with Christian's coin, the robes of a traveling friar. "As soon as we find rooms, you will stay with my lady while I seek audience with Cardinal Duise. Perhaps this may all be ended before it begins."

"My lord, you should not go alone."

"Nor will I leave Lady Anya alone. Better she should be well guarded. You have some knowledge of d'Auch's men and can be alert for them."

Anya spoke. "I would that he go with you, my lord. I am so weary I will only sleep. Can we not hire a woman to stay?"

Christian glanced at her, frowning. Her pallor had deepened, and he took a wineskin from his horse. "Drink much in this heat," he said, "but only weak ale and watered wine, else you'll be sick." He frowned, disliking the way her hand trembled as she lifted the skin to her lips. "Anya—would you like to rest before we go on?"

"Nay. 'Tis not weariness, but dread that weakens me." She wiped her lips and gave him back the skin. "I am afraid I have learned I am a coward."

Relieved, he grinned. "'Tis wise in a good knight to have a good measure of fear. Fear makes you alert."

He winked at her and gestured—they were nearly to the gates.

A trio of men on horseback, armed and in the uniform of guards, peeled away from the crowd. Christian glanced toward them, but turned to urge Anya along.

He didn't see the guards until they rode up in a cloud of dust, sending Anya's horse skittering as they galloped to a stop beside her.

"Anya of Winterbourne, you are under arrest for suspicion of heresy, at the order of the Holy Roman Church."

"No!" Christian shouted and rode toward them, drawing his sword. From the south, Jean-Luc galloped toward them, but was too late. As Christian rode toward the guards, his sword drawn, Anya tipped forward in a slump. Only by flinging down the sword and making a wild grab for her gown did Christian save her from falling in a dead faint to more disaster below the restless hooves of her nervous horse. He dared not let go of her. With a wild gesture toward Jean-Luc, he halted the youth's sword, close to splitting the head of one of the guards.

"She is no heretic," Christian said, "but a pilgrim going to the shrine of Saint Mary Magdalene to the south. 'Tis her penance and she is performing it."

The guard was unmoved. "She'll have a chance to tell her story before the cardinal. He will decide if the charges are true."

A fist struck his gut. "The cardinal?"

"D'Auch, who received a letter from a canon at Lichfield. The complaint comes from him."

Under his hand, Anya stirred. "Keep your head down," he said harshly, "else you'll fall off the damned horse." To the guard he said, "Let me come with you. She is not well and will need an attendant. Let me see her settled and—"

"Nay. The cardinal will see her at his apartments. If you so choose, you may come there this afternoon, when he sees petitioners."

A roaring screamed in his ears, and he was aware of the gathered peasants and the cadre of other guards no more than a few yards away. His mind raced with choices—he could grab her and fling her over his lap, then race toward the woods. Remus was strong and would outride the clumsy destriers of the knights, but not their arrows—if he were killed, she would have no hope at all.

He lifted his chin and narrowed his eyes. "Tell my father," he said in a low, dangerous voice, "that if he wishes to be pope, he will not harm one hair on this woman's head. And if he laughs, tell him I have been to the church in Donzère—and will tell all the world what I there learned."

The guard lifted a brow. "He's not an easily cowed man."

Christian stared. "Tell him. Jean-Luc!"

The youth rode forward. "My lord?"

"Go with them and see that she is well handled, and stay where they are. I will be there at Nones."

Anya lifted her head. "Christian," she whispered, and there was such agony in her voice, he could not bear it.

Harshly, he said, "There is no choice, Anya. Go with them and do not be afraid."

"He'll kill you."

He pulled up his reins. "No. He is the dead man, not I. That I promise you."

And before he could do something that would surely kill them both, he raced into the city to seek the help of John Duise.

Etienne sat at his desk, writing, when they brought the woman. In surprise, he put down his quill, for she was not as young as he'd imagined she would be—and far more beautiful, even through the pale mask of travel and fear that marked her dark blue eyes.

"I will not harm you," he said. With a nod, he dismissed the guards. One paused at the door. "What is it?"

"I have a message from the knight."

Etienne folded his hands, smiling faintly. "Let me see if I might guess. A threat, no doubt. He'll kill me if I harm her?"

The guard inclined his head. "He said he'd been to the church at Donzère and would tell the world what he learned there if the woman is harmed."

Etienne fought to hold his smile, but it faded. So at last, Christian had remembered the ceremony. It was what he had feared. He nodded heavily. "'Tis for just that reason I have taken his woman to be my guest." He waved a hand. "Bring him to me when he comes."

The woman swayed uncertainly, and Etienne remembered suddenly how the heat had bothered Rowena at first. "Sit, child. I'm too old to pick you up from the floor if you faint."

She ignored him, lifting her chin. "He'll kill you."

"No," Etienne said comfortably, pouring wine from a tankard on the table of his richly appointed chambers. He gave it to her and she was not foolish enough to refuse it. "He may believe he will, but he hasn't the heart to kill his own father. If you've spent any time with him at all, you know that well enough. 'Twas always his greatest flaw—a tender heart. Not a pretty thing in a man, but I let him spend too much time with his mother."

"You remember the boy," she said. With the help of the wine, she lifted her chin. "I know the man has killed often enough to have no qualms over killing you."

Etienne smiled. "We shall see." He admired her frankly. Hair the color of late afternoon sunshine, eyes the shade of the twilight sky, whole teeth and skin unflawed by pockmarks or poor food. Below her tunic was a body rather more slim than he liked—he'd heard of the poor harvests in England—but the breasts and hips were round enough. Women had never been his particular vice, save Rowena.

He moved closer and saw the sharp narrowing of her eyes. "Do you think he'd kill me the more if I took his woman?"

"You'd have to kill me," she said, and in the words was calm certainty.

He chuckled. "Ah. Well then, 'tis too much trouble."

A novice brought in a tray of food—strawberries newly plucked and shining with moisture, a loaf of bread sending its still-warm aroma into the air, a round of soft white cheese from Brie. Etienne nodded when it had been settled on the table he had placed nearby the wide windows of this high room. He settled and gestured for the woman to join him.

She did not move immediately, and with amusement he saw the war she fought with herself. To join him would be to admit defeat, but her eyes lingered on the food with an expression akin to passion.

"What will it cost you to eat my food?" he asked genially. "Sit. I will tell you of my plan."

She lost the war to her belly and crossed the room. At the table, she halted abruptly and gripped the edge of the table. "'Tis so high!" she said.

"The view is beautiful, is it not?" he agreed, gazing toward the green and yellow farmland in patches beyond the walls of the city. Between was another sort of patchwork, red tile and yellow thatch and brown timbers. Birds swooped through the white light of noon.

But she did not seem to gain pleasure from it. Gingerly she sank to a chair opposite him, sitting lightly on the embroidered pillow. Her knuckles were white from holding to the table. He watched closely as she jerked her gaze from the open vista and to the food.

As if she did not quite trust her balance, she let one hand go from the table, waited, and let the other go. Even then, her gestures were measured as she reached for the bread and cheese. "So," she said in a moment, "tell me your plan."

"Your brother," he said calmly, "most heartily wishes you dead."

She said nothing, but only looked at him

"What will you do to thwart him?"

She bit into a slice of bread thickly spread with soft cheese and stared at him as she chewed. When she swallowed, she said distinctly, "Live."

He laughed, and it startled her. The hatred and guardedness of her expression fled, to be replaced with a sort of wonder. He knew its source. "The resemblance is said to be uncanny." Lazily, he spread cheese on his own bread. "Must still be so. I have not seen my son since he was fourteen."

"You'll not be able to kill him," she said quietly. "When you look at him, you'll not be able to raise your hand."

Again he laughed. "I need not lift my own hand, Lady Anya."

She put down her food. "Why can you not leave him in peace? Let him live his life with me far from here?"

"Come now, my lady, surely you see how foolish a dream that is. He will not rest until I am dead."

"What do you mean to do with me?"

"Nothing at all, my lady. You will be locked in a comfortable room until that time I may rid myself of my son. Then you will be free to finish your quest and return to your home. I have no quarrel with you."

She folded her arms over herself in an oddly protective gesture, and with a start, Etienne saw the small swelling of her lower belly. "By the saints," he breathed, "you are with child!"

Anya stared at him. "And already once I bore a bastard, so I ask for my husband so I needn't do it again."

"'Tis touching, the way you plead for him. But I'm afraid the game is set. My son must die."

She rose from the bench with regal grace. "You are a monster, lord cardinal. I'll pray for your destruction."

In her eyes he saw the same accusation he'd always seen in the eyes of Rowena looking out from Christian's face. It enraged him. "Do not make judgments upon me, my lady!" he shouted, rising and rounding the table.

Instinctively, she backed away from him, but he pushed forward. "I was born to peasants as dull-witted as the cow that slept with us and meaner than the bull that chased us all through the fields. By my wits I raised myself from that hovel, in the only way open to me!"

Her hips bumped the lower sill of the embrasure and she made a soft cry as she glanced over her shoulder. Wildly, she flung out her arms, grabbing the air, and he saw her desperate loss of balance. She swayed and finally grabbed the edge of the stones, closing her eyes. He did not help her.

"You were manor-born and cannot know the struggle of my life. From that stinking hovel I rose—and I will not let any man or woman stand in my way."

"May God forgive you," she whispered, and carefully turned to face him. "All the things that are precious you have forgone."

Whirling to avoid slapping the bitch, Etienne called for the guard. "Take her to her chamber. I am done with her."

22

The chamber to which Anya was led was small but more than comfortable. In place of rushes, there was a carpet made of red and blue fibers. In wonder, Anya took off her shoes to feel it against the soles of her feet, walking back and forth on it happily. She'd heard of such things, of course, but had never seen one.

Here, too, there were embrasures, but they were small and not so daunting as the wide, wide openings in the main room. Remembering, Anya felt ill. She'd thought she might escape, but even in her most desperate hour she knew she could not attempt to climb down from a place so high.

Weary and nauseous, she lay down on the clean bed. A fat black fly buzzed around the room, bumping into the walls, lighting on the sill. She watched it, and found her thoughts buzzing around in her mind the same way, bumping and lighting and worrying about once again.

Christian . . . his father . . . Winterbourne—'twas June and the fields had been planted . . . Geoffrey—oh, Geoffrey! Playing music for the king . . . Mary . . .

She missed all of them. Missed her son with a dull, thudding ache. She wanted to hear him laugh, and hug his small, slim body, and ruffle his fine hair. She'd known always that he'd be fostered away from her, and at Winterbourne, she might have been able to bear the separation, for there were letters and the chance he would come to see her for a holiday. Now she was so very, very far from home. What if he fell ill or needed her and she was not there?

She wished she had told him that she was his mother. From such a distance, 'twas easy to see she'd made too much of the circumstances of his birth, thinking they would shame him. Now she knew he would be glad to know that his beloved Lady Anya was his own mother, born of her loins.

Christian.

The most vivid terror of her life had struck through her heart when she saw him lift his sword at the guards. With a sharp, pure certainty, she had seen his death in that instant, had seen the guards would gladly kill him and still take her, and she'd done the only thing she could—pretended to faint.

A coppery taste filled her mouth as she thought of it. Her hands trembled. The vision of him, run through with a sword, bleeding and no more to be hers—

Oh, sweet Mary!

Curling into a ball, she covered her face with her hands. Father and son—by the saints, but they were alike! Not only the arrangement of features, the fine cut of the mouths and the high, handsome cheekbones and the proud, tall strength of their forms, but a fierceness of spirit, an arrogant certainty that each had the truth of things. There would be no moving either.

One or the other of them would die. She had not known that until today, had still believed there was some answer, some compromise that could be made. Now she understood the truth: The battle was mortal and in motion and she had no hand in it at all.

Only their eyes were different. In Christian's cloud-colored eyes were the sky and rain and great gentleness. In his eyes were humor and mischief. And they must have been his mother's legacy, for Etienne's eyes were dark, almost black, as startling against his fairness as Christian's pale ones.

And there was no humor in d'Auch's eyes. There was ambition and determination and greed. She saw no gentleness or mercy or warmth, even when he laughed.

He said he would not harm her, but she didn't believe him. If it suited his purposes, he would sacrifice her—and her child—as easily as he'd slap a bothersome mosquito.

Dizzy and exhausted, she found her thoughts buzzing and bumping each other. Mary . . . Geoffrey . . . Christian . . . They chased her into sleep, but there at last, she found some peace.

Christian could not get an audience with Duise. The cardinal was beset with troubles, it seemed, and could not meet with an obscure man who could not state his business clearly. Reluctant to give his name, Christian said only that he would return on the morrow. The canon with whom he spoke said only there was a better chance then.

So it was at Nones that Christian rode to the apartments of his father. The streets of Carpentras—familiar to him from childhood—held no comfort. He avoided the noise of the fair by riding down alleyways in humbler sections of the city, where children with runny noses ran barefoot past dull-eyed women washing in the square.

In a tavern earlier, he'd heard that there was some quarrel with the pope's estate, that his family was unhappy with the disbursements. It had been plain that Cardinal Duise was attempting to head off some trouble.

Christian scowled. There was some answer to this, but he could not yet see it. In his gut was his subdued anger, boiling now and again in small explosions, but he tamped it down again with care. Anger made fools of the best men. To greet his father, he had to be calm.

And yet, as he reached the building and stared upward, he could had to clench his fists for a long moment. Here, Anya was trapped.

She did not know what the Church could do here. In England, there was not the same fervor for the Church as lived in this sunny, passionate clime. The English, for all their claims to civilization, yet held to their ancient pagan ways, cleverly disguising them in the clothes of Christian feasts. They had not ever truly been converted to the Faith the way these people had.

So close to Rome, and now Avignon, in the pathway of pilgrims traveling to Compostela and the Holy Land, the fervor of the Church was unbridled. Here they burned witches and heretics and were not content to let disbelief go ignored. Here, such things were serious.

But Anya would not know that. 'Twould seem to her only a guise for manipulating Christian. And for Etienne, it was just that. As long as Anya and Christian cooperated, there would be no danger.

But Christian knew his father, and he knew what would happen to Anya if his ire were raised, if Anya were sent to the courts.

His stomach went hollow.

Steeling himself, he nodded to Jean-Luc, who'd posted himself by the wall. "She is within?" Christian asked.

"Aye. They would not let me go with her, but none has been out again."

"Good." He frowned. "You say you are known here, and it was you who knocked me senseless in the borderlands. Does my father know your face?"

"Nay. The brigands hired me from a tavern."

"Come with me, then. While I am given audience, notice all you can of the design of the rooms, where lie the windows and roofs. Gossip with the servants and find out where Lady Anya is held."

Jean-Luc brightened. "Will we steal her, then?"

"We'll do what we must."

They were led up a twisting stairway, and outside the doors, Christian straightened his shoulders, aware of a thickness in his belly he refused to identify.

The door swung open. Behind him, Christian felt the warmth of Jean-Luc standing tall. He wished, ironically, for Geoffrey's endearing haughtiness at the church in Winterbourne. It seemed a long time since then.

And then there was his father.

Christian had prepared himself for this moment, for the time when he would look again on the face he had held so dear as a child. And for all the preparation, he could not stop the small stab of sorrow that struck his heart.

Etienne stood by the wide embrasures, and turned as Christian was led in. With a flicker of his gaze, Christian noted the dimensions of those wide openings—perhaps four feet high by six feet wide. They lent his father a grandeur in his rich cardinal's robes. Gold embroidery garnished the sleeves and hem and collar, and below peeked a finely woven wool tunic.

For a moment, father and son took each other's measure. Christian saw he'd outstripped his father's height by two inches or more, but had never gained the peasant bulk through his chest.

What Christian saw was that Etienne had grown old. Still vigorous and in good health by the look of his skin and eyes, but there was more gray than blond in the hair, and though the shape of his bones prevented many of the creases that would ordinarily garnish the face of such a man, there was loose skin below his jaw and softness in the once-chiseled cheeks.

Christian wondered what his father saw. A knight and a man, or a boy, still?

Annoyed with this softness, he spoke briskly. "Where is the Lady Anya?"

"Sleeping. We'll not bother her yet." He gestured toward a table. "Will you sit?"

Christian stared. "I would see the Lady Anya and conclude our business quickly."

Etienne folded his hands, a familiar gesture. "I vow 'tis as if your mother stares at me," he said softly.

Christian set his jaw, but not quickly enough to halt the rush of liquid memory the words brought to him. He did not speak, willing the past to leave him, not weaken him.

Etienne smiled, pouring himself a cupful of wine, and Christian saw that he knew he'd struck home. His father's greatest gift had always been his ability to read others, to guess before they knew themselves what was in their minds. And how much easier when it was his own son.

His next words made plain Christian was right. "You're very like her, in ways. That tender heart and need to serve others. Is the Lady Anya another of your broken birds?"

"I did not come here to speak of my mother, who was more woman than you deserved." With satisfaction, he saw the barb sting. A son, after all, also knew his father.

"Why did you come, Christian?"

"To see if I hate you as clearly as I thought." He nodded. "To see if I am as shamed by you as it seemed I should be. To see if you had changed." Tightly, he smiled. "You have not. You're still that rough peasant boy inside—not even the papacy will change that."

Again Etienne smiled, but there were daggers in it. "Only the pope can commute a sentence of heresy."

"You'll not be pope."

"Then your Lady Anya will die a gruesome death, and her babe with her, both of them burning in the flames." With a glitter in his eye, he lifted his cup. "They say it sometimes takes more than five minutes to die."

"Will you never cease?" Christian spat out, and knew he'd erred.

Etienne lifted a brow calmly.

He'd known he would not talk his father around, but there must have been some hope in him, for now he felt a bitter disappointment. "Let me see her."

"No." Etienne inclined his head. "You listen to me,

my son." The words dripped with irony. "'Tis only the grace of God that you stand here today at all. And I am willing to let you live. Anya will stay in my keeping until I am pope, then I will set her free and you may wander wherever your hearts take you."

Carefully he placed the cup on the table and folded his hands before him. "One word of our secret makes its way to anyone, and I'll send her instantly to the tribunals and you can watch her burn."

Rage leapt from its pen and erupted. In a trice, Christian crossed the room and backed his father to the wide embrasure. "One hair on her head, and I vow I will peel your skin from your body."

No fear flared in the black eyes, only a curious sort of satisfaction.

Behind the cardinal yawned the great opening, and for one blind instant, Christian thought of shoving his father over. His hands trembled at his sides—one push and it would be done.

Clenching his jaw, Christian stepped back. "One hair."

Etienne said, "One word."

It was finished.

Christian, for all his rage, knew he had lost.

In a noisy tavern, Christian drank heavily. Nearby him, Jean-Luc swilled ale and played dice with a pair of tanners. There were whores aplenty at the fringes of the room and sitting on laps; in the air was a great festiveness, a ring of bells and laughter and the heat of many bodies.

The whores steered clear of Christian, deep in his cups and a brooding mood. He thought of Anya locked in a room high in the building where his father slept, wondered how she fared, what things she had learned.

He lifted his cup and felt wine splash with a burn to his twisting belly. A coward and a fool was Christian de Morcerx—battered and beaten, a knight who could not even kill a man who threatened his woman and babe.

"My lord," Jean-Luc said hesitantly. "The hour grows late, and you must rise early. Mayhap 'tis time for you to put the wine away."

Defiantly, Christian lifted the cup. "Here lies my comfort," he said blurrily. "Cannot even kill my most loathed enemy."

"He is your father, my lord. I could not kill my father, either."

"Yours does not hold your woman and child," he said, his voice raw with the drink. "Nor aspire to lead the world as Christ incarnate, nor wish to kill you."

"Mayhap you are not meant to kill him, my lord," Jean-Luc said. "Mayhap the stain will wound you too deep."

Christian's eye twitched and the burn grew worse in his belly. He thought of young Geoffrey, so trusting and sure Christian knew best for him. Just so had he been with his own father. "How can a man kill his own blood?" he asked, and was not sure if he referred to his father or himself.

"Come, my lord."

Christian allowed himself to be led. His father had no such weakness as his son. "To bed, then."

He dreamed of a brace of flickering candles, and his mother bending her head, her great fall of hair spreading over her back. He dreamed of his father, laughing as Rowena danced in their small house. He dreamed of his father kneeling at Rowena's bedside, weeping as he held her lifeless hand to his lips.

The sound of that weeping tore him from sleep and he sat up, blinking, aware of a vague, nameless ache in his chest. He'd looked on as his father wept, the sound deep and hollow and dry. There had been anguish so deep in that sound that even at nine, Christian had known there would be no comfort for the man who felt it.

In the musty darkness, Christian rubbed his face, wishing to drive away the memories. Even at nine, he had understood the lifeless look in the dark eyes of his father, the regret and the sorrow. "I failed her," Etienne said. "All my light is gone."

And a boy who had lost his mother wanted to say, *But what of me?* He had not. Only stared at his dead mother and known he'd lost his father, too.

He rose in the warm room and paced to a small, shuttered opening. He flung open the shutters and breathed in the southern air, thinking of his own actions those long years before. A crescent of moon hung over the sleeping city, and the watch cried out as it passed. From a distance, a bell rang for Laud.

Etienne d'Auch had had nothing but the Church. Raised in the most miserable of poverty, he'd used his wits to rise. Often he'd told this truth to Christian, had explained he would have nothing if he left the shelter of career. There would be nothing for any of them, he told young Christian and his mother.

But Rowena had died of the shame. Her conscience, convent-nurtured, had at last eaten her love. By the time she died, she had spoken naught to Etienne d'Auch, who yet worshipped her.

After her death, the driven Etienne had become ruthless—mayhap, Christian thought now, leaning on the embrasure, even a little mad—in his pursuit of his ambitions. The change had chilled his son, but he'd known little of human nature then.

In the dark stillness of night with the weight of his years lending clarity, he understood what the loss of Rowena had done to Etienne. He did not condone it, but he understood.

With a thickness in his throat, he also knew he did not hate his father. He could not forgive him, but perhaps that was not his place. Etienne d'Auch would go to God with much on his conscience, but 'twas not given Christian to mete out his punishment in this life. If he were to be pope, so be it. God could choose.

There was no singing joy in him at the thought, only a resigned sort of sadness. All these years, the thought of his revenge had been held close like a promise. One day his father would see that he lived, would not overlook him as he had since his mother died.

Now Christian would walk away. Take Anya and go—live the life his father might have had. He, Christian de Morcerx, had a choice in his life, unlike his father and his king and the vast yawning lot of people sleeping below.

Tonight, he chose life over death.

He roused Jean-Luc. "Come. Get the horses. I am finished with this place."

"Where are we going, my lord?"

"To rescue the Lady Anya."

23

It was just past Prime when Anya awakened to a sense of someone standing nearby her. She started awake to see Christian at the edge of her bed.

"How—?"

He touched a finger to his lips and cocked his head toward the embrasure.

Anya leapt up and threw her arms around him, standing on the bed to embrace his broad, leather-covered shoulders. His hair touched her face, his strong arms fiercely circled her body. Very tenderly, he touched his lips to her neck, and buried his face in her shoulder. "By all that is holy," he said in a rough, low voice, "I have gone gray with worry over you."

In the streets below was a noise, and both lifted their heads. Frowning, Christian said, "Horses. A lot of them."

Urgently, he let go and went to the embrasure. He swore.

"Is it soldiers?" Anya asked, looking around for a place to hide him.

He shook his head, his face very grave. "'Tis a rough lot, coming here. You must go—now."

"What? Have you a key?"

He pointed to the window.

Anya's belly swooped and she backed up, shaking her head. "No, Christian—you know I—I cannot. . . ."

He grabbed her arm, his jaw hard. "You must. Here is your test as a true knight, Lady Anya. You must climb down to where Jean-Luc waits and ride to Saint Maximin. I will meet you at the church there when you are finished."

From below, the shouts and a clanking increased, the hooves loud on the cobbled streets.

He shoved her ungently toward the embrasure as a booming sounded through the building. "They're at the gates, Anya! Go, now!"

With a sob, she caught at his sleeve, one hip braced against the embrasure. "Christian, I do not argue to be foolish or stubborn!" Gingerly, she glanced over her shoulder. "I cannot abide heights, I've told you. I'll tumble down and be broken in the street."

Firmly he gripped her arms. "You must, Anya," he said, his voice implacable. "I suffer not the malady, so I cannot tell you how to resist it—but I tell you, you must go, and go now." Shouts sounded now from within and he glanced over his shoulder.

"Can you not come, too? Leave your father to his fate."

He shook his head. "There are some things I must say to him, else he'll haunt me always."

"Even at risk of your life?"

"'Twill be no life if I make no peace here, Anya.

This is my pilgrimage." A sound of crashing furniture and more shouts, perhaps even swords, rang into the room.

"Go!" Christian shouted.

Bracing herself, Anya looked out. A single rope hung from the embrasure, leading straight down two stories to a roof where Jean-Luc waited. "Hurry," he cried. "The light will soon illuminate us for the archers to pick off like flies."

Urgently, Anya turned. She grabbed Christian's hard, sunburned face in hers, feeling his beard prickle her palms, and kissed him. "I love you more than my life, Christian de Morcerx."

His cloud-colored eyes flickered. "In the church at Saint Baume we will be wed."

Now the sounds came from within the apartment itself, and Anya rushed to grab the rope, closing her eyes in a heartfelt and wordless prayer.

She fixed her eyes on the sky, refusing to look down as she gripped the rope in sweating hands. Her stomach bolted, turned and flopped, and a queer, unbalanced feeling rippled over her spine.

For one awful moment, she thought she would faint from fear. Darkness prickled the edges of her vision and threatened viciously. Hanging thirty feet above the ground, higher than the walls at the castle, she clung to the rope, her forehead against the cold walls.

And a bolt of memory came to her. The brigand with his filthy lips, tearing at her with his pawing hands.

Finally he had left her for dead in the fallen leaves of the winter forest. Her parents lay with slit throats in the snow, her brother John as if dead. She knelt beside him. His eyes fluttered open. "I'm sorry," he choked out.

Anya had stood and stumbled toward home, unmindful of the cold, the feeling of her deadened voice, and found help.

Setting her jaw, she opened her eyes. This was only height, not death. Jerkily, she lowered herself down, and her legs would not hold her when she landed beside Jean-Luc. He didn't let her linger, however, but pulled her toward a hidden ladder at the edge of the second roof.

"Wait!" Anya cried, and turned to look up—way, way up, to the embrasure from which she'd climbed. There stood Christian, bathed in the first fingers of gold morning light, his hair ablaze, his expression grim. Soberly, he lifted a hand in farewell.

She knew she would never see him again.

"Come, my lady," Jean-Luc urged.

Resigned, Anya gathered her skirts and followed him down to the street, where their horses awaited.

At the last moment, Jean-Luc seemed to be seized with the same fit of worry. He rode cautiously toward the open door of the apartments and whistled for Ysengrin. "Find him," he said.

The dog yipped and ran inside.

Within the chamber, Christian crouched by the locked door and listened to the crashing beyond, the frantic voices. Soon or late, someone would come to release the prisoner, and he would be ready.

'Twas not long before he was rewarded by the clank of the keys in the lock. Poised, Christian waited for the door to swing open, his sword in hand. From the climb up the rope, his arm ached, but a wild battle sense blotted out the stinging. When a guard entered, Christian grabbed him from behind, unhanding him of his dagger. "Where is my father?" he said urgently.

"I know not, my lord," the man gasped. "I was sent to get the girl."

Christian grabbed the keys from the guard's hand and flung the man forward. He landed in an ignoble sprawl, but did not seem overeager to get up. Christian closed the door and locked it behind him.

The fight seemed not to have come this far back, but in the main room, there were sounds of a struggle. Christian cautiously peeked around an arched stoneway, scanning the room for his father. Guards and brigands clashed, tumbling furniture and tearing hangings. The guards soon lost heart and darted for the door. Several of the brigands followed gleefully, their blood lust raised.

From a closed door, the cardinal emerged in his nightclothes, furious by the look of his red face. Only one brigand remained, riffling through the papers on the table, opening drawers and throwing them on the floor. "Halt!" the cardinal cried, and from one side came another bandit, rushing fast with his sword upraised.

Christian did not think—only bellowed as he ran forward, his weapon strong in his hands—rushing for the man who would kill Etienne.

It seemed to move with extraordinary slowness: Christian saw his father open his eyes wider as he spied the sword aimed for his gut, then saw Christian racing toward him like an avenging angel. The second marauder now joined the melee with a glad chortle. Christian narrowly missed the swipe of his sword with a hurried dodge. He turned back to halt the fall of the sword that would kill Etienne—

Christian's arm failed him with a great agonizing crack, a pain so disabling he heard it like a ringing bell in the room. He could not lift it more. Uselessly, it dropped. His sword clattered to the floor.

He whirled and rammed with his full strength into the second brigand who came at him again. The force knocked the man down, sending him off balance into his compatriot, who stumbled into Etienne, who seemed frozen, horror on his face.

With a mighty cry, Christian kicked the man with the sword backward, stunning him. And turned to grapple with the second one who came at Christian with dagger clutched in his fist, slicing the air with an expression like the mad foaming of a wild boar.

There was no choice. Fighting the weakness in his arm, Christian could lift no sword to defend himself or his father. Head down, he barreled into the man, and felt a sharp prick to his side as the smaller man struggled. Christian let the momentum carry him forward until the embrasure was at his back. The brigand gave an enraged yell.

"Christian!" came his father's cry. "Your back!"

Christian whirled as the other man came forward. He ducked and barreled forward again, finding less power in him now. His breath came raggedly and his shoulder screamed. Weakness soaked all power from his arm. A smell of sweat and fear and battle reached his nose. He stumbled and felt with a cold wash of fear the edges of the embrasure against his hips.

The snarling growl of a dog cut through the room. Confused, Christian thought it sounded like Ysengrin.

Then there was no wondering, for a man screamed as the creature leapt and tore the throat of the brigand holding Christian. Bright blood spurted from the wound and the man made a gurgling noise as he fell.

The other man cried out and ran from the room.

Breathing hard, Christian bent for a moment, hands on his knees. "Oh, I am old and weary of this life," he said heavily to himself. Slowly, he straightened and touched Ysengrin's head, pressing his forehead to the dog's furry head. "Brave Ysengrin," he said accepting his slurping tongue. "We'll have Geoffrey write a ballad of your bravery."

Only then did he fully straighten to look at his father. Braced in a sitting position against the doorway where he'd fallen, dressed in his nightclothes, Etienne d'Auch bled from a mortal wound to the belly.

"Son," he said.

Christian clenched his jaw at the blood. He'd thought his father safe. For one brief moment, he gazed at the mayhem around him with a bleak sense of futility.

"You fought to save me," Etienne said.

Christian gave into his exhaustion and sank to a squatting position. His shoulder was pure agony, and the pain seemed to rip down to his side. He touched the place and felt moisture. Blood, he saw, when he lifted his hand. Ysengrin whined.

"Aye," Christian said to his father. "As always, you were right. I have not the heart to kill you."

"You are so like her," Etienne whispered. "I see Rowena's eyes when you look at me." He groaned a little in pain. "I could not bear it when she died, that you looked at me all with her eyes."

Christian nodded heavily.

"I made the wrong choice," Etienne said. "I loved her, you know. She was all I loved in this life."

"I know."

"Forgive me, Christian. Grant me that one small measure of comfort before I go to hell."

Christian struggled to his feet, feeling in his wound the need for a surgeon to stitch the place. Too much blood soaked his hauberk, and he could feel the stickiness in his hose. Wearily, he said, "Long years ago did I forgive you, *mon père*. 'Twas you who did not forgive yourself." He turned and limped toward the door.

"Christian."

He paused, holding his side.

"Why did you come?"

Christian frowned, feeling more blood now trickle over his fingers. "To take my lady from you."

"But . . . she is . . . gone." The dark eyes grew hot and fierce. "You . . . came to find . . . me. Why?"

Dispassionately, Christian stared at the man who'd sired him. He felt nothing. "To be finished with it," he said.

Slowly, he limped out to seek out a surgeon.

For three days, Anya and Jean-Luc waited in Saint Maximin, sheltering at a small inn for pilgrims. Daily, Anya went to the church to wait for Christian, sure he would appear at any moment. How could he be so far behind them?

The first night, she was deeply worried. She told herself he might have been tired and need to sleep before he journeyed onward. But Remus was a fast horse, much faster than the two Jean-Luc and she had ridden. Christian should have overtaken them by now.

By morning, when there was no sign of him, she began to fret. And though Jean-Luc tried to hide it, she saw that he, too, wondered what might have happened in those apartments so high above Carpentras.

The second night Anya spent tossing and turning,

pushing away horrible visions of Christian lying dead, his father at last triumphant. A painful fear lodged in her throat and would not ease.

On the third morning after their arrival, Anya made her choice. Today she would go to the tomb, and they would return to Carpentras in search of Christian. Jean-Luc, visibly relieved, agreed to station himself at the church in case Christian came while she was gone.

So it was in the slow gold of late afternoon that Anya climbed the path to the grotto. Her heart was heavy. Loneliness wrapped her like a shroud. Everyone she knew was unimaginably far away; all that she loved was a wearying journey ahead. She thought on Winterbourne and wondered how the fields fared. Would the harvests be so poor again this year? How would the village look when she returned?

Gazing at the harsher vista about her, Anya for one moment saw Winterbourne as it might look in the warmth of an early July afternoon. Haze would gild the air above the fields, and in the baileys, women would be washing. The guards would be jesting over the fine swinging bottom of a young villager.

She ached to see it again.

As she made her way up the difficult path, she was not entirely alone. Other pilgrims traveled, too. Ahead walked a ragged man with shells and palms in his hat, a dark woman in strange dress walking with him. Behind her, Anya had glimpsed a single young girl, a local by the look of her. All of them climbing to seek the blessing of Magdalene.

Anya walked barefoot, her own contribution to making her quest holy. Her hair she left loose and unadorned on her back. It seemed oddly fitting to come here with a bastard child in her belly once again, a child that had, these past weeks, begun to dance and bump. The babe made her belly a small, roundish swell, more evident for the leanness of her body after the long winter and the journey following. Soon she would have to eat more, but it should not be hard now that the sickness had passed. Only last night, she'd dug into a mutton stew with relish.

As she neared the grotto, a strange emotion grew in her breast, fluttery and yet sober. It expanded as she made her way through the trees, thick and varied, and by piles of rocks. The day was hot, but a cool wind blew down from the mountains, as if in welcome.

But outside the grotto, Anya paused, her heart beating in a skittish pattern.

A long way had she traveled to stand in this place, with the sun slanting long streamers of dark gold into the hollows of rock. There was no sound but the buzzing of insects and the wayward song of a cricket. As she stood there, a great blue dragonfly swooped by and she stared at it in wonder, amazed at its size and sheen. It fluttered near the cave, the fairy wings glistening.

Here had Magdalene come for the last years of her life. Anya stared around her, wondering what she had thought of it, what it had been like, what things she had felt.

Mary Magdalene, the whore who became so holy the angels had appeared to her first when Christ had arisen. Anya felt a whoosh pass through her at the thought, and moved forward. She had been punished by this journey, but she stood here now for herself.

With a feeling of awe, she entered the dark grotto. Candles burned in the stillness, prayer offerings to the saint. Flowers and rocks and baubles were scattered over the altar. The two pilgrims who had come in before her moved back toward the entrance in the darkness. She kept her head lowered, unwilling to intrude upon them.

And for a moment, she was alone in the cool dim grotto, with only candles flickering in the darkness and a wild, pounding emotion in her breast, one she did not understand.

Kneeling, she crossed herself and whispered a soft prayer of supplication.

And here, now, the walls fell. Nine long years of holding back the shame of the awful thing that had happened in the woods poured through her. "I hated them all," she whispered, "the men who raped me and the priest and my brothers. All of them I hated."

But most of all, she had hated herself for allowing it to happen, for letting them take her, for not fighting to the death when that would have been the honorable thing. But she had not wanted to die!

Instead, she had fallen to the brigands and paid for her love of worldly beauty with their rape of her.

A fallen woman had Mary Magdalene been. Fallen and yet so pure at the end she could be visited by angels. Anya lifted her eyes and smiled. "I wanted to live," she said aloud. "So I might love."

There kneeling, she thought of her brave Christian. She thought of her brother William and breathed her forgiveness of him.

How she had hated being a woman these many years! How she had cursed God for it. Now she saw the sweet power, and in her belly, her child moved as if in celebration.

Light and calm filled her, and Anya rose as she heard the village girl come in behind her. Bemused, she ambled into the sunlight, peering out over the vista of hills and valleys.

She laughed, for where she stood was high above the earth, and there was no dizziness, no terror. She tilted her head back to the lowering sun and let it fill her.

"Anya of Winterbourne?"

With a startled cry, Anya whirled. It was the pilgrim who'd spoken, a rough man with a long, long beard. Puzzled, she stared at him. "I am Anya of Winterbourne. Who—"

The man stepped forward and Anya froze in disbelief, her mouth gaping as the man took off his hat, letting free a tumble of dark hair in curls as wild as Anya's own.

"John?" she whispered.

24

John of Winterbourne, late of Jerusalem, England, and points between, roared and scooped Anya into a massive bear hug.

Stunned, Anya allowed herself to be swept up. With one part of her mind, she noticed he'd grown even larger on his sojourn, if that were possible. Though even he would be dwarfed by Christian. He smelled of his journey, but Anya didn't mind it. She hugged him in return.

When he set her back down, she found her tongue still would not move. She stared at the bright blue eyes, at the ruddy health in his cheeks. "How—?"

He laughed and hugged her again. "I cannot believe it! How came you to be here? And are you all alone?"

"I . . . er . . ." She could not take it in. Her brother John, gone for so many long years, standing before her in the strong sunlight of the southern climes. Wildly, she glanced at the woman beside him.

John of Winterbourne? Aye, he married . . .

The woman was small and dark, with limpid brown eyes. She looked at Anya shyly, and Anya had the feeling she wanted to hide behind John before she could be judged. Anya's gaze swept over her odd dress, a sort of draped gown that included a veil over her hair. Her feet were bare. Anya swallowed. Brightly painted figures covered the flesh of the strong feet. Tattoos. Anya lifted her gaze to the woman's eyes, and saw she had bowed her head.

A prostitute. John had taken to wife a prostitute from the Holy Land.

Anya stepped forward. "Pilgrims told me you married," she said. "Please introduce me to your wife."

John turned and tenderly drew the girl forward. "This is Indihar. She wished to stop here on our way back to England."

"Welcome, sister," Anya said.

At last Anya could speak. She laughed, dashing away the tears of fullness from her face. "I can't believe it's you," she said. "I thought you dead till we met some pilgrims who told me they'd seen you."

"We?"

Anya nodded, worry swirling in. "Aye. My betrothed and I." She saw the curiosity in his eyes. "'Tis too long a story to give you now," she said, weary now with the walk and the surprise and the sheer weight of all that needed to be told. "Let us all go back to the inn and have supper, and trade our stories."

They walked down.

Anya tried to send John and Indihar to the inn, but John would not let her go alone. She smiled at him ruefully. "I have traversed the continent, brother, and

think I might manage the deserted streets of this
small town." She shook her head. "I am no longer the
child you left."

He smiled gently. "You were not a child even then.
How is Geoffrey?"

She sighed wistfully, but nodded. "He is well. William
tried to snatch him away to be a monk, but Christian
found him a place with the king."

"A page to the king?"

"No," she said, remembering John would not know
of Geoffrey's gift. "He is a musician. He's so like you,
John."

John nodded, obviously bemused. "'Twill be hard
to return after so long." He frowned as they paused
before the church. "I do not mean to go to Winterbourne, unless you wish it. I had thought we would go
to the castle."

Anya, looking anxiously for signs of Remus, only
nodded. A cluster of horses were stabled nearby, but
she could see at a glance there was no gray among
them. Her heart plummeted. Still not here.

The peace she'd known this afternoon shattered.
"Let me look inside," she said. "Then we'll take supper at the inn."

John nodded.

Inside, the newly built nave was dark and smelled of
rock dust. On the altar was the reliquary holding the
relics of Magdalene, and the usual brace of candles. No
one stirred. With a pang, Anya turned to leave.

Something brushed her skirts. Anya started, thinking a rat had scurried by, and squeaked in fear. One
would think they'd keep the rats from the church at
least.

In the darkness she couldn't see it and waited a

moment before she moved again, afraid she'd run into it again.

It came again, but this time, the creature made a sound. It meowed.

With a blaze of joy, Anya knelt and scooped Esmerelda into her arms. She whirled—

And there was Christian, coming toward her with the priest. His spurs clanged against the stone floor and his hair captured all the small light in the room. Her heart quivered.

He stopped before her. "Are you mad?" he bellowed. "Going alone to the grotto!"

Stunned at the anger in his voice, Anya straightened, opening her mouth to protest.

"You might have at least taken Jean-Luc with you!"

"But he—"

"Think you I traversed the world and fought soldiers and conquered at last the demons that haunted me to come and find you dead?" He gripped her arm fiercely. "I've been pacing here for hours, waiting for you."

Anya opened her mouth once again, but her words were smothered with a kiss. "I worried like a madman," he said at last, pressing his brow to her forehead.

A glimmer of joy, sparks only, began to twinkle in her heart. She thought of the scolding she gave Geoffrey when he'd taken a dare to walk the edge of the manor wall, and the whipping she'd given when he'd run off and been lost in the forest. 'Twas like that now with Christian.

"You love me," she said in faint wonder, the sparks growing now to a wide, glowing shimmer.

"Aye," he said softly. "With all that I am. How could you doubt it?"

She kissed him with joy, again and again, laughter rising like a fountain in her overflowing heart. "You might have said so."

"Nay," he said, touching her cheek, his gaze drinking in her face as if parched for the look of it. "You would not have believed."

Anya saw it so plainly now, that love in his face, and felt ashamed she had ever doubted him. "Will you love me when my breasts drag the ground?"

He laughed. "Aye."

"When I've lost every tooth in my head and cackle like a goose when I laugh?"

"Aye. And when you are sick and when you are well, and all the other times, God willing, we will share. I'm already old, Anya, with an old man's need for quiet. Will you love me when I'm no longer strong enough to lift my head, when all I can eat is stewed possets, and my belly is a giant thing pushing at the table?"

Said like that, she saw her worries for the shallow things they were. "'Tis your soul I love, my lord."

Gently, he kissed her. "You've appeased the saint?"

She nodded.

"Then we will marry now."

She laughed. "Now, my lord?"

His smile did not return. "Now."

They stepped out to the porch steps. There waited John and Indihar, not clear in the gloom. "Brother, will you wait while I marry?" she couldn't keep the mirth from her tone.

"Marry?" said John.

"Brother?" said Christian.

"I vow I'm near to dying with hunger," Anya said, waving away both their questions. "Let's marry and go eat."

The priest began the chant, and it was over quickly, so little that when all was said and done Anya felt dizzy.

Until Christian bent over her in the gloaming and cupped her face in his hands. "I love you, Anya of Winterbourne. My life and heart I lay at your feet." He kissed her with infinite tenderness.

And collapsed on the steps.

It was only exhaustion, coupled with the long, hard ride and the blood he'd lost in Carpentras. For half the day, riding toward Saint Maximin, he'd been near to delirious, and only his worry over Anya had kept him in the saddle. He'd eaten naught but black bread for two days in his haste to find her.

Sheepish he was to awaken in a small but clean room of the inn. Anya, her beautiful hair loose around her shoulders, sat nearby, smearing soft cheese over a loaf. "You've the appetite of a wolf," he said. His voice, rough with disuse, croaked.

"Christian!" She leapt up. "My lord, I was half sick myself with worry. How do you feel?"

"Hungry," he said, and shifted to one side. He took the bread she offered. "And dismayed."

"Dismayed?"

He gave her a rueful grin. "For all my struggle to get here and marry you by sundown so we might lie together this night, I find I will not be equal to the task."

She laughed, and he saw instantly the lightness of it, the clear joy in her that burned like a bright morning sun. "You love me," she said. "I'll wait to bed you."

He reached for her. "Come sit close, my sweet.

How I've missed you these past days. I grew used to having you at my side from dawn till dusk."

She complied, and he saw that his words struck tears in her eyes. "What have I said?"

"Nothing." She swallowed. "I thought I would never find happiness. Never find love or joy." She touched his face. "And in you, I find all and more."

So close she was. So beautiful. A restless stirring moved in his nether regions and he boldly reached out to touch her breast. He closed his eyes in pleasure at the softness, at the perfect molding of her to him. "I'll die of want before tomorrow," he said with a growl. "Come here and let me kiss you."

She smiled. "I'll do better."

He raised his brows as she bent over him and began to unlace his clothes, deliberately, freeing one thing after the other. The action aroused him.

Her face clouded when she saw his side. "So you are wounded again."

"'Tis not bad," he said. "Only a jagged flesh wound."

"And your father?"

"He's dead," Christian said shortly. "I will tell you all another time."

She stood there, gilded in candlelight, staring at him with a sad expression. He felt vulnerable in his naked arousal—and then she smiled.

Straightening, she lifted her hands to her own laces, shedding first her surcoat, then the good embroidered gown. With a coy smile, she stood there a moment in her thin linen kirtle, her body both hidden and revealed by the gossamer fabric. His arousal intensified.

Slowly, she shed it too, until she stood naked before him. He stared in wonder at the fullness of her breasts, the slight roundness of her belly, the long white thighs. His breath left him. "I cannot move well enough to do you any justice," he said in frustration.

"Then do not move, my lord." Wickedly, she lay down next to him, pressing their lengths together, her hands skimming over his flesh. "I have listened to the wise words of women who told me things you might enjoy."

He groaned at her caresses. "Oh?"

"Aye," she said with a wicked smile, and showed him.

25

On Christmas Eve at Winterbourne revelers sang in the Great Hall, lifting cups of ale and spiced wine to one another in great good cheer. John and Indihar had come for the feast from their fief, and Geoffrey too had been given leave by the king. William, to no one's regret, had been banished to a remote post in Wales.

Anya of Winterbourne labored to give birth.

Mary and the goodwife from the village soothed her as she struggled and sweated and gripped their hands, but in all, 'twas an easy birth, for she was well made for the business of children.

As the bells for Matins rang out from the church, Anya delivered a son.

The women helped her to her bed and nestled the babe at her breast. Anya trembled as she took him. She touched his head, fuzzy with colorless hair, and his cheek, which grew rosy as she held him. His wailing ceased as he recognized the pounding of his mother's heart, and he looked at her.

Anya wept and gave him her breast to suck. Her tears washed, unchecked, over her face as he latched on and eagerly drank.

Mary, standing nearby, shared her tears. "Oh, he's a strong one, milady."

She nodded and looked up, unable to speak. For a long, long moment, they looked at each other, thinking of all the things that had led to this moment, to this child being born in this bed. Mary smiled. "Ye've done so well, milady."

The door was flung open and Christian pushed his way in, past the protests of the women at the door. Behind him came Geoffrey, who'd come for the holiday. They strode toward the bed where Anya lay, fierce and straight and frowning like men.

Until they spied the little one. Both halted at the same instant, their faces showing perplexed expressions of stunned wonder.

"He's so small!" Geoffrey breathed. "Was I as small as that?"

Anya smiled, for she'd chosen to tell him the truth of his birth when they'd all returned from Carpentras. He'd wept and clung to her, and Anya had feared she'd made the wrong choice until he lifted his head. He kissed her cheek and said, "I'd always prayed for it to be so."

Now she looked at his lean, freckled face and remembered the night so long ago when she'd suckled him in this very bed, weeping then as now for the miracle of birth, for the wonder and power that came from a woman's body. "Aye," she said again. "You were even a bit smaller."

"Can I touch him?" Geoffrey asked.

"Gently."

The boy gingerly brushed the soft curls. As if he were a kitten, the babe closed his eyes. "Oh," exclaimed Geoffrey in a breathy sigh.

Anya looked up at Christian, and gave Geoffrey a nod. He stepped back, and with him went Mary and the other women, leaving husband and wife alone.

Anya stared at him and saw with wonder a single tear shimmering in his eye before he blinked hard to rid himself of such unmanly weakness. But his voice was rough when he spoke. "A wonder it is."

"You, too, may touch him," Anya said.

Christian knelt beside the bed. Very, very gently, he bent over her and kissed the babe's cheek. "Happy Christmas," he whispered, and kissed Anya, too.

A welter of powerful feeling rose in her and she clutched his hand when he made to rise. "Christian, this is the best moment in all my life," she said.

His mouth crooked in a teasing smile. "So you won't mind making a few more of these little creatures with me?"

She gave him a wicked lift of her brow. "Nay."

"At last my debt is paid."

She answered seriously. "More than paid."

"If you don't mind, my lady, I would like to stay awhile yet, in case you have need of a champion again." He kissed her fingers, his eyes filled with laughter.

"Well, I suppose there is room."

"Forever, then?"

She smiled. "That would be fine."

Then touching her and the babe, he pressed another

kiss to her mouth. Anya felt the swirling joy encompass them both like the magic snow beyond the windows. "I love you, Anya of Winterbourne," he said huskily.

And she knew that it was true.